TALES TOLD IN CANADA

TALES TOLD
IN CANADA

Edith Fowke

1986
Doubleday Canada Limited, Toronto, Canada

Copyright © by Edith Fowke
All Rights Reserved
Second Printing

Cover design by Dragon's Eye Press
Typeset by Compeer Typographic Services Limited
Printed and bound in Canada by John Deyell Company

Canadian Cataloguing in Publication Data
Main entry under title:
Tales told in Canada

Bibliography: p.
ISBN 0-385-25041-X (pbk) 0-385-25109-2 (bound)
1. Tales — Canada. 2. Folklore — Canada. I. Fowke, Edith, 1913-
GR113.T34 1986   398.2'0971   C86-094050-0

Contents

Introduction   vii

I. Myths   1
  1. Old One   2
  2. Crow Makes the World   3
  3. The Moon   6
  4. The Mosquito and the Thunder   6

II. Animal Tales   8
  5. A Wolf, a Fox, and a Lion   8
  6. The Race Between Turtle and Frog   10
  7. How the Agouti Lost Its Tail   10

III. Supernatural Tales   14
  8. Once Upon a Time There Was a Shepherd   15
  9. The Talking Nightingale   21
  10. The White Bear   25
  11. The Magic Chest   28
  12. The Blacksmith and Beelzebub's Imps   34
  13. The Fox Wife   36
  14. The Two Brothers   37
  15. The Green Flag and the Devil's Head   40
  16. The Shoemaker in Heaven   48
  17. Mac Crùslain   51

IV. Romantic Tales   56
  18. There Was a Lord in Edinburgh   56
  19. The Scotchman Who Loved an Irish Girl   59
  20. The Love Story of Laing Sanbo and Zhu Yingtai 60

V. Jokes and Anecdotes   63
21. Little Claus and Big Claus   64
22. Dickie Melbourne   70
23. Tall Tales from Northern Ontario   74
24. On the Trail of Joe Mufferaw   75
25. Humorous Stories from around Chapeau, Quebec   80
26. Jokes about Religions   85
27. Jewish Jokes from Toronto   91
28. The Lobster Salad   94

VI. Formula Tales   98
29. The Old Woman and Her Pig   98
30. A Catch Tale   100

VII. Legends   102
31. The Seal-Woman   102
32. One of the Thirty-Six Just Men   104
33. The Wrong Chill Windigo   107
34. Steer North and North East   109
35. The Ghostly Sailors   111
36. The Walker of the Snow/The Haunted Hunter   113
37. The Devil's Potato Field   117
38. A Miracle in Montreal   117
39. The Pot of Gold   118
40. Young Lad   120
41. The Vanishing Hitchhiker   121
42. The Blue Cardigan   122
43. The Pink Shawl   123
44. Old Man Gimli   124

VIII. Personal Experience Narratives   127
45. A Sasquatch Sighting   127
46. How I Learned to Make Bread   131
47. The Frank Slide Disaster   133
48. My Grandfather's War   137
49. St. Peter's Day   140
50. UFO Stories   142

Sources and References   145
Tale Types and Motifs   155
Bibliography   162
Acknowledgements   172

Introduction

THE ITEMS IN this collection are designed to illustrate the many different kinds of tales that have been told in Canada: myths, animal tales, supernatural tales, romantic tales, jokes and anecdotes, formula tales, legends, and personal experience narratives. They come from the many different ethnic groups that make up our population: Indian, Inuit, English, Scottish, Irish, French, German, Ukrainian, Doukhobor, Polish, Italian, Jewish, Greek, Swedish, Icelandic, West Indian, and some whose ancestry is mixed. There are examples from every region of the country, and they include some stories told in verse and song as well as in prose. The earliest were reported in 1898; the most recent in 1985. Some are drawn from books that are now out of print, some from early journals not readily available, some from archives, and some from colleagues and friends who have generously contributed tales from their unpublished collections.

A large proportion of the traditional tales told in Canada came here from older countries. Except for those of the Indians and Inuit, comparatively few originated in this country. Some of the older ones have been localized with names and details peculiar to Canada, but are still recognizable as international plots which can be located in Antti Aarne and Stith Thompson's *The Types of the Folktale*. Even the myths and legends, which are more apt to be identified with a particular region and often do not conform to international types, share motifs with stories throughout the world: details that can be identified through Stith Thompson's *The Motif-Index of Folk Literature*.

The stock of Canadian folktales is uneven. Tales of the native people have been collected and published in an enormous number of books and articles, and French-Canadian tales are almost as numerous. Bibliographies of these two groups are available elsewhere, and to discuss them in detail is beyond the scope of this book, which is limited to tales told in English or available in English translation. For listings of native tales see Fowke and Carpenter's bibliography, and articles by Penny Petrone and Robin Gedalof McGrath in *The Oxford Companion to Canadian Literature*. Gerald Thomas surveys French-Canadian tales in the *Oxford Companion*, my *Folktales of French Canada* has a substantial bibliography, and Luc Lacourcière has prepared a massive compilation, *Catalogue raisonné du conte populaire français en Amérique du nord*.

There are a number of books presenting French-Canadian tales in English, but most of these are rewritten versions rather than straight translations. Gerald Thomas's *Les Deux Traditions: le conte populaire chez les Franco-Terreneuviens* contains some stories that French Newfoundlanders told in English; Marie-Annick Desplanques collected some French tales in English from Angela Kerfont; and my *Folktales of French Canada* gives direct translations of a number of typical French-Canadian stories. Richard Dorson's *Folktales Told Around the World* includes a French-Canadian group translated by Margaret Low, and he has published some stories he collected from French settlers in Upper Michigan.

Most collectors of Anglo-Canadian folklore have concentrated on songs rather than tales, with the result that comparatively few tale collections have appeared, and even fewer contain tales as they were actually told by the folk. Most of the ones we do have are from the east coast: Mary L. Fraser's *Folklore of Nova Scotia*, Arthur H. Fauset's *Folklore from Nova Scotia*, and, more recently, Herbert Halpert's *A Folklore Sampler from the Maritimes* have substantial tale sections. To these may be added two Maritime books devoted entirely to tales: Creighton and Ives' *Eight Folktales from Miramichi* as *Told by Wilmot MacDonald* and Carole Spray's *Will O' the Wisp: Folk Tales and Legends of New Brunswick*. Helen Creighton has also published many supernatural legends in *Bluenose Ghosts* and *Bluenose Magic*, a few tales appeared in her *Folklore of Lunenburg County, Nova Scotia*, and she is currently preparing a book of other folktales from her collection.

More tales have been reported from the Scots than from the English. In addition to those in the Fraser and Creighton collections, there are two important books of tales that were collected in Gaelic and translated: Calum MacLeod's *Stories from Nova Scotia* and Margaret MacDonell and John Shaw's *Luirgen Eachainn Nill: Folktales from Cape Breton.* Also emphasizing the Scottish traditions are such articles as C.A. Fraser's "Scottish Myths from Ontario," James A. Teit's "Water-Beings in Shetlandic Folk-Lore as Remembered by Shetlanders in British Columbia," and MacEdward Leach's "Celtic Tales from Cape Breton."

Where the Maritime books are rich in *Märchen*, myths, legends, and jokes, the Western story collections from Anglo-Canadians all emphasize a single type, from Robert Gard's early *Johnny Chinook: Tall Tales and True from the Canadian West* to Herbert Halpert's "Tall Tales and Other Yarns from Calgary, Alberta," and Michael Taft's *Tall Tales of British Columbia.*

Among the more important collections from other ethnic groups are the black tales in Arthur Huff Fauset's *Folklore from Nova Scotia*, Jaroslav B. Rudnyc'kyj's *Readings in Canadian Slavic Folklore* and *Ukrainian-Canadian Folklore Texts in English Translation*, Robert B. Klymasz's *Folk Narrative Among Ukrainian-Canadians in Western Canada*, and André Elbaz's *Folktales of the Canadian Sephardim.* In *Prairie Folklore* Kay Stone includes tales from a number of different ethnic groups, and the Mercury publications of the Canadian Centre for Folk Culture Studies also contain a goodly number of ethnic tales.

A number of regional periodicals provide another source of tales: for example, *Cape Breton's Magazine, Them Days: Stories of Early Labrador, The Island Magazine, The Livyere, Inuktitut,* and older journals like *The Barrelman* and *The Newfoundlander,* have all published some traditional stories.

Folklorists are now progressing from collection to classification and analysis. Anthropologists have earlier analyzed Indian myths in books like Franz Boas's *Tsimshian Mythology* and Paul Radin's *The Trickster.* More recently French-Canadian folklorists at Laval have surveyed all the French tales in North America, and several have published detailed studies of particular tales in *Les Archives de Folklore.* Luc Lacourcière has described French oral traditions in North America in many articles, some in English; Gerald Thomas has written extensively of storytelling traditions among French Newfoundlanders, and Margaret Low has discussed "The Motif of the External Soul in French Canadian Folktales."

There have been surveys of certain tales and tale types. Edward Ives has studied the legend of the gorbey, Herbert Halpert has surveyed the tale of "The Cut-Off Head Frozen On," and I defended Paul Bunyan yarns. Robert Klymasz has analyzed "The

Ethnic Joke in Canada Today." Kay Stone wrote her dissertation and has published articles on characters in *Märchen*. Gerald Pocius has studied the skills of a Newfoundland joke-teller, and Richard Tallman has analyzed the style of Nova Scotia storytellers. Barbara Kirshenblatt-Gimblett wrote her dissertation and has published many articles on the context and function of storytelling among Jewish Canadians.

Other doctoral dissertations dealing with folktales include Joyce Coldwell's "Treasure Stories and Beliefs in Atlantic Canada," and John R. Scott's "Personal Experience Narratives Among Professional Sailors: Generic Keys to the Study of an Occupation." Master's theses include Jane (Dunsinger) Ardus's "A Comparative Study of Narrative Accounts of Visits Home Drawn from the Immigrant Ethnic Community in St. John's," Lawrence G. Small's "Patterns in Personal Experience Narratives: Storytelling at Cod Harbour — A Newfoundland Fishing Community," and Ruth Wooley's "A Comparative Study of Some French-Canadian Tales."

In this book the tales are all traditional, and are given as closely as possible to the way they were told traditionally. In a few cases the collector or translator modified the wording slightly, but they all came from the folk, and none has been retold or adapted in literary style. Where they were told in a language other than English they appear in translations that strive to preserve the style of the original storyteller.

The tales are grouped in seven sections according to their type, with brief introductions to each section and to the individual items. The appendix, "Sources and References," gives full documentation for each tale, along with types and motifs and a few comparative references. All the books and articles mentioned in this introduction and in the introductory notes appear in the bibliography. It gives a fairly complete list of publications of and about Canadian tales that have appeared in English, except for those of the native peoples.

While the emphasis is on the tales, the introductory notes include some details about the storytellers and the collectors, and, where possible, some comment on how the tales were told. That is a field that needs more study. A few folklorists have emphasized the context: for example, Barbara Kirshenblatt-Gimblett has analyzed the way Jewish tales were used in considerable detail, and Carole Spray gives an interesting account of her experiences with New Brunswick storytellers. Edward Ives has described storytelling in the lumbercamps, and Helen Creighton gives vivid pictures of Nova Scotia people telling ghost stories. As Canadian folklore develops, we can expect more description, discussion, and analysis of the tales, the way they are told, and what the storytellers think of them.

However, the tales themselves have an abiding interest for the listener and the reader. It is unfortunate that modern media have largely displaced the old custom of telling and listening to stories: a custom that held its own enchantment. As Charles Dunn described it in *Highland Settler*:

> *When the dusk of evening crept over the land and the tasks of the day were abandoned, the people gathered at the home of the most talented local entertainer. Their chief delight at such a* ceilidh *(gathering) was to lie in the warmth of the great fire, watch its glowing light play on the walls of the house, and listen to* sgeulachdan, *the ancient folk-tales of the Gael. Although the practised reciters have vanished from the land and the tales themselves can be recollected only by few, the impression they made still remains in the minds of the people who used to listen to them. Some remember the thrill of hearing a skilful story-teller as he worked up his audience with a favourite tale; others remember the terror they felt as they hastened home through the darkness and shadows of night after a particularly weird and unearthly story.*

Today few have the opportunity to hear stories in that way, and there is no doubt that hearing a good storyteller is far better than reading the stories in cold print. However, there is still enjoyment to be had from reading them. At present there is no book drawn from traditional sources that represents the widely varied tales that have been told across Canada by storytellers from our many ethnic groups. This collection is an attempt to provide a partial substitute for the *ceilidhs* that are now so rare.

Edith Fowke

I. Myths

THE TERM MYTH applied to a particular type of traditional tale is confusing because it has been used in many different ways. Folklorists consider myths to be tales told by people who believe them to be true accounts of a pre-historic world and of the activities of gods and demigods. Most of them deal with the origin of the world and its inhabitants, and with the origins of religious rituals.

Legends, which are also believed, are set in the world as we know it and usually feature humans. Tales that purport to explain the origins of geographic features, animal characteristics, or particular rites or customs are termed etiological, or explanatory, narratives, and may be either myths or legends.

While biblical narratives like the Genesis accounts of the Creation and the Flood fit the definition of myths, they do not conform to the concept of folklore because they have a set printed form and are taught rather than circulated orally. Thus the origin stories of formal religions are not generally classed as myths, although supplementary tales stemming from them may be.

The religious narratives of the native peoples do circulate orally and have many variants, so they form the main body of myths on this hemisphere. Indeed, nearly all Indian tales seem to have mythical elements, and the Indians themselves do not distinguish between tales of the present and previous worlds. However, the numerous tales that tell of their beginnings and feature creatures with supernatural powers are the ones normally classed as myths. The four that follow are typical samples.

1. OLD-ONE: AN OKANAGAN TALE

This creation myth, which James Teit noted from the Okanagan Indians of the West Coast, is unusual in that it postulates an original creator who makes an Earth Mother: she becomes the earth and from her flesh he makes the beings of the ancient world who are part human, part animal. It has a parallel in the myth of the Zuni of New Mexico whose creator made himself the Sun Father and from his skin made Earth Mother and Sky Father whose cohabitation produced all life on earth.

These tales differ from most of the Indian creation myths in beginning with one all-powerful being who creates the earth and its inhabitants, and whose nature is benevolent. The more common ones are less logical: they feature an animal hero who finds himself in a boat with other animals, creates earth from a bit of soil dredged up from the sea, and then creates humans and animals from clay or wood. He steals sun, moon, light, and fire, plays many tricks, fools and is fooled—quite different from the omnipotent and benevolent Old-One.

James A. Teit (1864–1922) was an important West Coast collector. In addition to contributing to *Folk-Tales of Salishan and Sahaptin Tribes* edited by Franz Boas, from which this tale comes, he published *Traditions of the Thompson River Indians of British Columbia* and numerous articles in the *Journal of American Folklore* on the Tahltan, Lillooet, Kaska, and Cree tribes.

Old-One

Told by Red-Arm

Old-One, or Chief, made the earth out of a woman, and said she would be the mother of all the people. Thus the earth was once a human being, and she is alive yet; but she has been transformed, and we cannot see her in the same way we can see a person. Nevertheless she has legs, arms, head, heart, flesh, bones, and blood. The soil is her flesh; the trees and vegetation are her hair; the rocks, her bones; and the wind is her breath. She lies spread out, and we live on her. She shivers and contracts when cold, and expands and perspires when hot. When she moves, we have an earthquake. Old-One, after transforming her, took some of her flesh and rolled it into balls, as people do with mud or clay. These he transformed into the beings of the ancient world, who were people, and yet at the same time animals.

These beings had some of the characteristics that animals have now, and in some respects acted like animals. In form, some were like animals, while others more nearly resembled people. Some could fly like birds, and others could swim like fishes. All had greater powers, and were more cunning than either animals or people. They were not well balanced. Each had great powers in certain ways, but was weak and helpless in other ways. Thus each was exceedingly wise in some things, and exceedingly foolish in others. They all had the gift of speech. As a rule, they were selfish, and there was much trouble among them. Some were cannibals, and lived by eating one another. Some did this knowingly; others did it through ignorance. They knew that they had to live by hunting, but did not know which beings were people, and which deer. They thought people were deer, and preyed on them.

Some people lived on the earth at the same time. They had all the characteristics that Indians have now, but they were more ignorant. Deer also were on the earth at that time, and were real animals as now. People hunted them. They were never people or semi-human ancients, like the ancestors of most animals. Some people say that moose and caribou were also animals, like the deer; and that elk, antelope, and buffalo were also animals, although stories are told of the last three as though they were ancients or semi-humans.

Old-One made each ball of mud a little different from the others, and rolled them over and over. He shaped them, and made them alive. The last balls of mud he made were almost all alike, and different from any of the preceding ones. They were formed like Indians, and he called them men. He blew on them, and they became alive. They were Indians, but were ignorant and knew no arts. They were the most helpless of all things created; and the cannibals and others preyed on them particularly. The people and animals were made male and female, so that they might breed. Thus everything living sprang from the earth; and when we look around, we see everywhere parts of our mother.

2. CROW MAKES THE WORLD: A TAGISH TALE

This is more typical of the Indian mythological tales which usually feature a culture hero who is also a trickster. Among the Algonkians of eastern Canada he is Glooscap, Manabozho, or Wisakeyjak; the plains Indians call him the Old Man; among the Salish Indians of British Columbia he is Coyote; among most of the Pacific Coast tribes he is Raven; among the Yukon tribes he is Crow.

Stories about the theft of light and fire are very widespread throughout North America, and are particularly popular along the West Coast. This tale, with Crow replacing Raven, is quite similar to Tsimshian accounts of the birth of Raven which Franz Boas analyzes in *Tsimshian Mythology*.

Mrs. Angela Sidney, born in 1902 of Tagish and Tlingit parents, has travelled throughout much of southern Yukon but now lives in the community of Tagish. Where most of the Indian mythological tales are found in early collections, Mrs. Sidney is a fine contemporary storyteller, having learned many stories from her parents, aunts, and uncles, in both the Tagish and Tlingit languages. Some of them appeared in *My Stories Are My Wealth* in 1977; the book from which this story comes, *Tagish Tlaagu: Tagish Stories*, was published in 1982. In 1985 Mrs. Sidney received the Order of Canada for her work in preserving the culture of her people. Her citation noted that she was one of the last living speakers of the Tagish language.

Julie Cruikshank, who recorded Mrs. Sidney's tales, writes in her introduction that:

> *People traced their family history through their mother's line and all clan names and affiliations followed this "matrilineal" descent. The society was divided into two groups (also called "moieties"): Crow and Wolf; membership in these was also inherited from one's mother. Throughout the southern Yukon, the rule was that Crow must marry Wolf and Wolf must marry Crow.*

Mrs. Sidney's story provides an explanation for this community pattern.

Crow Makes The World

Told by Mrs. Angela Sidney

One day there is a girl whose daddy is a very high man. They kept her in her bedroom all the time. Men try to marry her all the time but they say no, she's too good.

Crow wanted to be born. Wants to make the world. So he made himself into a pine needle. A slave always brings water to that girl. One time he brings water with pine needle in it. She turns it down. Makes him get fresh water. He brings it again. Again pine needle there. Four times he brings water and each time it's there. Finally she gives up. She spits that pine needle out and drank the water. But it blew in her mouth and she swallowed it. Soon she's pregnant. Her mother and daddy are mad.

Her mother asks her, "Who's that father?" "No, I never know a man," she says.

That baby starts to grow fast. That girl's father had the sun, moon, stars, daylight, hanging in his home. He's the only one has them. The world was all dark, all the time. The child begged for them to play with. Finally the father gives his grandchild sun to play with. He rolls it around. He plays with it, laughs, has lots of fun. Then he rolls it to the door and out it goes. "Oh!" he cries. He just pretends he cries because that sun is lost.

"Give me moon to play with." They say no at first. Like now if baby asks for sun, moon, you say, "That's your grandfather's fire." Finally, they give it to him. One by one they give him sun, moon, stars, daylight. He loses them all. "Where does she get that child from? He loses everything," her father says.

Then Crow disappears. Has those things with him in a box. He walks around. Comes to river. Lots of animals are there — fox, wolf, wolverine, mink, rabbit. Everybody's fishing. That time animals all talk like people talk now. The world is dark. "Give me fish," Crow says. No one pays any attention. "Give me fish or I bring daylight." They laugh at him.

He's holding a box — starts to open it and lets one ray out. Then they pay attention. He opens box a bit more. They're scared. Finally he broke that daylight box and throws it out. Those animals scatter, hide in bush and turn into animals like now. Then the sun, moon, stars, daylight, come out. "Go to the skies," Crow says. "Now no one man owns it," he says. "It will be for everyone." He's right, what he says, that Crow.

After Crow made the world he sees that sea lion owned the only island in the world. The rest was water. He's the only one with land. The whole place was ocean. Crow rests on a piece of log. He's tired. He sees sea lion with that little island just for himself. He wants land too. So he stole sea lion's kid.

"Give back that kid," said sea lion. "Give me beach — some sand," says Crow. So sea lion gave him sand. You know how sand in water floats? Crow threw that sand around the ocean. "Be world," he tells it. And it became the world.

After that he walks around, flies 'round all alone. He's tired. He's lonely. He needs people. He took poplar tree bark. You know how it's thick? He carved it. Then he breathed into it. "Live," he said. And he made person. He made Crow and Wolf, too. At first they can't talk to each other. Crow man and woman are shy with each other — look away. Wolf people same way. "This is no good," he said. So he changed that. He made Crow man sit with Wolf woman and he made Wolf man sit with Crow woman. So Crow must marry Wolf and Wolf must marry Crow.

That's how the world began.

3. THE MOON: A SALISHAN TALE

Myths that seek to explain cosmic phenomena are among the oldest and most widespread of tales throughout the world, and those about the moon have been particularly popular, especially among North American Indians. Most peoples have explanations for "the man in the moon," and such stories are common among the tribes of the West Coast.

This short tale, which James A. Teit recorded from the Thompson River Indians, incorporates the common motif of a sister who dims the moon's brilliance by sitting on her brother's face, and gives poetic explanations for other moon phenomena.

The Moon

The Moon was formerly an Indian, but was transformed to what he is at present. At one time his face was as bright as that of the Sun, if not more brilliant. It would be just as bright now, but his younger sister sits on it and darkens it. He and his younger sister now live together. Whenever it threatens to snow or to rain, he builds a house (the halo) and enters it. He is an inveterate smoker. The clouds are the smoke of his pipe. If the weather is quite clear and he begins to smoke, clouds arise. He always holds his pipe in his hand. Therefore we always see the Moon holding his pipe, and we also see the basket which he uses as a hat.

4. THE MOSQUITO AND THE THUNDER: A SALISH TALE

While there are various etiological tales about the origin of thunder, this explanation of why thunder strikes the tree-tops instead of people is rare. It is another item that Teit noted from the Thompson River Indians.

The Mosquito and the Thunder

Told by Nkamtci'nEmux

Once the Mosquito paid a visit to the Thunder. The latter, seeing that the Mosquito was gorged with blood, asked him where he obtained it, and told him that he had been wishing to get some for a long time, but did not know where to obtain it. The Mosquito answered, "I got the blood from somewhere." The Thunder was annoyed at this evasive answer, and said, "Why do you answer me thus? Don't you know that I can shoot you and kill you?" The Mosquito, being afraid, then said, "I suck it from the tree-tops."

By this lie the Mosquito saved the people, and that is the reason that the Thunder strikes the tree-tops at the present day. If the Mosquito had told the truth, then the Thunder would now shoot people and animals instead of trees.

II. Animal Tales

IN *The Types of the Folktale* Aarne and Thompson list "Animal Tales" as the first of their four main groups. These consist largely of fables — animal tales told to teach a lesson, which are among the oldest types of folktales, and stories from the animal cycle of Reynard the Fox that circulated throughout the northern countries of Europe in the Middle Ages. Other stories in which animals take on human characteristics were also common, especially those based on the concept of the trickster, a small or weak animal, often the rabbit, who manages to outwit larger animals.

Animal stories have not been very popular in Canada except among the Indians, and most of their animal stories belong with the mythological tales as they feature a culture hero. However, some Canadians do tell fables which they may have learned in school, and others remember animal stories that they brought from their homelands.

5. A WOLF, A FOX, AND A LION: AN ITALIAN TALE

Like many of the ancient fables, this is a tale intended to convey a lesson to the listeners: namely, that those who speak ill of others may suffer themselves. It is not as familiar as many of Aesop's fables: it is known in Italy and Spain but is not common elsewhere. Stith Thompson includes it in his motif collection under the heading of "Tit for Tat." Carla Bianco collected it from Antonio Carofano, a native of Cervinara, Campania, Italy, who emigrated to Canada in 1957 and settled in Toronto.

A Wolf, a Fox, and a Lion

Told by Antonio Carofano

The fox has always been known as a cunning animal. In the forest there lived lions, wolves, and foxes, no? One day the wolf and fox met and the wolf said to the fox: "My dear fox," said he, "do you know that our friend the lion is very ill? He is so ill. Are you going to visit him?" She replied: "When I have time I will also go and visit him." And so the wolf set off and went to the place where the very ill lion was, and the fox followed him to see what he would tell the lion.

The fox listened to the wolf and heard him say: "I met that impudent friend the fox. I told her that you were very ill and that she should come to see you here, to see if you needed anything, but she did not care and pretended as though it was nothing." And so the lion told him: "Well, my beloved friend the wolf, when I feel better again I will make that wretch pay for it!"

The fox heard everything and went off to find a puddle of water and blood. She threw herself in the puddle of water and blood and then went to the lion: "Huff! Huff! Huff!" When her friend the lion saw her he said: "What has happened to you?" "Oh, my dear lion, as soon as our friend the wolf here told me that you were ill I set off in search of a doctor that might procure me the medicine to cure you," said she. "That's why I am dirty like this. I have had to run too much. I have had to walk all the forest, all the woods, all this region."

"What did the doctor say?" "I can't tell you because it's a secret between you and I. When our friend the wolf leaves I will tell you." "Well, my dear wolf," said he, "would you go out for a while for our friend the fox has something to tell me." And the wolf left.

"My dear lion, first things first. Call your fellow lions to keep an eye on him. Have them keep an eye on our friend the wolf so that he does not escape." The lion said: "Why?" "I will tell you." And so the lion called his friends and told them: "Make sure that our friend the wolf does not move from here. Now what is it that you have to tell me?"

The fox said: "I have been to Trivento and there I found a good doctor. He told me that your sickness is harmless. You only need to keep warmer, and he told me that you would need a fresh wolf skin. A fresh wolf skin taken right from his body to put around you."

"Quickly," said the lion, "capture the wolf and take his skin for I need it to put around me. You must cover me with it in order that I might be cured." When the other lions were removing the wolf's skin, the wolf cried: "Ugh!" Meanwhile the fox looked on and said: "Remember to speak less at someone else's house!"

6. THE RACE BETWEEN TURTLE AND FROG: A SALISHAN TALE

While fables are the most familiar animal stories, this is a different kind of tale, in which a slow animal wins a race over a fast one by trickery. It seems almost the antithesis of the fables which teach moral lessons: here we are led to admire trickery rather than virtue.

There are several variations on this theme: in one a crayfish hangs on to a fox's tail and thus outwits him; in another a tortoise beats a hare because the hare stops to sleep; and in this one the turtle outwits the frog by having a series of relatives take places along the race track — the dupe sees them and thinks that each is the trickster outrunning him.

This particular form is more frequently told with humans as the protagonists, a version that is classified in the section on "Jokes and Anecdotes." However, this version, which comes from the Salishan Indians of the West Coast, is related to the various animal forms, and it also incorporates an etiological motif, explaining why the frog has no tail.

The Race Between Turtle and Frog

At one time there was a race proposed between Turtle and Frog. All the people bet that Frog would win. Mud-Turtle asked for three days to let his friends know about the race. The race-course was very uneven — low ground and high ground, rolling meadow. Turtle bet his back against Frog's tail.

On the third day Turtle was given a head start. Frog stood there taking more bets. Finally he started, and ahead in a low place he saw Turtle going out of sight. Each time he looked ahead he saw Turtle going out of sight. He hurried faster and faster, but did not overtake him. Just as he crossed the last low ground he saw Turtle over the line. He had to give up his tail.

It took six turtles to beat him, but he lost the race. Now the pollywogs have to lose their tails before they can become frogs.

7. HOW THE AGOUTI LOST ITS TAIL: A TRINIDAD TALE

"How the Agouti Lost Its Tail" is a good example of the stories that give animals human characteristics. It is also an etiological tale explaining something about the physical features of a particular animal, why certain animals are enemies, and how the dog came to live with man. It might therefore have been classified with legends, but as the main interest is in the interplay among the animals it fits best with the animal tales.

Many similar animal tales came to America by way of Africa. The best known are stories of the Tarbaby type, made famous through the Uncle Remus books, but there are many others in which animals are given human characteristics. Arthur H. Fauset noted a number of these from black informants in Nova Scotia.

Rita Cox, a Toronto librarian and a fine storyteller, came to Canada from Trinidad. She is one of the founders of the Storytellers School of Toronto. As a child she heard many stories from her parents and other relatives, and from different people in her community. She says that this one was particularly well known.

The agouti is a rodent about the size of a rabbit, brownish in colour, which is peculiar to South and Central America and the West Indies. The terms *Compère* and *Macumère* are French, emphasizing the multicultural nature of Trinidad's society and language. Rita says that these words are still common: that her godmother is referred to as her mother's *Macumère*, for example. She also notes that sorrell is a favourite drink made with the petals of the sorrel fruit — a red rosebud type of fruit that recalls the taste of rosehip tea.

How the Agouti Lost Its Tail

Told by Rita Cox

There was a time when all the animals were good friends.

Compère Dog and *Compère* Agouti lived near to each other. Dog was a handsome fellow, and so was Agouti, with his long beautiful bushy tail. They planted a vegetable garden together, sharing the crops. They hunted together and shared the meat. They were very good neighbours.

One day as Agouti was passing near a clearing in the forest, he came upon a crowd of animals talking and laughing. There was great excitement in the air. Agouti was curious. He stopped to greet his friends and heard *Compère* Goat addressing the crowd. "What's going on here?" he asked *Macumère* Cow. "What's all the excitement about?"

"*Compère* Goat is having a picnic next Sunday. We'll be going by boat to Gasparee Island and we're making plans for it," she replied. "I must hurry home and tell *Compère* Dog about this," said Agouti.

"Oh, no!" replied Cow. "You can't come. Only animals with horns are invited." Agouti's face fell. "But we have no horns — and we are your friends. How could he do that to us?" "Sorry, you just can't come," said Cow, moving away haughtily.

Agouti went home, sad and worried. He told Dog about the picnic to which only animals with horns were invited, and they both sat there, feeling very unhappy about being left out. Picnics were such fun and they did enjoy sailing. They talked about it for a long time, but nothing would console them. "Well," sighed Agouti at last, "I suppose we'll have to stay home by ourselves." Dog said nothing, just nodded his head.

Suddenly Agouti had an idea. "Why don't we get some wood and make two pairs of horns, one for you and one for me? We'll fasten them on with glue so they'd stay fixed; then we could go to the picnic." "What a wonderful idea!" Dog said. "Let's go now and find some wood."

It took a long time for them to find pieces of wood that were just right, but at last they did. Then they shaped and smoothed and polished them until they were just right.

Sunday came. They got up early, packed their picnic baskets with all kinds of good things to eat and drink — roasted breadfruit, peas and rice, curried chicken, sorrell, beer, coconut bread. Then they put on their horns and helped each other to fasten them into place.

First Agouti fastened Dog's horns carefully and neatly so that no glue showed and they were just right. Just as he finished they heard the voices of the animals coming from the boats. They were getting ready to cast off. "Hurry, Dog, hurry and get my horns on now, before they leave us behind!" cried Agouti. But Dog didn't even hear. He picked up his basket and ran away as fast as he could, not even looking back to see if Agouti was following.

Poor Agouti was left behind. Try as he could he couldn't fasten his own horns — he needed assistance, and Dog had gone and left him behind. At first he was sad, and then he got angry. Quickly he ran to a hill overlooking the harbour and he could see the boat full of animals just sailing by. Standing proudly on the deck with the other animals was Dog. Agouti ran up to the top of the hill and shouted as loud as he could:

"Examine the horns.
Examine the horns.
Captain Goat, hear me.
One of the animals has no horns."

Dog heard this and tried to distract the captain. He opened his basket. "Have some sorrell, Captain. It will keep you cool in this bright sun . . ."

Agouti ran higher up the hill and shouted even louder:

"Examine the horns.
Examine the horns.
There's a traitor on board
Who has no horns."

"Captain, do you hear that racket the wind is making?" said Dog. "Here, have some coconut bread." But Agouti shouted again, loud and clear:

"Examine the horns.
Examine the horns.
There's a traitor on board
Who has no horns."

This time Captain Goat heard. He stopped the boat and made all the animals stand in line. He tested all their horns — *Compère* Ram's, *Compère* Bull's, *Macumère* Cow's, but before he could reach Dog, Dog had jumped overboard and was swimming for shore. He was furious as he made for the hilltop from where Agouti had called out.

Agouti saw him coming. He ran as fast as he could to reach his hole, but he wasn't fast enough. As he dived into the hole, Dog made a great leap, got hold of Agouti's tail, and bit it off.

That is how the Agouti lost his tail, and from that day to this Agouti and Dog have been enemies. Dog pursues Agouti whenever he catches sight of him. He's still angry because Agouti had made him the laughing stock of the forest. The animals poked so much fun at him that he had to move away and live with man.

III. Supernatural Tales

TO MOST PEOPLE the term folktale suggests the kind of tales that the Germans call *Märchen*, the French *contes populaires*, and the English fairy-tales, even though many of them are not about fairies, and are perhaps better termed wonder tales. Although there are many other types, wonder tales — those that feature magic and the supernatural — continue to be the most familiar. Nearly all of them are old, many having their roots in a pre-Christian era, and their plots are widespread in Europe and Asia. Most of them have certain typical characteristics: repetition by threes, emphasis on trials and quests, supernatural adversaries, the triumph of the youngest son, magic objects and supernatural helpers, marvellous transformations, and happy endings.

The best known fairy or wonder tales — "Cinderella," "Jack the Giant Killer," "Snow White and the Seven Dwarfs," "Beauty and the Beast," "Rumpelstiltskin," "The Sleeping Beauty" — are part of the heritage of most English-speaking children. Similar tales of magic and the supernatural are found in practically every country of the world, and people from other lands have brought a great many of them to Canada. Today they are thought of as stories parents tell their children, but in earlier times they were told by adults to adults, serving much the same purpose in a pre-literate age as books of fantasy and science fiction do today.

Wonder tales usually tell fairly complex stories, although there is normally only a single plot line: subplots are characteristic of literary tales. Certain plots turn up in a wide variety of stories

14

from different countries, as Antti Aarne and Stith Thompson have shown in *The Types of the Folktale*. These form their second and largest section, "Ordinary Folktales," which they subdivide into "Tales of Magic," "Religious Tales," "Nouvelles (Romantic Tales)," and "Tales of the Stupid Ogre." As all of these except the "Romantic Tales" deal with the supernatural, they are grouped together in this section, with the "Romantic Tales" following in the next group. All of them, with the exception of "The Fox Wife," an Inuit tale, came to Canada from other countries.

These plots have a number of motifs: small elements of the story such as a magic wand, a speaking bird, a tabu, a fairy godmother, a test, or a deception, which are classified in Stith Thompson's massive five-volume set, *The Motif-Index of Folk Literature*.

While most people are interested in these stories for their entertainment value, folklorists, psychologists, and sociologists have been analyzing them in various ways. One of the best known discussions is Bruno Bettelheim's *The Uses of Enchantment* which exemplifies the Freudian approach.

8. ONCE UPON A TIME THERE WAS A SHEPHERD: AN ITALIAN TALE

This is a fine example of the tales commonly known as fairy-tales, and unlike many of them it actually includes fairies. It demonstrates beautifully one of the main characteristics of oral narratives: the importance of the number three. There are three fairies, three gifts, three girls in the beauty contest, three animals fighting, three gifts from the animals, three thieves, and three items stolen from the thieves. The story also illustrates many of the common motifs in tales of magic: the inexhaustible purse, the cloak that makes the wearer invisible, the magic table or table-cloth that produces food and drink, the magic boots that cover vast distances, and transformations from human to animal and back again.

"Once Upon a Time There Was a Shepherd" comes from a substantial body of Italian-Canadian folklore that Carla Bianco collected in Toronto in 1968. The narrator, Antonio Carofano, was one of the best storytellers she found. Before telling this, he commented: "The true significance of this tale can be summed up in a few words: A vain man or a vain woman is worthless. You always have to pay for the consequences, and never gain."

Once Upon a Time There Was a Shepherd

Told by Antonio Carofano

Once upon a time there was a boy, a boy that was a shepherd. He was a shepherd and every day he would go to the woods and to the mountain to graze his lambs, his goats, and his sheep. He had very few of them. One day, in the middle of the woods, he found a glade with nice grass, beautiful and cool, and discovered three girls sleeping in the sun there. The boy saw that the girls were beautiful and said to himself: "But you are so beautiful! Why are you sleeping in the sun?" He had brought an axe with him and so he cut the branches from the trees and made a sort of small hut to shade the girls from the sun, and then hid. The first girl awoke and said: "Oh, what beautiful shade! If I knew who had done it I would present him with this purse so that every time he wanted money he would find as much as he wished." The second girl said: "Oh, what beautiful shade! How wonderfully I have slept! If I knew who had done it I would present him with this table-cloth so that every time he felt like eating he would find whatever he wished on top." The third girl awoke and said: "Oh, what beautiful shade!" (She was the most beautiful of the three.) "What beautiful shade! What a beautiful dream I have had! If I knew who had done it I would present him with this ring. Every time that he touched the ring I would appear at his side and he would become my master and do with me as he wished." The boy finally said: "I did it." And so the girls gave him the purse, the table-cloth, and the ring. Then the three girls disappeared.

[Were they fairies?]

They disappeared. They disappeared because they were fairies. And so the boy went on his way with his flock and arrived under a beech tree in the shade. He sat down and said: "I would really like to see if what they told me is true." He took the purse and said: "One hundred coins." And one hundred coins in the purse he found! One hundred coins! And he put them in his pocket. He took the table-cloth and put it on the grass and said: "Now I would like a nice plate of spaghetti, a flask of wine, a cutlet, and some fruit." He ate the food and found it to be very tasty. He drank the wine and soon began to feel stimulated, more than before, as he was a young lad. And so he touched the ring and the girl appeared. He kissed her and then they made love. Of course you can very well imagine what happens between a man and a woman. Then the girl disappeared.

The girl left and he went back to his village. He had already accumulated one hundred coins in his purse. He had the table-cloth and so he began to lead the life of a lord. At night he would touch the ring and the girl would reappear. The girl would reappear and she would voluntarily make love to him. One day she said to him: "Do not take advantage of your wife's beauty because if you take advantage of me and look at other women you will lose me. You will not only lose me, but you will also lose the other things that my sisters have given you." The three were sisters. This went on day after day until he finally forced her to live with him.

And so the people could see a castle outside of the village. She had built a luxurious castle but no one ever saw her. Her husband began to act like a lord and associated with lawyers and doctors. He knew how to play cards, and whether he lost or won was of no consequence as his purse provided him with as much money as he wanted. Therefore, he began to become vain. He started talking about women and noted that one man had a beautiful woman, the other had a lover, and so on and so on. In the end, he was asked to judge a sort of beauty contest. He went home and his wife already knew about it and said: "You have done wrong. I warned you." He said: "No. You must come. You must come to the piazza. You must come down to the piazza." And so he convinced her to go down to the piazza. The first girl that passed by was beautiful. She was the wife of one of the others there. They had a jury just like a beauty contest. Another girl passed by, and she too was beautiful. When one particular girl arrived and passed through the piazza her beauty blinded everyone, and he won the wager with his friends. He won the wager with his friends, and his wife returned home while he remained to play cards with his friends and lost everything. He returned home and went to bed.

In the morning, when he awoke, he found himself on top of a pile of straw. The house had disappeared. He no longer had the purse, or the table-cloth, or the ring. He was poorer than before. And so he said: "I will not stop looking for her until I find her again." And he started roaming the mountains and valleys, mountains and valleys, deserts, walking and searching.

One fine day, while walking in the middle of a glade in the woods, he met three animals. There was the carcass of a dead animal and three animals fighting with one another. They were fighting because they had to divide the dead animal amongst themselves in order to eat it. There was a lion, an ant, and an eagle. The shepherd approached them and said: "Do not fight. I can satisfy the three of you."

When the three animals saw how the creature had been

divided the ant was quite content because she had received meat. The eagle was also happy because she received the intestines and the liver, which was her preferred meat; and the lion was the happiest of the three because he received all the flesh and all the bones. And so as a token of her appreciation the ant said: "Since you have been so honest with us, I give you this small leg. Take care of it and when you find that you are in difficulty, as soon as you touch it, you will be transformed from a man to an ant." The lion took a tuft of hair and said: "And I, as a token of my appreciation, give you this tuft of hair so that when you find yourself in difficulty in the middle of the woods and are confronted by animals, guide this tuft and you will become king of the lions and everyone will respect you." The eagle took a small feather and gave it to him. She said: "Whenever you wish to travel from one mount to the other, because there are many ravines, touch this feather and you will become an eagle and will be able to conquer lakes and valleys."

He took these three things and set off again, but he was always thinking of being able to meet his wife, whose real name was the Fairy Rubina. He walked, walked, walked, walked, walked, and walked, and after three, four, five, six months of walking he met three men wandering about. They were three thieves. One of the three thieves had stolen a pair of boots that, when worn, would enable a person to travel as many leagues as he wished. The other had stolen a cloak that, when worn, would render the person invisible. And the other had a napkin that, when placed on the ground, would give him whatever he wished to eat.

The shepherd approached them and said: "Why are you fighting?" The three thieves were not in agreement with one another because they could not decide on who would take the napkin, the boots, or the cloak. And so the shepherd said: "Would you like me to distribute these things? You should all be quite satisfied. Decide." They said: "All right." "Let's see how we can handle this matter," said the shepherd. And so he put the napkin on the ground and said: "Well, I would like a nice bowl of soup, with a small piece of bread." And so there appeared a bowl of soup and a small piece of bread. "Good! This works." He put the boots on and said: "Ten paces." And the boots took ten paces, far away from the others, and then returned. He said: "These also work very well!" But he never took them off. He said: "The cloak." And he put on the cloak and said: "Now you see me, now you don't." He took a pace one hundred miles long and disappeared. He disappeared and took the napkin, the boots, and the cloak with him.

And so he began to cross the world from North to South, East and West, in search of the famous castle of the Fairy Rubina, his wife, with the magic boots. One day he saw a small mountain over the horizon. This mountain was [covered with] a forest, like a virgin forest. And so with his famous boots and the eagle's feather he flew over towards the light in the forest. He went towards the light, but it was still nightfall, and [he] saw an old woman. He saw the old woman and decided to go to her for information; to ask her if she knew where the famous Fairy Rubina lived. He approached her and asked: "Dear grandmother, dear mother, dear lady, could you tell me where the Fairy Rubina lives?" "My son, what can I say? Only my children would be able to tell you. I am the mother of seven winds. Only they who run about all the continents might be able to tell you. But it's too dangerous, because if they find out that you are here, they will eat you." "Yes, but if you want, dear lady, you can convince them not to touch me. You can defend me, no? I would only like some information." She said: "All right, then. Come here." And she hid him. The old woman hid him.

The first son arrived and had a craving. As he arrived he said: "Oh, what a smell of human flesh, what a smell of human flesh!" The mother had prepared a bucket of food and said: "Eat. You must have brought the smell from whence you came. There is no one here except me." And so the wind believed her and started to eat what was in the bucket, and then went to the chimney to find a place to sit. The second arrived, making so much noise that it seemed as though he would never cease. The third arrived and it was even worse — the fourth arrived, worse still. The fifth arrived, worse still. The sixth arrived, worse still. The last to arrive was the "Tramontana" (the North wind), the earth wind as we say in our dialect. This wind tears trees, plants from their roots, everything. When he arrived it seemed like a tempest. He said: "Oh, what a smell of human flesh!" His mother could in no way convince him. He did not want to leave. She finally made him eat and after he was satiated, he sat around the chimney where the other six brothers were and he [was] the seventh.

["Do you remember the names of the other six winds?"]

One was called "Bornia," the other was "Tramontana," and the other was "Stocco." The seven winds, you know.

And so after they had all eaten, the mother sat with them.

Each one started to tell a story. One said: "I have been to a certain village and I dried out everything. I dried out all the farm lands. I would say that they have very little to eat this year." Another said: "I was on the beach and all the boats that were anchored there were untied and many of them sank." Another said: "I have been to the woods and tore down all the branches and the trees there and all the birds fell down." The last to speak was the earth wind, the most terrible of them all. He said: "I have been to the end of the world where the Fairy Rubina lives. I turned the castle upside-down. There is no roof or chimney left. There is no longer any roof or bricks left. I crushed everything." And so the mother said: "Well, I have something to say, also." One of them said: "What is it that you have to say?" She replied: "You know, here there is — " "Ah, ha! I told you that someone was here!" "Well, if you interrupt me I won't tell you what it's all about," replied the mother. She convinced her sons to keep quiet and said: "Well, there is a young man here who is looking for the castle of the Fairy Rubina. He has been wandering about the world for five or six years." And so the earth wind said: "I've told you that I have been there. If you want, I can accompany him there." But he was thinking to himself that he would not eat him tonight but rather tomorrow morning. He said to himself: "When I accompany him along the road, I will eat him."

And so they decided that very early the following morning they would set off together, the boy and the earth wind, to go to the end of the world where the castle of the Fairy Rubina was. The mother of the winds called the boy and advised him on what he was supposed to do. She said: "Look, you take this with you," and she gave him a supply of meat and water. She said: "As you are walking along and hear cries of 'water,' you throw meat in his mouth. If he cries 'meat,' you throw water." And so they left from the summit of the mountain, a very high summit, and he had his boots with him in order to travel as he wished. When the wind cried "Water," he gave him meat. When the wind cried "Meat," he gave him water. They arrived at a certain point and the supply of meat and water had run out. The supply of meat and water had run out and so he remembered about the napkin. He remembered about the napkin and asked it for meat and water. When they were finally about to reach the castle the earth wind was so full of water and meat that he left the boy on his own.

The shepherd could see the castle on a peak at the end of the world. When he saw where it was situated he began to think of how he was going to get in. When he arrived, he found that the castle was barred like a tower. It resembled a fortress. And so he touched the feather and became an eagle. He became an eagle and flew over the roof of the castle. Once on the roof, he began to think once more of how he would get in. And so the eagle transformed itself into a man again. He touched the leg of the ant and he became an ant. In this way, he was able to go into the castle through a small opening. Having entered into the castle, the ant transformed itself into a man. He became a man again and put on the cloak, the cloak that made him invisible. He started wandering about the rooms looking for the Fairy Rubina, and finally found her. At night, as she was going to bed, he transformed himself into an ant and crawled into her bed. Thinking that it was some sort of flea, she changed beds. She changed to still another bed and then changed rooms. She finally realized who the ant was and said: "For the great pains you have taken and all the sufferings you have endured during these six years in order that you might find me, I forgive you. You can come out now." He came out and they lived happily ever after in the castle at the end of the world.

9. THE TALKING NIGHTINGALE: A SEPHARDIC TALE

Like the previous narrative, "The Talking Nightingale" is typical of the stories we term fairy-tales, featuring a talking bird, a witch, a magic ring, and a happy ending that punishes the villains and rewards the virtuous. It is an international tale known as "The Three Golden Sons," and is quite popular among French Canadians. Laval University has more than thirty versions in its archives.

"The Talking Nightingale" is one of eighty folktales, legends, and anecdotes that André E. Elbaz published as *Folktales of the Canadian Sephardim*. These are part of a larger collection that he made for the National Museum of Man in 1976. The stories, told by Moroccan Jewish immigrants in Toronto and Montreal, stem from the rich heritage of the Sephardim: the Jews of Spain and Portugal whose culture reached its peak in the twelfth and thirteenth centuries and then was carried to Africa and other countries when the Jews were expelled from Spain in 1492. The term Sephardim is now used for all Jews living around the Mediterranean. Their culture differs considerably from that of the Ashkenazim, the Jews of Central and Eastern Europe, whose lore has survived mainly in Yiddish. The Sephardic stories were told in three languages: Judeo-Arabic, French, and Judeo-Spanish.

This tale came from Jacques Cohen, a forty-year-old business representative living in Montreal who had immigrated to

Canada in 1972. He told it in a combination of French and Judeo-Arabic. Professor Elbaz, who translated it into English, was born in Morocco, studied in France, and now teaches French and Comparative Literature at Carleton University, Ottawa.

The Talking Nightingale

Told by Jacques Cohen

Once upon a time there was a Sultan who had ten wives, and lived peacefully in his palace, reigning over his people who loved him greatly. But this Sultan was very unhappy because his wives were all barren and none of them had given him a child. Above all, he wanted a son, so that he might have an heir. He had married his ten wives, one after another, for this purpose but none of them had as yet brought him this happiness. The wives would often pray and weep on the tombs of *marabout* saints,[1] but they remained childless, and the Sultan was in despair.

One day, the Sultan decided to consult a famous sorcerer who lived in a cave in the desert. After accepting a number of handsome gifts, the sorcerer traced certain lines in the sand with his finger.[2] Then he told the Sultan what he should do.

"*Ya Sidna*,[3] this is what you must do to have a son. You will go unescorted, very early in the morning, to the sacred spring which flows near the tomb of the holy *marabout*, and you will ask the hand of the first woman who comes to fill her jug at the spring."

The very next morning, the Sultan followed the sorcerer's advice and went to the designated spring. There came a very beautiful girl who immediately pleased him. He sent for her parents who were very happy to learn of the Sultan's choice. Great celebrations were organized at the palace for the Sultan's wedding with his eleventh wife. The people were not forgotten; alms were distributed to all the beggars in the town.

Shortly after, the young bride became pregnant, and the Sultan's joy knew no bounds. But the ten other wives in the harem became extremely jealous, and decided to avenge themselves on this intruder who had stolen their place in the Sultan's

---

1. *Marabout*: Moslem ascetic, who spends his life in contemplation and study of the Koran. The word *marabout* sometimes refers to the ascetic's tomb. The cult of *marabout* tombs is very common in Morocco.

2. Magical practice, which enables a sorcerer to pronounce an oracle, in Morocco.

3. *Ya Sidna*: O, Our Lord! (Arabic).

heart. During the confinement, the neglected women pretended to be caring for the young mother but, without her knowledge, they substituted a little dog for the new-born baby boy. When the mother regained consciousness and asked to see her baby, her cruel sisters presented her with the little dog. The unfortunate mother broke into sobs and tore her hair in despair.

The Sultan was aghast when he learned that his wife had given birth to a monster. He fell into a great depression and decided to send away the poor woman of whom the whole harem was now making fun. The first ten wives were triumphant, and entrusted the baby to a servant with orders to kill it. However, the servant took pity on the child and, instead of killing it, abandoned it in a cave in the mountains, confident that some wild animal would carry out his sinister task.

Now, near the cave, a shepherd was minding his flock of goats. That day, a goat by chance entered the cave and found the baby lying on the ground. To dry its tears she suckled it, and the hungry child was able to feed. The goat came back the next day, then every day for the following week, so the baby had enough to eat. One day, the goat attracted the shepherd's attention and drew him into the cave where, to his great surprise, he found a plump and smiling baby. He immediately took it home to his cottage, and decided to adopt it and bring it up as his son. He called it Mess'ud so that it might bring him happiness.[4]

Mess'ud became a big boy, then a fine intelligent young man, for the shepherd gave him an excellent education. When he came of age, his adoptive father wanted to marry him, as was the custom, to the daughter of a *sherif* of the town.[5] But the Sultan's wives heard about this marriage and discovered Mess'ud's existence. Out of spite, they wanted to prevent the proposed marriage, and succeeded in convincing Mess'ud that his future happiness depended on three conditions that he must fulfil if he wanted to marry the girl he loved.

Very much in love, Mess'ud accepted all the conditions stipulated by the Sultan's wives: "You must first of all build, with your own hands, a fine and fully-furnished house, to accommodate your future family." Mess'ud immediately set to work, and very skilfully built a fine house at the foot of the mountain.

"You must now surround your house with a large garden fit

---

4. *Mess'ud*: literally, of good omen (Arabic).

5. *Sherif*: title of nobility (Arabic) given to the descendants of the Prophet Mohammed.

for your future wife. This garden must contain all the species of trees and all the species of flowers that grow on earth,'' commanded the old women. Mess'ud worked day and night to collect all these plants, and he surrounded his house with the finest garden in the world.

Finally, Mess'ud was ready to face the third and last task imposed on him by the Sultan's wives: "You must now go in search of a talking nightingale and, when you find it, you must bring it back and put it in your garden so that your wife may hear its songs and words, for nothing is too fine for her. But be warned. Several young men have tried before you to catch this marvellous bird, but none has succeeded. All have perished, for the bird lives in a far-off country and the road is strewn with obstacles. There is still time to change your mind and abandon your marriage plans."

Mess'ud paid no attention. On the very next day he mounted his horse, took provisions with him, and left in search of the nightingale. After crossing several unknown countries, Mess'ud reached a great forest where he was stopped by a witch. When he asked for her help in finding the nightingale, she laughed at him, reminding him that men much braver and more important than a shepherd's son had already tried, but that they had all failed. To discourage him, she showed him the severed heads of his wretched predecessors, but to no avail.

Mess'ud continued on his way until he was once again stopped. Another witch tried to keep him prisoner in her cottage, but Mess'ud succeeded in escaping and galloped away.

His attention was soon attracted by loud cries that came from a clearing in the forest. He turned his horse in the direction of the screams, which sounded nearer and nearer. He very soon found the reason. A lion had knocked an old woman to the ground, had already torn her with his claws, and was just about to devour her when it fell, struck down by Mess'ud's arrow. With the help of the young man, the old woman got up painfully, and thanked him in these words: "Generous Mess'ud, you have just saved my life. Know that I too am a witch, and that I was getting ready to bar your way and kill you to stop you reaching your goal. But to show my gratitude I shall spare your life, and even help you in your search. The nightingale that speaks lives near here, but it is guarded by a fierce ogre who has devoured all who have tried to catch it. You must therefore first of all get rid of this ogre. I will give you this magic ring which will protect you and enable you to kill him."

Thanks to the advice of the last witch, Mess'ud was able to

kill the ogre and take possession of the nightingale. He brought it back to his garden where it charmed all visitors by its songs and wonderful tales. The Sultan was soon informed by his servants of the existence of this extraordinary bird that had been brought back from a far-off land by a shepherd's son. He too wanted to see and hear the marvel.

When the Sultan asked the nightingale to tell him a story, it gave him a detailed account of Mess'ud's adventures since his birth in the royal palace and his kidnapping by the Sultan's wives who had been jealous of his mother. The Sultan was filled with joy when he learned that Mess'ud was the son he had always wanted. He immediately named him his heir. Mess'ud's marriage to the *sherif*'s daughter was held in the palace amid great rejoicings to which the people were invited. The Sultan magnificently rewarded the shepherd who had brought up his son so wisely and generously. He also brought back Mess'ud's mother, begging her to pardon his injustice. The Sultana forgave him for everything, so happy was she to find her beloved husband once more, and a son who made her forget all her years of suffering.

As for the unworthy wives of the harem, the cause of all these ills, they received the punishment they deserved. According to custom, the Sultan had them tied to the tails of several camels, and they were torn apart. It was thus that the nightingale re-established truth and justice in the kingdom.

10. THE WHITE BEAR: A FRENCH TALE

This old French tale has some variations on the common motifs found in the wonder tales. The cruel stepmother is a familiar figure in a number of stories, but the cruel mother is less common. However, in a time when reports of battered children are in the news almost every day, it is not too hard to believe that a woman might find her children a nuisance and want to get rid of them. The motif of children saved from death by a servant or a good-hearted shepherd occurs in many tales, but here the saviour is a white bear. However, the motif of talking birds or animals who save their owners at a critical moment conforms to the usual pattern.

Angela Kerfont, a French Canadian living in the Newfoundland outport of St. George, told this old French tale and several others to Marie-Annick Desplanques during the winter of 1983. Mrs. Kerfont, now over eighty years old, is a famous storyteller in her community, although she belongs to the private rather than the public tradition of storytelling, relating her tales mainly to members of her family.

Although Mrs. Kerfont learned the stories in French, she told them in English, and Marie-Annick Desplanques, who was studying English-French bilingualism in Newfoundland, notes that in her editing she has attempted "to preserve the specific style of Mrs. Kerfont's delivery as far as language is concerned. Her French origins are not to be denied and the reader will notice them through several patterns and sentence forms that seem to derive from literal translation from French into English." Another point of interest is the colloquial language of much of the tale: for example, "My mistress told me to drown her kids," and "Well, king, that's the most beautiful castle I've never seen." ("I've never seen" is one of the literal translations from the French.)

The White Bear

Told by Angela Kerfont

One time there was a king and a queen. They had no children, but the queen was pregnant. On her last month, the king went to another town. While he was gone she gave birth to twins, a boy and a girl. But soon she had enough with the children, and she said to the servant, "I'm tired with them kids. I'm putting them into a basket, and you will go and drown them!" So she washed them, dressed them to go to sleep, and she put them into a basket. She gave the basket to the servant who took off for the river.

When she arrived by the river, she sat down and talked to them. They were asleep and so pretty. "What a mountain sin that I have to throw you in that water!" she said. By and by, she saw a big white bear coming. "What are you doing here?" he asked. "Well," she said, "my mistress told me to drown her kids, and I find it sin, they are so pretty!" She was crying. "Calm down, and give them to me!" He put the basket in his mouth and he took off for his place. He reared them to a big girl and a big boy, and they grew up prettier than they were.

Meanwhile, the king had come back from town and he asked his queen, "Where is your baby?" "Don't ask me!" she said. "I had a dog and a bitch, I drowned them!" He believed her.

A long time passed and the twins had grown up. One day the white bear told them, "You're old enough to go by yourself now. I am going to build you a little castle outside the road, and you will have everything you want!" The white bear built them the most beautiful castle they had never seen.

One evening the king's servant boy was going down that way. He passed by the castle. He said to himself, "That's funny. This castle was never there before!" He came back home and told that to the king. "I saw something today I never saw before!" "What is it?" the king asked. "Well, it's a castle on the lower side of the road that was not there before. No, there was nothing there before!"

The next morning he went back the same way again and when he came home he told the king, "Well, king, that's the most beautiful castle I've never seen. It hurts your eyes!" The queen was stunned. She said, "I'm gonna go and see what kind of castle is that. That's your eyes that are doing that!" "No, it's not my eyes," he said.

The queen knew what was going on. So she went down to see. The girl saw the queen passing by and she said to her brother, "My! The queen is coming here!" She was right. The queen came and visited them. She spent the whole day with them, chatting and everything. Anyway, before she left, she told them how beautiful their castle was. "You have a nice castle there, and if you had a blue bird in a golden cage, it would be ten times prettier!" So the boy said, "I'm gonna go to look for a blue bird in a golden cage, and if I am not here in a year and a day, well, I am lost."

He took off. She waited for him. A year and a day had passed and she said to herself, "I've got to go and find my white bear!" So she went and she told the white bear, "My brother's gone for a year and a day and he is not back yet. He must be lost!" The white bear asked, "Where has he gone?" "Well, he's gone to get the blue bird in a golden cage." "Well," said the white bear, "it's not him who is going to get that. It's only you." The white bear went to get a big mirror and gave it to the girl. "When you're gonna get down there, the door's gonna be open about ten inches wide. You will turn the glass back to your face and you'll walk right in," he said. "The little bird is going to open the door and will say 'I am yours.' Then you will go upstairs, you will find a big bottle of water, and drop some of it on every lump you will see!"

So the little girl took off. She walked through the woods, and she arrived at the castle; the door was open, she turned the glass back to her face and walked right in. She saw the bird who said, "I am yours." She went upstairs, took the bottle of water, and dropped some of it on every little spot she could see. All kinds of people jumped off the ground: kings, queens, princes, princesses, my God! She had one drop left and her brother was not there yet! Well, she dropped it — and there he was! "Where were you?" she said. "Well, it's not my fault," he said. "Now come on home!" They took the blue bird in a golden cage and went home.

Anyway, one morning the king's servant boy went down this way again. He was about to pass by their castle but he couldn't. It was ten times prettier. Then he turned back to the king's. "King!" he said. "There's something there. It's too pretty, I can't pass it. When the sun strikes on to it, it's a lot prettier than yours!" "I want to go and see that castle!" said the king. He took his horse and gig and went for the castle.

When he arrived the girl saw him through the window and she told her brother, "Look! The king is coming here." He came in and she gave him some dinner. He had never eaten so well in his whole life! They spent the whole day chatting about everything. Now, by the time he was to go home, he said, "Well, I had dinner with you, now you have to come and have supper with me." "Well," said the boy, "we'd better go." "I'm not going if I don't take my cage and my bird," she said. "Sure, take your cage and your bird with you, I don't mind that," said the king. Anyways, they arrived at the king's, they put the bird on the wall, and the king said, "Let's go down to the garden and see my flowers."

Meanwhile, the queen was preparing supper, and when supper was ready she raised the table. She put poison on the twins' plates. She knew they were her children and she wanted to get rid of them. "Supper's ready!" she said. They came back from the garden and sat down, the twins on one side and the king on the other. So they started to eat, they took a spoonful and were going to put it in their mouths when the blue bird in a golden cage said, "Mistress and master, don't eat what's in your plate, it's poisoned!" The king said, "What?" And they were going to eat another spoonful when the blue bird in a golden cage said, "Mistress and master, don't eat what's in your plate because it's poisoned!" "Oh!" The king jumped up, grabbed his wife to cut off her head. He killed her right there! Then he stayed with his girl and his boy. And if they're not dead, they're living yet.

11. THE MAGIC CHEST: A UKRAINIAN TALE
This Ukrainian story illustrates several more aspects common to wonder tales. The triumph of the poorer, weaker, or younger hero over the richer, stronger, or older rival is a very common theme that shows the folk's desire to redress the unfair balance

in worldly affairs. The downfall of the rich man through greed
lends a moral note, and the magic box with its commands adds
a supernatural element.

This tale is one of many that Robert B. Klymasz collected as
part of the work for his doctoral dissertation, and later published
in *Folk Narrative Among Ukrainian-Canadians in Western
Canada*. He has also published two collections of Ukrainian-
Canadian songs, and is currently the Slavic curator for the Centre
for Folk Culture Studies, National Museum of Man, Ottawa.

Although tales of rich and poor men in which the poor man
triumphs are common in folklore, the two are not usually brothers.
However, Mr. Klymasz notes that there are several similar stories of poor and rich brothers in the Ukraine.

The Magic Chest

There were two brothers, one was a wealthy man but the other
was poor. That poor one came to the wealthy man, to his brother,
and says, "Brother, you have much grain to thresh. Let me do it,
let me earn at least a sack of flour. Easter Sunday is coming soon
and my wife has not money to buy enough flour to even bake a
paska [Easter loaf] for the food-blessing ceremony at church,
and there's just no place that I can turn for help." So then the
brother led him to the barn and gave him a flail. And so the other
threshes and threshes, but finally he says, "Brother, give me the
flour! Let me take it to my wife (for it was Easter Saturday)! Let
the wife bake a *paska* for tomorrow 'cause it has to be blessed."

But he says, "O, so you want me to give you flour, but what
makes you think that you've earned it? You have to work for a
few days to earn it." And he took and sent him home without the
flour, saying, "I didn't make any agreement with you about
flour!" And that poor one went home weeping. And he comes to
his wife and tells her this and that happened, that "I worked
hard," and so forth.

And she advised him, saying, "You know what, my husband,
we'll manage somehow. Go into the forest and cut down a linden
(that's a kind of tree that's called a linden) and cut out a *paska*.
The wood's smooth and yellowish, so make a *paska* out of that
and we'll go and have it blessed. Whatever comes out we'll have
it blessed, as long as it looks like a *paska*."

He went to the forest, cut himself down a tree, and carved it
out nicely, just like the designs that there are on real *paskas*. She
smeared it nicely, just like they used to with egg in order to have
it nice and yellow. And it was as smooth as anything. On Easter
Sunday they got up and took that wooden *paska* to have it

blessed. And there everyone had placed their *paskas* around the church and he put his wooden *paska* there, too. But that rich one, his brother, couldn't go himself to look at what he had, for he knew that he didn't have flour, that he didn't have a *paska* and won't have one. He was so envious, and he says to his boy, "Go and walk among the people, see if your uncle's there and what he has to bless. I know that I didn't give him any flour — what's he going to have blessed?"

And so the boy went around and found his uncle there standing by his *paska*, such a nice, smooth *paska* — no one had such a *paska*! The boy returned and tells about it. "Father," he says, "by uncle there was such a beautiful *paska* that I've never seen such a *paska* before! And I was walking around, looking at the kinds of *paskas* which all the people have, and there isn't one as nice as his. So nice and so smooth, nowhere was it split, nothing, nor was it scorched (for sometimes when it's baking it will become scorched) — and [it was] so delicate, just like an ornamented Easter Egg."

But now the priest finished consecrating everything and the *paskas*. Unable to endure it any longer, the wealthy brother came up to him and says, "You know what, brother," he says. "You have a fine looking *paska*," he says. "Come over to my place for the feast and sell me your *paska*. I'll pay you for it."

And that one says, "But I, this here . . ."

But that one asks, "Where did you get such a nice *paska*? Well, forget it. You sell me that *paska* and I'll pay you, and I'll invite you over for dinner after the mass, after it's all over." Then he gave him something, five or six gold coins for the *paska*. And the rich man rode off with the *paska* home, leaving the poor one behind — by the time he got home on foot!

And he waits, thinking that perhaps the rich one will invite him over for dinner, as he said he would. But he actually fooled him. And it happened that the poor one went among the people and the people got together on his behalf and brought him [some food] after the blessing of the food ceremony was over. And he, along with his wife and children, had enough to eat. But the rich one comes and says to him, "Why aren't you coming over to my place for the feast?" And he says, "You said that you'll send a boy to get me! You said that you'll call me over. I can't go just like that."

And that poor fellow bought some things for that money and spent it all on the household and on food for the children. And what's there to a couple of gold coins? It all went. And again the poor one has nothing to eat. And so he was walking by the water—there was a kind of river passing by there — and he wept.

But a crab comes out of the water and says, "Why are you weeping, my man?"

And he began to tell him about how he was threshing for his brother and how his brother didn't want to pay him and didn't give him any grain. "And Easter Sunday came and the wife didn't have anything with which to bake a *paska*, and I made myself a wooden *paska*. And that brother bought that *paska* from me, gave me something like a couple of gold coins, and all that went. And now again there's nothing. And again I'm poor, and so I'm weeping."

And that one says, "Don't weep. I'll bring you something that will make you satisfied." The crab went into the deep and brings him out a nice little chest and says, "Take this chest, my man, go home and say, 'Little chest, open!' And it will open for you and there you will have everything. And then say, 'Little chest, close!' And it will close for you."

And so he brought the chest home. The children, the wife, gathered about, asking, "What is that?"

And he says, "Wait. I myself don't know what's here." And he says, "Little chest, open!" And the chest opened up and there's all kinds of good, fine clothes for the children, all kinds of things for them. And there was more and more in that chest, all kinds of things. And they all rejoiced.

And then after the children had eaten their fill, they went outside and played. But the children of that wealthy one came to play with those poor ones. [They were told:] "Go and see what those children are doing." And they were playing outside, so well dressed that people were asking "Why are you so raucous, so joyful?"

And they say, "Our father brought home such a fine chest! When it opened up there was food, all kinds of things, clothing. They dressed us and we ate our fill. And that little chest closed and there's still much more inside!"

Those other children come home and tell their father about it, that rich man. "Such and such a thing happened . . ." Impatient, he himself went over.

"Glory to God!"

"Glory for ever!"

"What's new, my brother?"

"Oh, everything's fine, thanks be to God!"

"And how are you making out?"

"Well, fine."

"I heard—my children were off with yours and were saying that you got some kind of little chest from somewhere, that there's everything in it, food and clothes."

"So it is."

"Where did you get it from?"

"God gave it."

And then that one says to him, "You know what, I'll give you five hundred gold coins for that little chest. Give it to me, sell it to me!"

That poor one thought it over and went and sold it to him. And the other one brings it home. There was everything and the rich one took everything for himself. There was food and clothing. But it all came to an end.

Meanwhile, the poor one used those five hundred gold coins to buy something there, a cow and a piece of land, some things like clothes for the children and things like that. And it all went. And again he went to that place and again he weeps there where the crab had emerged. And the crab comes out and asks, "Why are you weeping, my man?"

And he says, "Such and such a thing happened. You brought me out a little box, and the children found out about it while my children were playing with my brother's children. And those children told that such and such a thing happened, that I have such and such a little box. My brother came over and gave me five hundred gold coins and bought it off me. I sold it and that money's gone. And again I'm poor."

The other says, "Wait, I'll bring you another little chest, but there won't be any more." And that crab went into the water and brought another little chest.

The other says, "How should the chest be opened?"

"Just say, 'Out of the drum, boys!' And to close it: as soon as you whistle it'll close."

And he brought the chest home and says, "Out of the drum, boys!" And out of that little box there jumped out Cossacks, something like little devils, kinds of Cossacks with whips and lashes. They beat that young poor one. The man's wife and children—they all ran out, so thoroughly did they beat him up! But he recalled that he was to whistle. So he managed to whistle somehow and that box closed up. Now things were calm. And he began to think, "I'll sell it to my brother for he is very much tempted by such things." And somewhere his rich brother learned about this, and he came to him.

"Well, brother, how are things going with you?"

And he says, "Fine, thanks be to God. I again bought such a little chest, and again I have enough of everything since I've gotten the little chest."

And he says, "Would you sell it to me?"

"And why not? I'll sell it, for I need money, anyhow."

"Well, how much do you want for that little chest?"

And he says, "This one now is more expensive. If you give me a thousand gold coins, I'll sell, and if not then I'll keep it for myself. There's everything here that's necessary, even more than the other one. There are all kinds of garments, costly rings — there are such valuable things that you'd never estimate the value it has."

And that one became very enticed, that rich man. "Well, I'll give you already those thousand gold coins, give it here to me!" He counted out a thousand gold coins and the other one took that money.

And he brought the little box home and put it on the table and says, "Out of the drum, boys!" O, Lord God! Those Cossacks jumped out of that little box! And they begin to beat that rich one up, and they were beating and beating those children, they were lashing away with the whips! And that wealthy man went to the hospital. The children ran out onto the yard, and not a single one was able to stop that little box! And so those children of the rich man escaped into the yard and to the uncle, to that poor one, saying, "Come to our house, for some kind of Cossacks are jumping out of that little box and they're beating up our father terribly! They've already cut him down so with the whips that I don't know if they'll probably kill him, cut him up completely! It's luck that we escaped, but they're still beating up father there!"

And that poor one was sitting barefooted in the house. "Well, wait a minute, let me put my shoes on!" But he was whiling away the time so that they would give that rich brother a good thrashing.

"Oh, for God's sake, come along, for we'll not find father there alive!"

And so he had hardly managed to put something on his feet and went. He came and looks — and he was indeed slashed up, bloodied, barely breathing, and he whistled and that box closed up. And the brother was completely unable to talk. The rich man lay in bed for several days, and that poor one went on along home. The other one sends his wife and says, "Please go, wife, and call that brother of mine over, for I'm thinking that I'm going to die, for I am so wounded that I even don't have any strength now." And so she called him over. The brother came with his wife and he talked to him a little. The other one began to complain about the fact that he had sold him the Cossacks who had attacked him so.

And that one says, "That's right, brother, you earned that for yourself. For I worked hard for you. I threshed for a whole day and you didn't want to give me enough flour for even a *paska*. And I myself made a *paska* for myself and you paid me for it. But I didn't gain too much from that. And then I brought that little box, and you found out that I have that box with all kinds of food and clothing and you bought that from me. And that came to an end. And then, finally, I didn't have anything, the money went; and I went again to the water and began to weep by that river. And that crab came out of the water a second time and asks what I want. And I told him that again everything of mine had gone and that I was again poor as I was. And he gave me that little box, the same one that you have, that you bought. And those little Cossacks beat me up for nothing, just on account of you. And I sold you the little box so that they would beat you up because you cheated me."

The whole matter came to an end and he died. That rich man died, and that's the end of the story.

12. THE BLACKSMITH AND BEELZEBUB'S IMPS: A GERMAN TALE

This is one of the many stories about men who sell their souls to the Devil. It belongs under an international tale type, "The Blacksmith Outwits the Devil," although it has some interesting differences. While the other versions include the devices of the seat and the tree that have power to trap a person, the motif of the nails in the shoeing-box is not usual. The appearance of both the Devil and Beelzebub, the Prince of Devils, is also unusual: normally Beelzebub is considered another name for the Devil. Beelzebub sending his imps to collect the man's soul is another variation from the pattern: His Satanic Majesty usually likes to perform that function himself.

W. J. Wintemberg collected this tale in Ontario's Waterloo County, which was settled originally by Pennsylvania German Mennonites. As the opening of the story indicates, this was transplanted to North America from Alsace, which in the nineteenth century was part of Germany. Versions have been found in practically every country of Europe and throughout North and South America.

Wintemberg, who was born in Waterloo County in 1873, was an archaeologist by profession, but he took a great interest in the folklore of his native region, studying and writing about the folk traditions of his cultural group, the German Mennonites. He also collected more generally in other Ontario counties and published several regional collections in *The Journal of American Folklore*.

The Blacksmith and Beelzebub's Imps

Once upon a time there lived in a certain town in Alsace a blacksmith who had sold himself to the Devil. This Devil gave him the power to hold the person who picked nails out of his shoeing-box, sat in a certain chair in his house, or ascended a high pear tree in his garden. Wishing to obtain some more money the blacksmith again sold himself, but this time to Beelzebub, the Prince of Devils, who was supposed to be fabulously rich. The blacksmith was to get several thousands of dollars, Beelzebub having the right to claim him, body and soul, at the end of twenty years.

When this time had expired, Beelzebub sent one of his imps to claim the blacksmith. The latter asked the imp if he would help him, for he was very busy. The imp was willing, so the blacksmith told him to pick the bent shoenails out of his shoeing-box, but as soon as he put his hand into the box he became powerless and could not move. Then the blacksmith, in great glee, heated a pair of tongs and began to pinch the imp. After torturing him to his heart's content he released him from the spell, and the imp returned to Beelzebub.

Beelzebub then sent another imp, and the other one having related his experience, this one was a little more cautious. When the imp arrived, the blacksmith was just going into the house to eat his dinner, so he invited him to come in also, and told him to sit down while he washed and got ready for dinner. The unsuspecting imp, seeing no other chair in the room, sat down in the magic chair, and thereupon came under the influence of the blacksmith's spell. The blacksmith returned to his shop and heated some irons with which he tormented the unlucky imp more than he did the other. Then releasing him from the spell, he sat down and ate his food, confident that Beelzebub would now be willing to let him live in peace.

But the fiend, undaunted, sent another imp. The blacksmith had still another method of escape — the high pear tree. At this particular time the topmost branches bore some large juicy pears. When the imp appeared the blacksmith told him about his pear tree and the pears that were ripe and which, owing to the fact that he and his apprentice were busy, and also because his wife and daughter were unable to climb to such a height, would spoil if they were not soon picked off the tree. So he asked the imp if he would kindly undertake to pick them for him. The imp, eager to claim this troublesome soul for his master, climbed the tree, but as soon as he was up amidst the branches he became powerless. The blacksmith then called his apprentice and they heated some long iron rods with which they tormented him until they thought he had enough. Beelzebub could not get another imp to go for the blacksmith, and so he was left in peace.

13. THE FOX WIFE: AN INUIT TALE

Transformations of an animal to a person are very common in Inuit tales. This particular motif in which a fox is transformed into a woman is also common in Asia: it occurs in stories from China, Japan, and Korea.

Robin Gedalof, who published this tale as "The Faithless Wife" in *Paper Stays Put: A Collection of Inuit Writing*, notes: "The story of the fox-wife is one of the best known in the Arctic. Children from Greenland to Siberia know it, much as southern children know 'Red Riding Hood' or 'Hansel and Gretel.' Like European fairy-tales, this story has an ending that is violent enough to satisfy even the most bloodthirsty child."

The Fox Wife

Told by Leah Tataniq

A man who was living alone with his wife noticed that she often left the place without his knowing where she went. On his return home from his day-work, he seldom found her at home. This made him suspicious; and one morning he feigned to be going far away, but when he went out in his kayak he only paddled to the nearest point, and went on shore again and hid himself behind some rocks. After a little his wife emerged from the tent in her best attire. He now stole up behind her, and followed her till she reached a lake; there he observed her throw off something into the water, upon which a masculine being appeared and she, undressing, went out to him in the water. At this sight the husband got into a great rage, and set about gathering all kinds of vermin; and one day when he was quite alone with his wife he stuffed them into her, and in this manner killed her. From that day he was all alone, but did not wish to go out in his kayak minding his usual business.

One day, on his returning to his lonely tent, he was very much surprised to find his supper cooked and the smoking meat served up. The next day the same thing happened again; the meat, smoking hot, was served up on his dish, and his boots were dried and ready to put on; and all this was repeated every day. One day he only paddled a little way off the coast, and then he went on shore to hide in a place whence he could keep a look-out on his tent; and he soon observed a little woman, with her hair dressed up in a very large tuft, come down the hill and enter his tent. He now quickly made for his kayak, paddled home, and went creeping up to his house. Having softly lifted the door-curtain he noticed a strong unpleasant smell, and saw the little woman busily trimming his lamp. She was really a fox transformed into the shape of a woman, and this accounted for the strong smell. Nevertheless, he took her for his wife.

Once day he met his cousin out at sea, and told him about his new wife, praising her loveliness, and next asked him to come and see her. "But," added he, "if thou shouldst happen to notice a rank smell about her, be sure not to make any remarks about it." The cousin followed him at once, and having landed together they both entered the tent. But when the visitor observed how nice and pleasant the wife of his cousin was he grew jealous, and in order to make mischief exclaimed, "Whence comes this nasty smell?" Instantly the little woman rose to her feet. She had now got a tail wherewith she extinguished the lamp; and like a fox [she] cried, "Ka, ka, ka!" and ran out of the tent.

The husband followed her quickly, but when he again caught sight of her she was transformed into a fox, running uphill as fast as possible. He pursued her, and at last she vanished into a cave. It is told that while he stood outside calling for her she first sent him a beetle, and then a spider, and at last a caterpillar. He then grew quite enraged, heaped some fuel together at the entrance, and burned her alive; and once more he was quite alone, and at last killed himself in a fit of madness.

14. THE TWO BROTHERS: A GREEK TALE
This is a version of one of the most familiar of all fairy-tales, identified internationally as "Open Sesame!" The Grimms collected it, it is known in practically every country of Europe,

and it was carried to the Americas by French, English, and Spanish immigrants. This version is close to the standard form except for the ending: usually the rich brother enters the cave and then forgets the formula for opening it. The poor brother's generosity is an added motif that emphasizes the familiar contrast of good and evil.

G. James Patterson collected this while working with Greek Canadians in Vancouver for the National Museum of Man's Centre for Folk Culture Studies. He notes that the Greek immigrant from whom he got it told it to his Canadian children.

The Two Brothers

There once were two brothers who lived in a village; one was very rich and one was very poor. The rich brother was greedy, and he refused to help his poor brother who, for some reason, just could not earn a decent living for himself and his wife.

One day the poor brother spoke to his wife and said: "Wife, I must leave our village and go to seek my fortune, for we cannot live on what I earn here." And with that he took leave of her. He set off into the forest and walked and walked until nightfall. When it became too dark to continue on the path, he looked about for a place to spend the night. To protect himself against the wild animals in the woods he climbed a large tree and settled down among the branches.

Almost at once he heard a loud rumbling sound; he looked about him and saw a big rock moving sideways, revealing a large cave. As he sat watching, horsemen came galloping out; they were huge, ferocious *draculas*.[1]

The man in the tree counted forty-one of them as they passed beneath the tree where he sat. The cave door slid closed behind them and they disappeared into the night. The man was extremely frightened and remained hidden in the tree through the night. Toward dawn the *draculas* returned to the cave, their horses laden with gold and jewels and food which they had stolen during the night. They paused at the cave entrance and shouted, "Cave, open!" With that the rock slid open and the men disappeared inside.

The man was overwhelmed by all the riches the *draculas*

---

1. Barbarians: giants, flesh-eating men who rob and terrorize villages and carry off the riches to hidden caves. They live on the goods they steal; murderers of the worst sort.

had carried into the cave with them; so he decided to remain in the tree another night to see if he could get a closer look. The next night the cave door opened as it had the previous evening, and the man counted the forty-one horsemen as they passed by. After they had disappeared he stole up to the cave and shouted, "Cave, open!" and the rock slid aside. The man entered and was positively overwhelmed by the sight which he beheld: gold, jewels, beautiful cloth everywhere! He filled his pockets and his boots and carried as many sacks of gold as he could. And he slipped out of the cave.

Later that night the *draculas* returned to their cave. Immediately, they detected the smell of human flesh — and soon after, they discovered that some of their riches were gone. They became infuriated and vowed to find out who had dared to steal their gold and jewels.

In the meantime, the man had returned to his village with more money than he and his wife had ever dreamed of. When his brother saw all of the gold he became very jealous, and he demanded to know where the man had found such a fortune. No sooner had the man told the wealthy brother his strange tale than the brother set off for the cave himself. He waited in the tree until nightfall and he saw the horsemen gallop out of the cave, just as his brother had told him they would. However, the rich brother was careless. He didn't count the *draculas*, and so didn't note that forty, not forty-one, had left the cave. The rich brother approached the entrance, recited the magic phrase, and entered the cave. He, too, was overwhelmed by the riches and began to fill his pockets; however, he soon heard a terrifying roar. The *dracula* who had remained in the cave to guard the treasure had caught a whiff of human flesh and set out to find the intruder. The man tried desperately to escape and then to hide, but he was unsuccessful. The *dracula* caught him and held him captive. When the other forty men returned to the cave they decided to punish the man for his crime; so they chopped him up in pieces, put the pieces in little bags tied to his horse, and sent the horse back to the village.

When the horse appeared in the town, the people were horrified at what had happened to the rich man — his brother was particularly grief-stricken. In spite of his brother's cruelty to him and his stingy behaviour with regard to the sharing of his wealth, the former poor brother took his brother's family under his roof and provided for them in every way. And they all lived happily ever after.

15. THE GREEN FLAG AND THE DEVIL'S HEAD: A FRENCH TALE

This lengthy tale is a good illustration of no less than four very common themes in *Märchen*: the quest of the hero, the three tests, the supernatural helper, and the magic object. Luc Lacourcière collected it from a fisherman, Johnny Larocque, who had a large repertoire of stories, including both *fabliaux* and *Märchen*, and Margaret Low translated it into English.

It combines elements from two tale types and includes a remarkable number of motifs. It is closest to a very popular tale, "The Prince and the Arm Bands," which is known in practically every country of Europe, as well as in Turkey, Arabia, India, Indonesia, French and Spanish America, Chile, Puerto Rico, and the West Indies. It seems to have been particularly popular among French Canadians: some forty-three versions have been reported, and Luc Lacourcière has published a study of them. It is interesting to note that it was a version of this tale found among the Chipewyan Indians of the Alberta-Saskatchewan border that inspired Stith Thompson's doctoral dissertation, *European Borrowings and Parallels in North American Indian Tales*, and launched his outstanding career in folktale research.

While Johnny Larocque's tale is obviously a version of "The Prince and the Arm Bands," it varies in several ways. The magic object is a flag rather than arm bands. In the usual plot, the mother's betrayal is intentional; here it is not. The supernatural helpers are usually lions rather than an old man. The motif of the ring broken between the lovers is not part of this type, although it turns up in some other tales and is a very common motif in ballads. A ring used for identification is usually dropped in a glass of wine, but here it is put in a bowl of soup. An interesting link is that European versions have the princess going to Arabia, which probably explains the reference to the Red Sea.

The tale also shares some motifs with another type known as "The Monster's Bride," in which the hero wins the princess after finding certain objects that she hides, and killing the monster (or, in this case, the Devil), of whom she is enamoured, with the help of a "grateful dead man" (in this case simply an old man).

The Green Flag and the Devil's Head

Told by Johnny Larocque

Once there was an old woman and she was a widow. She had only one boy. But when the old man died, he had forbidden his boy to disobey his mother. Well, the boy went about the city from one end to the other, begging. People got tired of that and they didn't want to give them anything more. So the little boy said to his mother, "We'll have to go away, move to a new area, try to find another place where they don't know us; they speak English there. Perhaps we could beg for a bit longer, just until I'm man enough to earn my living."

Well, they decide to go away. They walk all day and in the evening they come to a castle. They ask the king if they can sleep there and the king lets them both stay the night, and he gives them breakfast the next morning. They would have to walk the whole day again before reaching the forest where they were to take a highway.

"You can walk all day today," the king says. "It's going to take you the day to reach the highway near the forest, but," he says, "I forbid you to go into the forest because there are all kinds of giants and wild animals there to devour you."

So they thanked the king and set out walking again. Before they reached the forest they passed by a tall flagpole they had in those days, and they called that a banner, what you'd call a flag. The lad had his heart set on that flag as soon as he saw it. Anyway, they went on as far as the forest — it wasn't very far from the flag — and they made a fire there to spend the night. The little boy says to his mother, "You, you're going to lie down and me, I'm going to keep watch, and then when I'm tired I'll wake you up and I'll sleep, and you'll keep watch until morning." "That's all right," she says.

So he gets the fire going pretty good so she could have a good sleep. The old woman was pretty tired — they had been walking for two days — and she slept like a log, as they say.

When the lad saw that his mother was sound asleep there he went back to the flagpole, climbed up and took that green flag, and climbed back down with it. Then he bent forward and wound it all around his body and attached it with a big pin. When he had that on him then, he couldn't feel the ground under his feet. He had so much strength that he could have destroyed anything!

He gets back to his mother. She had slept something like an hour so he wakes her up. "Mummy, are you tired?" he says. "Well," she says, "I had a good rest and I'm pretty well rested now." "We'll walk on then," he says. "You know what the king told us?" [she says.] "Oh, that doesn't matter," he says. "We'll go on anyway."

They set out walking. They come to some fairly hilly country, and when they reach the top of a hill they see a giant at the bottom of the hill coming towards them. "Do you see," she says, "what's coming there?" "Oh, that," he says. "That doesn't worry me much."

The giant comes up to them. "Why, my little worm," he says to the lad, "I'll eat you tomorrow morning for breakfast." "Oh," he says, "I'm not easy to eat." Anyway, the giant goes to grab him but he hits the giant on the forehead and sends him flying into the tree stumps. Then he pulls him back out of there, you know, and he throws him back on the road.

Well, the giant found himself in such a tight spot that he thought to himself, "I'd better not try it again. He's going to kill me." "Oh, that's all right," he says to the lad. "You and your mother will come along with me. I've got a castle," he says, "and the three of us will stay there. We'll be fine there." "Oh, well, that's all right," the lad says.

So he took them to his castle. They went to bed at night, although it wasn't long before daylight came. Then the giant made breakfast. He cooked a quarter of a moose for each meal. The lad didn't eat too much.

The giant's work was clearing land. "Me," he says, "I'm going to go and clear some land. I'm making a clearing for a farm." They called the giant his grandfather. [The giant had married the lad's mother.] "Grandfather," the young lad says, "do you want me to come with you?" "Well," he says, "you can come along and watch me work."

The giant pulled out large cherry trees and big maple trees by the roots and when he had pulled out enough of them like that, he put them all in a big pile. The young lad watched him working. The giant threw down one tree and pulled out another one just the same then as you'd pull out hay. Then he grabbed them all around the middle and carted them away and piled them up there. But he was beginning to get tired.

"Grandfather," the lad says, "it would go a lot faster if I gave you a hand." "You're much too small to do that," he says. "But take the top of the tree and I'll take the trunk."

Every time the lad swung a tree, he threw the giant right along with it! Well, that went on all day. In the evening when the giant gets home, he says to his wife, "There must be a lot of strong people where you come from." "Ah, well," she says, "he's not a man yet; he's just a little boy. He's not very old; he's only about twelve years old." She didn't know how strong he was.

That begins to bother the giant and it bothered him a lot. So he says to his wife, he says, "You're going to pretend you're sick and after you're sick I'll tell you what to do then." So the old woman consented just to please the giant but she didn't know what her little lad would have to do. The next morning, then, the old woman was complaining that she was sick. When he got up, he says to his mother, "Well," he says, "what's wrong with you?" "I'm awful sick," she says. "Go find your grandfather and he'll tell you what to do."

So he goes and finds his grandfather, the giant. "Mummy is sick," he says. "What can I do?" "Well," he says, "it'll take the golden apple to save her." "The golden apple? What's that?" "Listen," he says. "Come here." He shows him the road. "Follow that road," he says. "It'll take you to the castle where the golden apple is."

The lad sets out and he walks, my friend. He walks the whole blessed day and part of the night. There was a small camp just before you came to the castle. He sees it well enough and stops there. There was an old man there. I don't know how many hundreds of years old he was, but he had never seen anyone come there before.

When he sees the lad turn in, he says, "Hello, little boy. Where are you going?" "I'm going to get the golden apple for Mummy. She's sick." "Yes, the golden apple," he says. "It's hard to get. A lot of men have passed by here," he says, "but they didn't consult me, not a bit. They've sure gone and tried but thousands and thousands of them have been killed. No one has been able to get it. Well," he says, "you're going to rest a bit anyway, and early tomorrow morning I'll tell you what to do."

Anyhow, he goes to bed and rests. Then when it's getting on to daylight and he's well rested, the old man gets him up. "If you can reach the castle just as the princess is bathing and if, at the moment she throws her water through a flagstone that runs outside the castle, you can wash yourself in that water, you're ready to get the golden apple right away; but if you can't you'll have a lot of things to do." "Well, I'll try," he says.

So he runs as fast as he can but when he reaches the castle she had already emptied the water and he can't even get a couple of drops of it. So he can't wash.

He goes into the castle. A beautiful princess! "Hello, little boy." "Hello, princess." "Where are you going?" she says. "I've come to get the golden apple for Mummy," he says. "She's pretty sick." "Yes," she says. "The golden apple is here but you'll have to work to get it." "What do I have to do?" he says.

"Well," she says, "I'll tell you this evening what you'll have to do tomorrow morning to get the golden apple."

So he spends the day with her. At six o'clock in the evening she takes the keys to the castle and gives them to him. "Tomorrow morning at six o'clock," she says, "you'll have to give me back the keys to the castle." He takes the keys and puts them in his pocket. Then the princess goes away.

The old man arrives. He had a little invisible hat on his head; when he wore his hat, he was invisible. So when he arrives, the young lad was sitting in an armchair. "Well," he says, "what'd she give you to do?" "She gave me the keys to the castle," he says, "and I have to give them back to her tomorrow morning at six o'clock." "Will you be able to give them to her?" "I'm going to try," he says.

Well, for a young lad that's not too intelligent! So this one gets drowsy and falls asleep. At a quarter to six there's a sort of earthquake, and who enters? The Devil! He came to take the keys of the castle away from the lad, but the old man is faster than the Devil and he takes the keys and sticks them in his pocket. But the Devil can't see him! He searches the lad thoroughly and then goes away.

Anyhow, at six o'clock the old man wakes the lad and says, "Do you have the keys to the castle to give to the princess this morning?" He sticks his hand in his pocket. He doesn't have any keys. Ah, he's pretty sad. He doesn't say a word. The old man puts his hand in his pocket. "Here," he says. "You'll give them to her."

When the princess arrives, she says coldly, "Do you have the keys to the castle this morning?" "Yes," he says. "Yes." He pulls them out of his pocket and gives them to her. "Well," she says, "you're pretty good but you still have two more penances to do."

She spends the day chatting with him. At seven o'clock in the evening, she takes a gold saucer and gives it to him. "You'll have to give me back the saucer at seven tomorrow morning," she says. He takes the saucer and sticks it down the front of his shirt.

When the princess leaves, the old man comes back again. "What penance did she give you?" he asks the lad. So he tells him that she gave him a saucer and that he has to return it at seven o'clock in the morning. He chats with the old man and then falls asleep again. The old man keeps watch all night long. At a quarter to seven then, the Devil makes so much noise coming to get the saucer that it's as if the castle were going to rise up off the ground!

Anyhow, the old man wakes up the lad. "Are you asleep?" "Yes," he says, "I'm sleeping." "Do you have the saucer to give her this morning?" "Yes," he says. But the old man had it. The lad sticks his hand down the front of his shirt. No saucer! He was awfully sad. So the old man takes the saucer and gives it to him. "Here," he says. "You'll give it to her." Well, he takes the saucer and he gives it to the princess when she arrives. "Ah," she says, "you're pretty good but those weren't your two worst penances. You'll get your big penance tonight."

Well, in a tale things happen quickly. The day goes by and at eight o'clock in the evening the princess comes to find the young lad. "I'm going where the Devil lives," she says, "to the Devil's place. And you'll have to have the Devil's head to put in my gold apron tomorrow morning at eight o'clock." Then she goes and gets ready to leave.

The old man arrives right away and goes to the lad. "What did she say to you? What penance did she give you?" "Well, she said I had to have the Devil's head to put in her gold apron tomorrow morning." "Look, that's pretty tough. Are you going to be able to do it?" "Don't know," he says. "I'll do what I can for you," [the old man says].

The princess comes down not long after. She opens the door. "I'm going now," she says. The old man goes out behind her. "I'm going now, too," he says. She looks behind her but doesn't see anything. "Am I alone?" she says. "No, there are two of us," he says. She crosses a forest and then she says, "I'm crossing the Red Sea." "I'm crossing the Red Sea, too," he says. She turns around and says, "And yet I'm all alone!" "No, there are two of us." She crosses the Red Sea and then crosses a forest there on the other side. "I'm crossing a forest." "I'm crossing a forest, too." She turns around. "How can that be? Seems to me I'm all alone." "No, there are two of us."

She continues on her way and comes to a cabin there. "I'm going in," she says. "I'm staying outside," he says. He stays outside behind the door. She goes in.

"What penance did you give the lad to do tonight?" the Devil asks. "Well," she says, "I told him he had to put your head in my golden apron tomorrow morning." The Devil shakes his head — and he had pretty big ears! "Oh, no," he says. "He'll not get my head!"

Ah, well, they chat for quite some time. At midnight they

were still talking. It was a nice night; there was lovely moon-light. "Ah," she says, "it's time I was going. I've got a long way to go."

She comes outside. The Devil sticks his head a little ways out of the door and says, "You'll have a nice evening. It's nice out." The old man who was hidden there gets hold of the Devil's head and he pulls it right off his shoulders — Cr-rack! — and he takes the head.

"I'm going now," she says. "I'm going, too, and with the Devil's head," he says. She turns around. "I'm all alone," she says. "No, there are two of us."

She was travelling along so quickly that the bottom of her dress trailed out stiffly in the breeze. "I'm crossing the Red Sea." "I'm crossing the Red Sea, too." She turns around. "How can that be?" she says. "I'm all alone." "No, there are two of us." "I'm crossing a forest." "I'm crossing a forest, too." "I wonder how that can be. Seems to me I'm all alone." And on she goes. She is back home at seven-thirty in the morning. "I'm here," she says. "I'm going in." "I'm going in, too."

Then the old man goes up and wakes his young lad. "Do you have the Devil's head to give her this morning?" "No," he says. "Ah, well," he says. "You're finished. But you still have half an hour. Go and get washed up."

When the lad is washed, the old man takes the Devil's head and gives it to him. The head is still snarling! If they had dropped it, it would have gone back to the body. "Here, you're a lot stronger than I am," he says. "She will come with an apron of yellow cotton but be sure you don't put it in that. She'll go back and get her gold apron and then you'll throw the head in the apron so that the horns stick in the floor. The head will be dead then. You're the only one who can do it."

He was very strong, you know. He had the head there behind him and the head was snarling away. She arrives with a yellow cotton apron. "Do you have the Devil's head to give me?" "Yes." "To throw in here?" "Go and get your gold apron," he says.

She thought he didn't have it. She goes up and puts on her gold apron and comes back with it on. Ah, there, my friend, he swings the head in it! He sticks the horns in the floor there! "Oh," she says. "You won me. I'll be your wife for ever now that you won me."

Well, he stayed there for a couple of months but he thought about his mother all the time. "My mother who's sick there," he says, "I'll have to go and take her the golden apple." She gives him the apple and says, "Go then." She takes off her wedding ring and cuts it in two and then gives him half and keeps half. "When the two halves of this ring are joined," she says, "you'll have found me." Then she says, "You're going to be betrayed!" Anyway, he goes home and his mother is still in bed. He gives her the golden apple and she recovers quickly.

When the giant saw that he had taken all those steps to get the apple, he pretty well knew what he had to do to get it. He says to his wife, "There's something. I pretty well suspect that he has the green flag on him. So try to get him to take it off. You'll tell him that you're going to wash it. Put it outside to dry in the sun and if I can get my hands on it, I'll be well off. It's because of the flag," he says, "that he's so strong."

Anyway, the lad was pretty tired. The old man, the giant, goes off to clear some more land. His mother tells him that then. She says, "While your grandfather isn't here you're going to give me your flag that you have on you and I'm going to wash it, then I'll put it out to dry, and when it's dry you'll put it back on."

He takes his mother's advice. He didn't think his mother was going to betray him! She washes it and puts it outside on the clothesline. The giant wasn't too far away and when he sees the green flag on the clothesline he comes back and grabs the flag and puts it on. Now with his own strength and that flag, he was pretty strong.

The lad was asleep and he goes and wakes him up. The young lad only weighed about as much as a fly in the giant's hand. "Ah," he says, "I knew you had that flag. Now, come over here!" The giant takes the lad and leads him fairly far out in the forest. He takes out his two eyes and leaves him there.

The young fellow made himself a trail by going from tree to tree. He reached the coast and then the sea, but when he saw that he had reached water he stopped. He stayed there on the shore.

There was a captain who travelled by ship. He was forever watching the shore through his telescope. He sees this object that is there and orders his ship turned around and brought into shore as close as possible. He throws a small boat into the water and says to his sailors, "There's a blind man there. Go and get him." They go and get the lad and bring him on board ship.

Then the captain, who was a king, says, "We aren't far from home, so we'll turn around and take him back home. We have servants there and they'll take care of him." So the king takes the lad home and tells the servants to look after him until he gets back. The servants were to take turns looking after him. And the lad's wife, when she saw that she was all alone at home, had gone to the king's and she had become first servant there.

It was the last servant who brought his first meal. He spoke well and was an intelligent man. After the meal the servants talk about him among themselves. The second servant fed him the second day and he told the servant everything, how he had come there and everything. The next day the third servant, who was his wife, came. He starts to talk to her. She takes the half of her ring — he was eating soup that day — so she takes the half of her ring and puts it in his bowl of soup. Anyway, he takes a spoonful of soup and when he goes to eat it he finds half of a ring. He takes it out and sticks his hand in his pocket and pulls out the other half and joins the two halves together.

She knew him then. "You're my husband," she says. "And just as I told you, the two halves of the ring are joined together. You're my husband." "Well, we won't stay here," he says, "even though I'm blind." "We have all we need to live on," she says, "so we'll go away." She goes and finds the queen to tell her that, and that made the queen awfully sad.

Anyway, on the way to their place there was a road which led to a spring and the water from that spring could heal any disease. "We'll take that road," she says. "It takes longer to get home that way but we just have to take that road." When they reach the spring there were crutches and glasses and all sorts of things hung there! "Kneel down here," she says, "and ask the Holy Virgin to give you your sight back by washing your eyes with water from the spring." So he does what his wife tells him and when he stood up he had his sight back!

"I'm in good health again," he says, "and I have my eyesight back. We'll go back to our castle and we'll have a good life," he says. "We'll live together in peace."

Well, he went and got his old man, you know, the one who had done so much for him, and he lives with him now.

When I left there, they had a good life. They had two or three babies, I think. They sent me here to tell their story.

16. THE SHOEMAKER IN HEAVEN: A POLISH TALE
This story is a fairly well known type, usually with a tailor rather than a shoemaker as the main character. The Grimms found a version of it in Germany, and it has been told in Scandinavia, Scotland, and Russia. It belongs in a subsection of "Ordinary

Folktales" which the Aarne-Thompson Index lists as "Religious Tales."

Kay Stone, a Canadian folklorist who teaches at the University of Winnipeg, collected this and other stories from a Polish-born Canadian in her early twenties who had left Poland when she was about twelve. Dr. Stone included it in a volume of *Prairie Folklore* and wrote of the storyteller:

> *Both her father and her maternal grandmother told stories, her grandmother favoring moralistic or religious tales, her father preferring the adventurous and humorous ones. She had heard the tales only in Polish, of course, and at first had difficulty retelling them in English. She began by telling the English version as almost a word-for-word translation of the Polish versions. As she became more confident, the English versions began to be true recreations rather than translations. In other words, she was beginning to make them her own stories rather than her grandmother's or father's.*

The woman herself commented:

> *You lose something in the translation in English. I don't think this one would make as much difference as in some of the longer stories. I tried to make it very close to the Polish, like as close as possible. The only difference that I feel is that you don't get the same feeling of the story. I don't think I'm convincing the other person that I'm telling it in English so that it's really natural. Maybe it's because I heard it first in Polish, and it has more meaning to me. I remember them in Polish now.*

The Shoemaker in Heaven

Like I told you, the whole family sat around with my grandmother, and my father listened to them, too. It was a family thing. So it's still my grandmother's story. I just asked my father to remind me because my grandma wasn't around. This is a short one, kind of funny. This shoemaker's soul comes to heaven, comes to the door and knocks on it and Peter comes out. So he says, "Well, I'm just a poor shoemaker's soul and I'd like to come into heaven." So Peter says to him, " Well, I can't really decide right now. I don't know if you belong in heaven or hell, because God is just out for a walk with the angels. He's not around and I can't decide for Him." So he says to him that he can come in and sit down in a corner and wait till God will talk to him. "And He'll decide whether or not you should go to heaven or hell."

So this soul of the shoemaker is crunched up and everything like that, you know, petrified and worried, with this big man [Peter] standing over him. Well, anyways, he hides in the corner in the big room, and all he sees in this room is one big throne, like a big chair, and a little footstool. He looks around, gets used to the place, and sees that there's no one around, so there's nothing to be scared of. So he gets up and he says, "Well, why should I sit on the floor? I'll go and sit on the footstool." So he sits on it for a while and is comfortable. Then he looks around, and says, "Well, there's no one here who's going to see me, so I'll try the big chair."

As soon as he sits on the big chair, you know, he sees the world beneath, and he sees everything that's going on. In one spot he sees a man and wife arguing, and she's throwing things at him; and then he sees the cities and all the things that are going on there. And this one thing that really caught his eye is there's some women washing shirts — shirts belonging to a noble. His servants, you know, washing his shirts. So one of them takes one, goes in the bush and hides it. She looks around and nobody's looking, and she washes some more, takes one, and goes again to hide it. Well, that shoemaker just couldn't take it anymore. You know, such injustice; stealing right in front of his eyes. He just couldn't control himself, so he just picked up the footstool and threw it down — down to earth.

At that time, you know, God walks in, and a party of angels. So he hears Him coming and he runs back into his corner and hides. So as soon as God walks in and sits on this throne, He says, "Now where is my footstool? Who's been around here? Where is it?" So everybody's looking around in search of the footstool. They found him in the corner. So they drag him forward, and he's kneeling down and he says he's just a poor shoemaker's soul seeking entrance to heaven and he hasn't done anything wrong or anything like that. So God says, "Have you seen my footstool around here?" So he says, "Yes, I have." This he admits, because he figures, you know, that if God can see everything on earth he's sure He knows that he did this too, so he'd better admit it. So he admits it, and he says, "Well, I was sitting in your chair and I saw these bad things going down there, and I just couldn't help myself!" He says, "I just wanted to stop that woman from stealing, so I threw that footstool at her."

So God says, in His wisdom and glory and everything: "So you see what sort of a problem I have. I've been sitting here for centuries judging people and seeing them sin and do all these outrageous things, and you see, I have to control myself!" He says, "You know, by this time I'd have nothing left in heaven. I'd throw everything down, even Peter himself!" You know, to stop people from sinning, if He could. So He says, "Well, what do you think? Do you deserve to go to heaven or hell?" So the shoemaker says, "Well, I have been a very honest shoemaker. The only thing I ever kept for myself was the trimmings that came off the shoes when I was making them." He says, "I've led a good life and everything like that, and I never did any harm to anybody." So he deserves he should go to heaven, he says. And then he says to God, "Well, why do you ask me? You saw what I did!" So God says, "Well, I just wanted to find out whether you were telling the truth or not." But, He says, "You sort of saw that I knew what you did during your life anyways, because you sat on my chair."

17. MAC CRÙSLAIN: A GAELIC TALE

Mac Crùslain is a well-known character in Highland Gaelic tradition, and tales about a man who fools a giant with tricks, like those in the episodes of the heavy axe, the throwing contest, and the eating contest, are also popular in Ireland. There are so many tales like this that the Aarne-Thompson Index has a separate section under "Ordinary Folktales" for "Tales of the Stupid Ogre."

Sister Margaret MacDonell collected "Mac Crùslain" and many other stories from Hector Campbell of Hillsdale, Inverness County, Nova Scotia. Mr. Campbell, who was born in Cape Breton in 1888 and died in 1976, has been described as "one of the finest traditional Gaelic storytellers in Cape Breton during our time." His family came out from the Scottish Highlands in the 1840s and, as the collector notes, "In his home, as in almost every other Highland home in Cape Breton, there was Gaelic singing, fiddling, and piping." He learned his stories from an older Gaelic storyteller, Hector MacEachen, who died in the mid-1920s.

Sister Margaret MacDonell is chairman of the Department of Celtic Studies at St. Francis Xavier University, Antigonish, Nova Scotia. She is fluent in Gaelic and has provided the translations of Hector's tales. She has also published *The Emigrant Experience: Songs of Highland Emigrants in North America*.

Mac Crùslain

Told by Hector Campbell

There were once two men called Mac Crùslain and Prabaileas who lived together. They were only poor men and they owned nothing in the world but one milk cow. They killed the milk cow and they were going to share her between them.

"Which do you prefer?" said Mac Cùslain to Prabaileas. "Which do you prefer: what is between the four limbs of the cow or the manyplies [third stomach] of the hundred hairs and tatters?"

Prabaileas thought it over and he heard the word "hundred." So he preferred to take the hundred hairs and the hundred tatters.

"Oh, you will get that."

So Mac Cùslain took the manyplies out of the cow. He dressed the meat and kept it for himself and the manyplies went to the other one — to Prabaileas. Prabaileas was not very pleased with that. At last Mac Cùslain shared the remaining part of the meat until it ran out and then they were in a bad way. They had nothing at all.

"What we had better do," said Mac Cùslain, "is to go to seek our livelihood."

"Yes, we had better," said Prabaileas. "We must set out."

They went off to seek their livelihood. They spent a good while travelling by foot but towards nightfall they entered a place with a king's palace nearby. They decided that they would look for work somewhere around there. They went looking for their livelihood then and a man there — a big giant — said that he would hire one of them. Well, that was fine. But Mac Cùslain [said] then, "You had better take service with him," he said to Prabaileas. So Prabaileas hired on [with him].

Well, Mac Cùslain departed. He went to look for another place and found [work] with a farmer nearby. And the work that they gave Mac Cùslain was threshing. So, Mac Cùslain began threshing. As for the big giant, Prabaileas was with him and the big giant was nettling Prabaileas; Prabaileas was having a hard time with him. Finally he decided that he could not stay with him and that he had to leave him: he could not get along at all and the giant would do away with him. He went down to where Mac Cùslain was working. Well, he said to him, "The place that I got there," he — Prabaileas — said, "I can't stay there. The big giant is so hard on me that I can't stay there."

Mac Cùslain said to him, "You stay here, then, and I'll go and hire on with the giant." Oh, that was fine. Prabaileas stayed at the threshing with the farmer. Mac Cùslain went and took service with the giant. The big giant was getting ready and he had to go to the well. He said to Mac Cùslain, "You must go to the well. There is a vessel out there to bring home water."

Mac Cùslain went out and he could not lift the handle of the vessel, let alone the vessel itself with the weight of it. He came inside and said to the big giant, "It's not worth my while to go there like that with the vessel. If I go down, I'll bring up the whole well."

"Oh, no, you will not," said the big giant. "That will empty the well. You mustn't bring it up. The water will run out of it and I will be without a well at all."

"Well, then," he replied, "you had better go there yourself." So the big giant set out and went to the well himself and brought up the vessel full of water.

Things were going very well. But where they were sleeping inside, there was a cow on one side of the fire and the giant himself was close by it, too. Mac Crùslain slept on the other side of the fire. But after he retired for the night Mac Crùslain began thinking that maybe the giant would do something to him. When he thought that the giant had fallen asleep he got up and pulled the cow over on the other side where he himself slept, and he went to sleep in the cow's place. And on towards the end of the night the big giant awoke and got up. He looked around and he found a large hammer and he went and delivered some blows to Mac Crùslain; he supposed that it was Mac Crùslain who was in the bed. He struck the cow and dispatched her with the first blow and there wasn't a sound out of her so he returned to sleep.

He slept until day dawned. Then he arose. He got up and he came over and began to kindle a fire. Mac Crùslain stuck his head out from under the bed clothes.

"I believe," he said, "that it rained last night." "What makes you think that?" said the big giant. "It must have been the leak here that I felt, just as if three drops were falling on my forehead." "Is that how you felt it?" "It is." "Oh, well, well. That was me with the large hammer." "If it was, you're not much good."

But they were going to go on that day: they arose and made their breakfast. "Well," said the giant, "we had better go to the woods. We are getting short of firewood."

"I am sure we are," said Mac Crùslain. "I'm going to fetch a load of firewood. If I go to the woods," said Mac Crùslain, "I'll bring home the whole forest."

"Oh, you mustn't bring home the whole forest. It will go to waste," [said] the big giant.

"Oh, it will not," he said. "I have to bring it all back home if I go there at all."

He set out with the big giant and the giant started to make up a load. He pulled up the large trees and put them into a pile and Mac Crùslain was going around the tips of the trees in the forest.

At last the big giant had the load made up. He took hold of it and put it over his shoulder and Mac Crùslain went and rode amongst the tree-tops that the giant was carrying on his shoulder. The giant brought home the load with Mac Crùslain coming along in the tree-tops.

When he reached the woodpile Mac Crùslain appeared and said, "That won't last long for you. If only you had let me bring home the whole forest."

"Oh, I certainly would not," the giant replied. "That forest would rot and I would be without a forest at all."

Well, they were going ahead on their way home and they were getting along very well. But anyway, the big giant asked him, "Are you good at throwing stones?" The big giant went out. Mac Crùslain went and got a mixture of stuff — curds or something — which he plastered onto a chunk of stone. The big giant began. He got a large stone and he was throwing it and they were aiming at a tree in the woods facing the house. Mac Crùslain threw his stone and hit the tree, making a white mark on it. Said Mac Crùslain, "You're no good at all. See how I made a spot on the tree."

"Well, yes," said the big giant. "I was throwing as well as I could."

"Well, you're not much good at all." So that was over.

"How are you at throwing the hammer?"

"Oh, I can throw the hammer all right," [said] Mac Crùslain. The big giant got a large hammer and he cast it and threw it a fearful distance.

"Oh, you must bring it back now," said Mac Crùslain. "Since you're the one who threw it, you must bring it back."

The great giant went and he brought back the hammer. There was a fair-sized inlet a short distance across from them and Mac Crùslain began calling to the people on the other side of the inlet to be careful — that he was going to throw the hammer.

"Oh, son of the world," said the great giant, "you mustn't throw the hammer out there."

"Well, I'm going to throw it," said Mac Crùslain, "and they had better watch out. If it goes across they will be badly off."

"Oh, I'll lose the hammer if it goes into the sea. You had better not throw it at all."

"Well," [said] Mac Crùslain, "I'll leave it alone if you wish."

He left the hammer and the big giant was pleased that he did. But then the big giant told him that he was going to make a large pot of porridge and that they would have to try to see who would eat the most porridge. Oh, that was fine. Mac Crùslain went and got a sack and sewed it all up on himself to make a place where he could put down the porridge. When the pot of porridge was ready, they sat down beside the pot and the eating began. Mac Cruslain [was] driving it into the sack and the big giant did not realize that he had no intention of eating it—that he was putting it into the sack. He filled up the sack and he had [what looked like] a great stomach bulging out.

"We'll try jumping," said the great giant.

"Oh, I can jump as well," said Mac Cruslain.

The great giant prepared to make a leap. He leapt and hardly went any distance at all.

Mac Cruslain [was] watching him and could see how hopeless he was at jumping.

"Well, I will do better than that," said Mac Cruslain. "But I must let out some of the porridge that I ate," he said.

He ripped open the sack and he let out the porridge. He took a run and jumped and he went farther than the giant.

"Oh," said the giant, "you are good at jumping."

"Oh, yes," he answered, "when I am light. I let out the porridge."

"Oh, if I were that light myself," said the big giant, "I could leap just as far as you and even further."

"Indeed you could. If you let the porridge out of yourself, you could jump just as far."

"Oh, I can't do that," said the great giant.

"Well, I'll let the porridge out of you."

He then went [to work] and the big giant was ripped open [and the] porridge was taken out of him. He was done for then.

["The big giant was done for?"]

He was done for then.

In any event, he had finished the big giant and if the giant had a ransom, he had left it inside. And Mac Cruslain got the ransom and there was silver and gold. He sent for Prabaileas and he gave him part of the gold and part of the silver which the big giant had in a cave. He was rich forever after and I parted from him.

IV. Romantic Tales

SOME FOLKTALES ARE more realistic than the wonder tales, relying less on magic and the supernatural than on the character of the heroes and heroines. Although they are commonly termed "romantic tales," they do not necessarily involve romantic love. They often emphasize the cleverness of the protagonist in winning contests, solving riddles, or outwitting enemies.

Among them are the plots from which Shakespeare shaped *The Merchant of Venice, Cymbeline, King Lear*, and *The Taming of the Shrew*. They include also such other well-known plots as the story of Oedipus, the judgement of Solomon, the prodigal's return, and what is probably the most widespread of all international tales, "The Shepherd Substituting for the Priest Answers the King's Questions," known in England as "The King and the Abbot of Canterbury."

In Canada this group seems less popular than the tales of the supernatural, but collectors have noted some stories of cuckolded husbands, riddle solvers, romantic elopements, and tragic love affairs.

18. THERE WAS A LORD IN EDINBURGH: A BALLAD
19. THE SCOTCHMAN WHO LOVED AN IRISH GIRL:
*   A CANTE-FABLE*
These two items tell the same story in different ways. The plot is related to the very widespread one of the husband or lover who returns from a long absence to find his wife or sweetheart about

56

to wed another: the theme of endless tales from *Ulysses* to "Hind Horn." Here the long absence is not an element, but an extra dramatic feature is added with the bride being carried off from her wedding feast. The pattern is probably best known through Sir Walter Scott's poem "Lochinvar"; and his inspiration came from an old Scottish ballad, "Katharine Jaffray," which in Ireland became "The Lord (or Squire) of Edinburgh."

"There was a Lord in Edinburgh" is one of a number of old British ballads that have survived better in North America than in their homeland. It has been more popular in Canada than in the United States: Helen Creighton collected numerous versions in Nova Scotia, Maud Karpeles and Kenneth Peacock both found it in Newfoundland, and the version used here is one of two Ontario versions.

"The Scotchman Who Loved an Irish Girl" is told as a prose story, with interspersed lines from the ballad, thus turning it into a cante-fable, while "There Was a Lord in Edinburgh" is a typical Canadian version of the ballad, printed here as sung by a traditional Ontario singer, LaRena Clark. The prose version, which Arthur Huff Fauset collected in Nova Scotia from an eighty-seven-year-old black woman, Caroline Reddick, illustrates how ballads are turned into tales when someone does not remember all the verses. As the ballad was known to Anglo-Canadians in Nova Scotia, Mrs. Reddick had probably heard it sung and just remembered the story with some of the lines. She has embroidered her version with many interesting details that are only hinted at in the ballad, and her ending, implying that she had been present, is typical of the way storytellers try to add verisimilitude to their tales. For another example, see Johnny Larocque's ending of "The Green Flag and the Devil's Head" (No. 15).

There Was a Lord in Edinburgh

Sung by LaRena Clark

There was a lord in Edinburgh
    And he has one only son.
He had courted a girl in the lower countree
    Till he thought he had her won.

He got consent from old and young,
    From father and mother likewise,
Till "Oh," she cried, "I am undone!"
    With the salt tears in her eyes.

She wrote her love a letter
    And she sealed it with her hand,
Saying that on her wedding day she would
    Be wed to another man.

He wrote her back an answer,
    And he sealed it with a ring,
That on her wedding day she would
    Put on a suit of green.

"A suit of the same I will put on,
    For your wedding I'll prepare,
And I'll wed you, my gay lady,
    In spite of all that's there!"

Then he rode east and he rode west,
    And he rode all around.
He rode till he'd got one hundred men,
    All for the Highlands bound.

He seated them, he placéd them
    All in the streets of Brock,
And then away to the wedding house
    This gentleman did walk.

They welcomed him both old and young
    And asked him how he'd spent the day,
And if he'd seen those Highland troops
    Who'd just rode out that way.

He laughed at them, he scornéd them,
    And unto them did say,
"It might have been some Highlanders
    Who'd just rode out for play."

He filled up a glass of the new malt wine
    And he tossed it round and round,
Saying, "Happy, happy is the man
    Who now they call the groom,

"But happier, happier will be the man
    Who shall enjoy the bride,
For if anyone loved her as I do,
    He'd take her from his side."

Up stepped the groom all in a rage,
    And an angry groom was he,
Saying, "If for fighting here you came,
    I'm the man that will fight thee."

"It's not for fighting here I came;
    Good fellowship I'll show.
One single kiss from the bonny bride,
    And away from here I'll go."

He took her by the lily-white hand,
    And by the grass-green sleeve,
And he led her straight from the company,
    Of the company asked no leave.

Yonder she rides close by his side,
    Dressed up like any queen.
She's guarded by one hundred men
    All dressed right up in green.

Come all young men both far and near,
    A warning take by me,
And don't be tricked as I have been
    All on your wedding day.

The Scotchman Who Loved an Irish Girl

Told by Caroline Reddick

Once there was a young Scotchman, an' he went to see an Irish girl. Her parents didn't like the Scotchman, because the girl was Irish, an' they wanted her to marry this Irish boy. So the Scotchman went away to make some money. The girl used to go to her bedroom an' cry an' cry. She didn't want to get married to no Irish boy. What did she do? She set down an' wrote a letter to her Scotch fellow, an' said on such a day her father had appointed for her to be married, an' try to be there if he could, three o'clock in the evening. So he answered back: "I'll be there. Don't worry, I'll be there."

The hour come. She had to dress. First thing here comes the Irish chap with all his grooms an' all, an' all dressed, an' he set in the parlour waitin' for the clergyman. He looked out the window, an' then he said, "Oh, my, look at the crowd of people. Who are them? They're all dressed in green, an' on white horses. An' all the horses' heads is trimmed off in green an' flags. They're all men, too." So they rode up to the gate. It was a big swing gate, an' one man opened it an' they walked in. They had swords on 'em, an' they glittered like new steel. So they come to the door an' rapped. Then the Irish fellow went to the door an' told them all to come in. They set chairs about an' told them to set down. The marriage was halted a while, 'cause these fellows was comin' in. The intended groom come around with the wine, treating all the company. He treated the strangers first. Every man gave a toast. This was the Scotchman's toast:

> *Here's to the health of the bonny bride.*
> *Who sets beside the groom,*
> *A man who loved her as well as I,*
> *Might take her from your side.*

The groom then kind o' saw what was up. He said:

> *Was it for fightin' you come here?*
> *If it was for fightin' you come here,*
> *I am the man for thee.*

The Scotchman said:

> *Not for fightin' I came here,*
> *But good fellowship to show,*
> *Give me one kiss from your bonny bride*
> *An' away, away, I'll go.*
>
> *He took her by the lily-white hand,*
> *An' led her out o' the room,*
> *No more for you an Irish bride,*
> *Away, away I'll go.*

Out he went, an' all the soldiers followed. They mounted on white horses, an' had a horse for her, all trimmed in green. The intended groom said:

> *Come all ye noble Irishmen,*
> *Take warning now by me,*
> *Never go to Ireland*
> *To choose yourself a wife.*
>
> *For if you are served as I was served,*
> *All on my wedding day,*
> *A ketchin' frogs instead o' fish,*
> *I always got foul play.*

I had my drink with them, an' a piece of weddin' cake, an' I left the groom fine.

20. THE LOVE STORY OF LAING SANBO AND
ZHU YINGTAI: A CHINESE TALE

This Chinese tale of tragic lovers has many counterparts in Western literature, including *Romeo and Juliet* and the numerous old ballads in which the doomed pair are buried together, with intertwining plants growing from their graves. The motif of a woman who disguises herself as a man turns up in many ballads and other tales, as well as in several real-life stories.

This plot is one of the most common in China, and is often told in considerably more detail. The longer versions sometimes lack the poetic description of the money paid for the betrothal contract which gives this one the form of a cante-fable. The story has also been dramatized in theatre plays dating back to the Ming era of the fourteenth century. The plays usually concentrate on the early episodes of the story rather than on the tragic ending. However, the folktales emphasize the tragedy, and are sometimes titled "Faithful Even in Death."

Ban Seng Hoe, the curator of Asiatic folklore at the Canadian Centre for Folklore Studies, has collected Chinese lore all over Canada and has published a study of Chinese tales told in Montreal. The woman who told him this one, Mrs. G. Chan, was born in China, and educated there and in the United States. She came to Canada in 1957 after her marriage to a Canadian-born Chinese.

The Love Story of Liang Sanbo and Zhu Yingtai

Told by Mrs. G. Chan

Liang Sanbo and Zhu Yingtai were classmates and studied together. Zhu was a woman disguised as a man; even though they studied for three years, Liang had no idea that Zhu was a woman.

Zhu once confided to her sister-in-law about her good friend Liang. Her sister-in-law told her she would plant a pot of hibiscus and if the plant died she would start to menstruate. Her sister-in-law did not wish Zhu to study too much so she killed the flower, and Zhu started to menstruate. So she had to return [home].

Liang missed Zhu so much that he came to look for her. When he reached Zhu's residence, he sang: "Looking at a distance there are several tall buildings. I wonder which one is the house of Zhu?" When he was at the gate, he asked for a man named Zhu Yingtai but he was told there was no man by that name. However, there was a woman by the name. Zhu heard him from upstairs and she came down immediately to see him. She asked him to stay for a meal and treated him with fat chicken and goose.

When Liang realized that Zhu Yingtai was a woman, he asked her to marry him. But she told him that her parents had already betrothed her to Mr. Mah; therefore she was not free. Liang asked her how much money Mr. Mah had paid for sealing the betrothal agreement. She said:

> *Two mountains of gold and two mountains of silver,*
> *Hundred pairs of gold and silver bricks,*
> *One ounce of pearl followed you to the door.*
> *Bamboo branches and of gold and silver countless baskets,*
> *Also a huge amount of betel-nuts;*
> *Lots of beautiful leaves and streams of pots,*
> *And also three big jars of evening wine,*
> *Every one of them is filled up to the top.*

When Liang heard that Mr. Mah was such a rich man and he himself was only of average means, he despondently bade her goodbye. After he returned home he was so heart-broken and love-sick longing for Zhu Yingtai that he died not long after.

On the day of the wedding, as the sedan chair carrying the bride Zhu Yingtai passed by the grave of Liang Sanbo, some mysterious power strangled Zhu with her red veil, and she died. So the families of these two lovers decided to bury them in one grave.

V. Jokes and Anecdotes

WHERE THE PLOTS of the supernatural and romantic tales are usually fairly complex, involving a series of incidents, most of the jokes and anecdotes are simple, featuring only a single incident. These are the kind of stories most frequently told today. While the older complex stories are comparatively rare, nearly everyone occasionally tells some jokes or anecdotes.

Of this type, bawdy jokes, tall tales that depend on exaggeration for their humour, jokes ridiculing some minority group, and anecdotes about famous or local characters are the most common forms circulating in Canada. Many of these parallel those told in other countries, but they are usually more distinctively Canadian than the ordinary folktales.

Although most jokes and anecdotes are brief, some international tales classified in this section are fairly lengthy and are more akin to the "Ordinary Folktales" than to the usual jokes and anecdotes. These more extended tales, told throughout the world over the past centuries, are mostly about the misadventures of married couples and the tricks clever individuals play on stupid ones. They are much less common than the shorter tales, but some, like "Little Claus and Big Claus" and "Dickie Melbourne," have been popular in Canada as well as in a great many other countries.

21. LITTLE CLAUS AND BIG CLAUS

This is a very popular and widespread international tale classified as "The Rich and the Poor Peasant" in a group of stories about "The Stupid Man." It is known in every country of Europe, in Turkey, India, Japan, Africa, the West Indies, and South and Central America, as well as in the United States and Canada, and it has even turned up among the Inuit and the Micmac Indians.

The versions normally begin with the rich peasant killing the poor man's horse and go on to the episodes of the oracular hide and the rich peasant being fooled into killing his own horses, and they normally end with the trickster escaping from a sack by exchanging with someone who wants to go to heaven. Some, like the following, include additional incidents in which the poor peasant manages to fool the rich one, and sometimes the various incidents exist as separate stories.

Helen Creighton collected this tale from Edward Collicutt in Lunenburg County, Nova Scotia. He was a guide who gave her a sample of a moose call before telling this story which he had heard in the Maine lumberwoods. This was the first long folktale Dr. Creighton collected: in fact, she noted that until she found Mr. Collicutt she "doubted that folktales in English were told at all." However, she later published eight tales from the Miramichi storyteller Wilmot MacDonald, and collected a number of others, including more from Mr. Collicutt, which she is currently preparing for publication.

Mr. Collicutt's style is a good example of oral storytelling, and his language gives a colourful tone to the narrative with phrases like "riz up the cover," "skun the horses," and "skinned him up on his back," and little details like the references to the picket fence, the "nice hymn," and the "white cows, red cows, black cows."

Little Claus and Big Claus

Told by Edward Collicutt

This is the story of two men who lived in the sandy desert. Their name was Claus—Little Claus and Big Claus. Big Claus was a man who was well off and owned five horses. Little Claus was poor and only owned one horse. Their land was hard and clayey, and Big Claus couldn't plough his land with his five horses and he didn't want to buy any more. He went over to Little Claus and said, "Will you give me a lend of your horse? I'm a little short of money now." Little Claus said, "I don't know. I'll tell you what

I'll do. You can have the horses for the ploughing six days if I can have them one."

On Monday morning he went over and rigged the horses up. When he took them to plough he ploughed Monday, Tuesday, till Saturday night. On Sunday morning Little Claus went over and said, "I've come over for the horses." Big Claus thought he had him trapped and said, "Why, today is Sunday." Little Claus said, "It's a bargain," so they harnessed up the horses. But Big Claus said to Little Claus, "If you call the horses yours, I'll kill your horse."

Little Claus didn't say anything but he went to work ploughing. Big Claus was very fond of going to the meeting and the road they took went right across where Little Claus was ploughing. As he came abreast of the land, Little Claus said, "Get up, all my six horses." Big Claus went on to the meeting and didn't say anything. When he came back Little Claus was farther back. Just as Big Claus was passing again Little Claus said, "Get up there, my six horses." Big Claus didn't say anything but kept walking.

Little Claus ploughed and finished the day and that night he took Big Claus's horses home and Big Claus helped put them in the barn and everything seemed to be going good. Monday morning, over walked Big Claus with a pole-axe on his arm and hauled off and killed Little Claus's horse.

Now Little Claus was poorer off and thought he couldn't say anything because he had said he wouldn't do it. He wondered what to do, so he skinned his horse and he stretched the skin and dried it. About a month afterwards he took it to a tanner to sell it and rolled it up.

"I won't go in the morning," he said. "I'll wait till the afternoon, and I'll go as far as my uncle's and stop the night and go in town in the morning." So he did that, and when he got to his uncle's he carried the horse-hide with him and slid it on the doorstep. His uncle's wife came to the door and he said, "Could I stay here tonight?" She said, "No, we don't keep no old tramps." So he picked up his horse-hide and he started away.

When he got out around a bend of the road by the barn where he couldn't be seen, he doubled around and went in the barn door and looked around and saw that overhead there was a loft and a window hole, so he said, "I'm going to go up there." So he went and took the horse-hide with him and he lay down so he could look out the window. He was looking away and a face came to the window and he said, "There's my uncle now," and he thought he'd take a sharp watch.

He kept looking and he saw in the kitchen window and saw

his aunt come upstairs and go on to a bed on that side of the house, and by and by he saw this man come up. "I must keep a sharper watch now," he thought. Then his aunt went downstairs and set the supper table. She put on roast beef and potatoes and carrots and pickles and everything that was nice.

Only a few minutes afterwards Little Claus heard the barn doors open. "That's my uncle now," he thought, and he went to the edge and said, "Hello." His uncle said, "What are you doing up there?" Little Claus said, "I wanted to stop overnight but my aunt wouldn't keep me." So he said, "Come with me and we'll go to the house." So he fired the horse's hide down on the barn floor. His uncle said, "What's that?" He said, "That's my goddess." So his uncle said, "Come in the house," and he said to leave it there; but Little Claus said no, he had to have it with him.

They went in and put the hide on the floor. The woman put some bread and apple stew on the table. They were sitting at the table and the uncle said, "Our supper ain't very good." Little Claus said, "That's all right." Now when he went to the table he had put the horse-hide under the table and he put his foot on it. By and by he pressed his foot on it and it said, "Cr-unch," and he said, "You keep quiet there." His uncle said, "What does that say?" Little Claus said, "Oh, whatever that says, it's true." "I wish you'd tell me what it said." "Oh, I don't like to." So again he pressed it and it went, "Cr-runch." His aunt went into the room again and his uncle said, "You've got to tell me what it says." "Well, it says over there in that cupboard in the corner there is roast beef, potatoes, carrots, and everything that's good to eat."

The uncle said, "No, we've got everything that's good to eat here." But when she came out of the room he said, "You go over in that cupboard and get the roast beef and the mashed potatoes and things that's in that cupboard." She didn't say a word but went and got them.

They talked and chatted and ate their supper and they sat back in their chairs and filled their pipes. Little Claus took the horse-hide and set it in front of him, and by and by he put his foot on it. "Cr-unch." "Look," said Little Claus, "you be still there." His uncle says, "What's he saying now?" "I wouldn't dare tell you." "Cr-unch." "Be quiet there," says Little Claus. The uncle said, "You've got to tell me what's there." Little Claus said, "If I tell you you'll faint." His uncle said, "Nothing will make me faint." So Little Claus said, "You go upstairs to the room on the south side and go into the red chest, and the devil is inside."

So up went the uncle as big as life and riz up the cover and here was this man. Down he came as white as a sheet and says, "Can you take the devil out of the house with that?" "Oh, yes," said Little Claus. "I can do anything with it." "I'll give you five hundred dollars if you can take the devil out of the house." "Oh, yes, I can do that," he says.

So Little Claus took his horse-hide and he sailed up the steps and he says to this man, "Look, they're going to kill you and I'll save your life." "All right," he said; so Little Claus shoved him into a big bag. He started and come downstairs, bump, bump, bump, bump, and pulled him outdoors and skinned him up onto his back, and when he got to the river he got on a bridge and he says, "I'm going to drown you." "Don't do that," he says. "You let me clear and I'll give you five bushels of gold." "Where are you going to get five bushels of gold?" "I can't give it to you here," he says. "But I've got a cheque and the ink and I'll write it out now." So Little Claus told him to keep to the side of the river where they couldn't see him from the house. Then he went back to the house and got his money and stayed overnight.

Next day he took his horse-hide and went to town and sold it for a dollar. Then he went to the bank and the cheque was good for it so he got his five bushels of gold measured out. Then he hired a team and put it on and brought his gold home.

When he went to unload, Little Claus was doubtful if he had the five bushels so he went over to Big Claus and borrowed his half bushel. He said to Big Claus, "Will you lend me your half bushel?" Big Claus was puzzled to know what he had to measure, so he smeared some tar in the bottom of the bushel. Little Claus measured his gold and he had five bushels so he took Big Claus's half bushel home. After Little Claus was gone Big Claus picked up the bushel and picked out seven hundred dollars worth of gold. He didn't say anything but he went to town and got his gold cashed and got seven hundred dollars for it.

Then Big Claus went to Little Claus and said, "Little Claus, where did you get your gold?" He said, "I got it out of my horse-hide." "Your horse-hide? How did you get five bushels of gold out of your horse-hide? If I killed my horses could I get five bushels of gold if I took the hides to town?" "Sure," said Little Claus. "All you got to do when you get to town is to stand up in your wagon and swing your arms and say, 'Horse-hides for sale. Horse-hides for sale. Five bushels of gold apiece,' and they'll bring your money right there."

Big Claus went home and took the pole-axe and killed three of his horses and skun them and put them on his wagon. Next morning he started to town and thought he would be a rich man. In town he stood up in his wagon and sung out, "Horse-hides for sale. Horse-hides for sale. Five bushels of gold apiece." People began to look at him and said, "That's Big Claus. He must be crazy." At last they began to gather around him and said, "What have you got?" He said, "Horse-hides." "Well," they said, "the only place to sell them is the tannery. He'll give you a dollar apiece for them."

Big Claus went back home. He only had two horses left, and he said, "I'll get even with you, Little Claus." Big Claus was very ugly and mad, and next night along about twelve o'clock he walked over and went into Little Claus's house. It happened that night that Little Claus and his grandmother traded beds. She slept downstairs and he slept up. He walked into Little Claus's room and took the pole-axe and let it go whang-oh, and it was the old woman. He went home and said, "You won't fool me anymore."

Next morning when Big Claus got up he looked over and saw Little Claus up working around his yard. He said, "There's Little Claus and I killed him last night."

Now when Little Claus got up that morning he saw his grandmother was killed and didn't know what to do, because if he said anything they would think he did it, so he decided to say nothing. Instead he went to town and borrowed a nice horse and covered cab and came home bright and early, and he had the old woman set up in the carriage and she sat there as if she was alive. He went to town and when he came to the front part of the town he came to the barroom and saw people there drinking, and he stopped the horse and went in. He said to the bartender, "Pour me out a drink; no, two drinks." One was for himself and the other for the bartender. Then the bartender took the treat.

The next time Little Claus asked for three drinks, and he said, "You take the third one out and give it to my poor grandmother. She's getting cold out there." The bartender said no, but Little Claus gave him twenty dollars. So he took it out and said, "Here, drink." But she didn't say anything and he was pretty drunk himself by then, so he threw the glass at her and she fell over and down between the shafts, and he ran in and said, "I've killed your grandmother." Little Claus said, "I'll have to have you arrested." The bartender said, "No. I'll give you three thousand dollars." So Little Claus said, "All right."

Then they sent for the undertaker and gathered the old woman up and buried her. Little Claus paid the expenses and stayed that night and the next day came back home, but before he came back he bought the carriage. Big Claus saw his nice horse and carriage and thought, "Where does Little Claus get money to buy such rigs as that?" He asked him and Little Claus said, "My money? I got it out of my grandmother. I sold her." So Big Claus knew he had killed the grandmother. "How much did you get for her?" he said. "Three thousand dollars." Big Claus said, "If I kill my grandmother and take her to town would I get three thousand dollars?" "Oh, yes," said Little Claus. "All you've got to do when you get to town is stand up in your wagon and swing your arms and say, 'Grandmother for sale. Grandmother for sale. Three thousand dollars.' "

Out went Big Claus and killed his grandmother and put her on an old express wagon and put a rug over her. Next morning he started for the town to sell her. He stood up in his wagon singing, "Grandmother for sale. Grandmother for sale. Three thousand dollars for grandmother." People gathered round and said, "Big Claus is crazy," and sent for the mayor of the town; and they lifted the rug and there lay the old dead woman with her head smashed in with the axe. They arrested him and buried her, and he had to pay seven thousand dollars, all the money he had. Then he came back home.

"Well," he said, "the next time you won't trick me." He went to the tanner and he bought a side of leather with a lock on it. When night came he grabbed Little Claus and shoved him into the bag. After the meeting was through and everybody had gone past he shoved the bag on his back and started to the river. He tugged along and when he came by the church they were singing a nice hymn and he thought he'd like to go in, so he put the bag down behind the picket fence. He went in, and after church he stayed behind until all the others had gone home.

Now while he was in church an old farmer had come along with twenty head of cows and Little Claus heard them and he began to moo. The old farmer heard him and Little Claus was saying, "I'm going to heaven." He stopped and went into the churchyard and asked, "What's that you say?" "I'm going to heaven." "How old are you?" "I'm thirty-five." "Well, I'm seventy-two and I never expect to go to heaven. Now if I'd open that bag and you fasten me up, could I go to heaven in your place?" "Yes," said Little Claus. "Anybody could."

So the farmer let Little Claus out, and he said that if Little Claus would let him go to heaven in his place he'd give him the twenty head of cattle. Little Claus told the farmer he mustn't speak or he wouldn't go to heaven. Then he put him in the bag, gathered up the cows and got them home ahead of the meeting, and tied them all over his barnyard, and after the meeting, Big Claus came out. He skinned the bag on his back and when they got to the bridge, away he threw the bag in the river.

Now Big Claus was happy. That night he went to bed and slept late; and by and by he looked up and there in Little Claus's yard was white cows, red cows, black cows, and there was Little Claus himself. "And I put him in the river last night!"

He went over and said, "Where did you get all your cows from?" "I got them out of the river you threw me in last night. As I floated down the river a mermaid picked me up and gave me these cows and told me to go home." "If you threw me into the river would the same thing happen to me?" asked Big Claus. "Yes, it would happen to anybody."

So Big Claus went home and made another bag and Little Claus had to rest three times before he reached the river. He walked out to the middle of the bridge and away went Big Claus down the river, and Big Claus is going yet.

22. DICKIE MELBOURNE: A CANTE-FABLE

Like "Little Claus and Big Claus," this amusing yarn is a well-known international tale classified as "Old Hildebrand," although it is called "Dicky Melbourne" in both England and Ireland as well as in Canada. It falls in a group of "Stories about Married Couples," most of which deal with adultery or other hazards of the married state, and it is an excellent example of a cante-fable with the storyteller singing the rhymed inserts.

The theme of the cheating wife has long been popular with storytellers and ballad singers. Chaucer and Boccaccio both delighted in such ribald tales, and "Our Goodman," who is repeatedly cuckolded, is one of the few Child ballads still common in oral tradition.

The "Old Hildebrand" story is known in practically every country of Europe as well as in India, North America, and the West Indies, and the plot is remarkably constant wherever it is told. It seems to have been most popular in Ireland (Stith Thompson reports 148 versions from there), and Leo O'Brien, a Newfoundlander, is obviously of Irish descent. (So was Mrs. Walsh from whom Helen Creighton recorded a very similar version.) Kelly Russell taped Mr. O'Brien's story and issued it on a Pigeon Inlet record.

Mr. O'Brien's version is very similar to the usual "Dicky Melbourne" texts except that he has an introduction about Dickie's parents and childhood which was apparently added to explain why Dickie was small enough to fit into the pedlar's pack. Old World storytellers were not too concerned about implausible details, but North Americans are more likely to try to rationalize their tales.

This is a good example of the way oral storytellers punctuate their narrative with repetitive words or phrases. Mr. O'Brien uses "he says" or "she says" a great many times, and where there is no conversation he uses "and so on" and "anyway" as punctuation. Such repetition is rather obtrusive when reading the tale, but passes unnoticed when listening to it.

Dickie Melbourne

Told by Leo O'Brien

Many years ago there was a boy and a girl growing up in a village, and when they grew up to be around the age of seventeen or eighteen they fell in love with each other, and after a period of courtship they wanted to get married. And the boy's name was Melbourne. So they got married anyway, and after they got married for a period of time, they noticed that Mrs. Melbourne was pregnant. So when the time of delivery arrived Mrs. Melbourne gave birth to a baby boy. And after he became two or three days old they had him christened, baptized and christened, and they named him Dickie, so his name became Dickie Melbourne. After Dickie became two or three months old they discovered he wasn't growing very fast, so they had to get some special food to try to make him grow. But in spite of all Dickie was very slow in growing, so he only ended up to be a very small man.

When Dickie grew up to be eighteen or twenty years of age he decided he would go around the world to see if he could earn some money, so he went to this place and some other different places and so on, and he earned a lot of money. And in one particular place he met up with a beautiful girl, and after a period of courtship they got married. Now Dickie was happy. He had plenty of money to build a lovely home, and he had a lovely woman, and oh, he was very, very happy.

So as years went on, Dickie was going to work and so on, and one day he came back and he said to his wife, he said, "I feel sick," he said. "Today I had difficulties at the work." His wife said, "Well, you'd better call the doctor." So he said, "Yes, I think it'd be wise." So Dickie phoned the doctor and the doctor came and examined him and said, "Well, Dickie boy, you're not serious," he said. "I'll give you some treatment," he said, "and in a few days you'll be able to get back to work again."

And while the doctor was there examining Dickie he took a fancy to Dickie's wife, and Dickie's wife took a fancy to the doctor. So when Dickie was able to go back to work again Dickie's wife phoned and told the doctor Dickie had gone back to work now, and the doctor came and paid Mrs. Melbourne a visit. And every day when Dickie went back to work the doctor would come, and Mrs. Melbourne and the doctor got very, very fond of each other.

And there was a pedlar living in the same village. So one day the pedlar said he thought he would go out and see if he could sell something; so he went around here and there, and he went to Dickie's house. And when he went to Dickie's house there was nobody there but the doctor and Mrs. Melbourne, and the pedlar took notice of what was going on between the doctor and Mrs. Melbourne. So anyhow the pedlar went home.

By and by Mrs. Melbourne and the doctor got very, very fond of each other, but the only thing was now Dickie was in the way. If only they could get rid of Dickie; but they didn't want to kill him or anything like that, but get rid of him some decent way. So they talked it over and the doctor said to Mrs. Melbourne, he said, "I got a plan," and she said, "Yes, what is it?" "Well," he said, "when Dickie comes from work, when you see Dickie coming, you set down in the chair; and when Dickie comes in you say, 'Dickie boy, something happened to me very, very quick just now,' and you say, 'I'm getting sick very, very fast.' You sit in the chair. You won't sit in the chair very long before you say, 'Dickie boy, I can't sit any longer, I got to go to bed.' " And he says, "You won't be in bed very long before you say, 'Dickie, I'm getting sick very, very fast, you'd better call the doctor.' And," he says, "I'll come and I'll know just what to say."

Dickie came home from work and Mrs. Melbourne sat in the chair and she said, "Dickie boy, I don't know what happened. I got sick very, very fast just now," she said. And finally she didn't sit in the chair very long. She said, "Dickie boy, I've got to go to bed." So she went to bed. She called Dickie in and she said, "Dickie boy, I can't stand it any longer. I'm getting sick very, very fast. You'd better call the doctor."

So Dickie rushed out and he called the doctor and the doctor came. He went into Mrs. Melbourne's room and finally he sat down with his head down, and Dickie said to the doctor, he said, "Doctor, what do you think of my wife?" he said. The doctor said, "Dickie boy, in fact," he said, "your wife is dangerously ill," he said. "She's going to die." But he said, "There's one thing in the world will save her and that is a bottle of Sweet Absalom. But you'll have to go to the end of the world to get it." Dickie said, "Go to the end of the world! Will I ever get there?" The doctor said, "Yes, boy, sure you'll get there and you'll get back again, too," he said. "And you'll save your wife."

My God! But Dickie would do anything to save his wife! So he set off for the end of the world. On his way he met this pedlar and the pedlar said, "Hello, Dickie, where are you going?" And Dickie said, "Boy," he said, "my wife is dangerously ill. The doctor tells me," he said, "there's only one thing in the world is going to save her and that's a bottle of Sweet Absalom, and I got to go to the end of the world to get it." And the pedlar said, "Ah, Dickie," he said, "you're foolish. Ah, God, you know you'll never get to the end of the world," he said. "You'll die before you get there." Dickie would hardly believe that. The pedlar said, "You know, Dickie, your wife is trying to get rid of you." Dickie would hardly believe that. The pedlar said, "I'll prove it. You crawl in my knapsack and I'll take you to your home so you'll see all that's going on for yourself." So Dickie crawled in the pedlar's knapsack and the pedlar threw it on his back and took him to Dickie's house.

Dickie was gone and Mrs. Melbourne was all dressed up and smiles, and the doctor was all smiles and everything. So Mrs. Melbourne prepared a lunch now for the three of them. So when the lunch was ready and set on the table, Mrs. Melbourne and the doctor sat at the side of the table and the pedlar sat at the end. And the pedlar said, "I think it would be wise now," he said, "for the three of us to sing the verse of a song before we eat. If we're going to have a good time," he said, "let's have a good time," he said. "Oh, yes, oh, yes, we agree!"

"Well," the pedlar said, "I call on Mrs. Melbourne to sing the first verse." So Mrs. Melbourne said she'd do her best anyway, and so she sang:

Oh, little Dickie Melbourne, you're far, far from home.
You're after a bottle of Sweet Absalom.
May God send you long passage and never to return,
And it's way for a bottle of ale, more ale!
This way for a bottle of ale!

Oh, they clapped their hands and said, "That's wonderful. That's a wonderful verse, a wonderful verse!" Now the pedlar said, "Doctor, it's your turn for the next verse." So the doctor said he'd do his best, so the doctor sang:

Oh, little Dickie Melbourne, you're far, far from home.
You're after a bottle of Sweet Absalom.
If God spares me my life I will sleep with your wife,
And it's way for a bottle of ale, more ale!
This way for a bottle of ale!

Oh, they clapped their hands. "That's wonderful! That's a wonderful time!" Now the doctor said to the pedlar, "It's your turn to sing the next verse." The pedlar said he'd do his best anyway, so the pedlar sang:

Little Dickie Melbourne, you are very nigh,
And out of my knapsack you may present fly,
And if you'll attack I will stand to your back,
And it's way for a bottle of ale, more ale!
This way for a bottle of ale!

Oh, Dickie began to shiver and shake in the knapsack. Up jumped the doctor and up jumped Mrs. Melbourne from the table, all excited. Dickie comes out of the knapsack and Mrs. Melbourne starts running away. Dickie threw a golden pennant to Mrs. Melbourne and he threw an old boot to the doctor. That separated the doctor and Mrs. Melbourne for ever afterwards.

23. TALL TALES FROM NORTHERN ONTARIO
Tall tales are especially popular in Canada, far outnumbering the more complex wonder tales. Herbert Halpert, Michael Taft, and Robert Gard have all published substantial collections, and most general folklore books include some. Quebec and Ontario have stories of Joe Mufferaw, and nearly every province has its Paul Bunyan yarns as well as other types of tall tales.

Many of them describe the fantastic exploits of hunters and fishermen, and others dwell upon our weather, which in reality is extreme enough, and hence lends itself readily to the type of exaggeration characteristic of tall tales. The cold winters and insect-ridden summers of northern Ontario inspired these short anecdotes that Forrest Sandberg heard in the Swedish community of Fort Francis. Sounds that freeze and later thaw out turn up in many yarns, as do oversize mosquitoes and blackflies.

Tall Tales from Northern Ontario

Told by Forrest Eugene Sandberg

Northern Winters
It's so cold in this here area that the coldest winter a mortal will ever have was on a summer day.

In this here country it's so cold that you just start a fire and when you're ready to leave you break off some of the frozen flame to start your next fire.

Nobody goes anywhere the first day of spring. All the sounds freeze in the winter and that spring day when they thaw out is one hell of a noisy day.

To hold a conversation up here in this here country in the winter, you need a large fire and two big frying pans. After you say a word you put it in the frying pan and thaw it out.

Paul Bunyan had an ox called Babe. He found her in the snow. It was such a cold winter that she'd turned blue. She never did thaw out completely, and that's why she's the blue ox.

Northern Insects
Only a greenhorn would try to shoot a mosquito with a 30-30. Anybody else knows that a wounded mosquito is dangerous.

[I] remember a man got lost, walked for twenty miles afore he saw he was atop a deer-fly.

Hell, the mosquitoes up here are so big and so fierce that as you walk through the woods you find a pile of big bones. That's where a mosquito chews up a whole village, pauses to digest his meal, and spits out the bones.

Mosquitoes get so bad in the spring that you have to swing an axe to cut out a square so you can breathe.

I've heard other places complain about horse-flies, about they fly right into a man and take a chunk out. Up here they fly right into a man quick as a dip and leave a little chunk.

24. ON THE TRAIL OF JOE MUFFERAW
Joe Mufferaw, like Paul Bunyan, was a favourite character in the tall tales popular among lumbering men and, like Paul, he was credited with prodigious size and strength. However, he differed

from Paul in that he had a real-life counterpart: Joseph Montferrand, a famous French-Canadian athlete whose career Benjamin Sulte described in *Histoire de Jos. Montferrand: L'Athlète canadien.*

Although Joe Mufferaw is more definitely Canadian than Paul Bunyan, he is not as popular in oral tradition. Still, he is a very familiar figure in the Ottawa Valley, largely because Bernie Bedore of Arnprior, Ontario, has popularized him in a number of books. He has some hold in tradition and has travelled beyond Canada: Richard Dorson collected several Mufferaw tales from French Canadians in Michigan's Upper Peninsula.

As these anecdotes from a mother and daughter indicate, Mufferaw is well known and much talked about in northern Ontario. Their stories differ from the usual tall tales, being more personal and inspired by the local setting. Jeanne Pattison, who collected them as part of a project for a folklore course at York University, got a photograph of the giant heel Mrs. Parcher talks about — which is indeed huge, and is definitely a heel. It might be explained prosaically as an artifact produced for an advertising display, but Mrs. Parcher's explanation is more attractive.

On the Trail of Joe Mufferaw

A. Told by Mrs. Simon Parcher

The first I heard about Joe Mufferaw was from my grandfather, my mother's father, and he lived along the banks of the river for a certain length of time, the Madawaska River, and then he finally turned into buying a farm. And it's about half a mile back from here, and he farmed on that and raised four children; and he used to log still when they took out the timbers, and he was a great shingle maker. He made shingles by hand and he claimed that he was in territory that Joe Mufferaw was in and cut timber. And at that time they didn't have any horses, but that Joe Mufferaw was strong enough fer to put those logs onto his shoulders and carry them out of the bush to the river banks!

So I said, oh, oftentimes, well it couldn't all be true. He couldn't be that big. They said, "Well, yes, because he took a number twenty-one boot and it had to be made by the shoemaker and such a huge man you never saw the like. He was just a real giant." They used to call him a giant, Joe Mufferaw, and they said he would go into a bar and ... people, they'd get into fighting condition and he'd just clean the whole bar. And he'd just take them by the back, each man like that, and bang them together until they were ready to quit fighting. So that his name was quite a legend around the whole country because of one thing would happen and it was pretty big and they would say, well, Joe Mufferaw had to be there because such and such couldn't have been done without Joe Mufferaw.

I [Jeanne Pattison] asked: What was your relative's name who told you Joe Mufferaw tales?

Hemon Townes. He come up there in 18 and 60 [1860]. And he was only a young man and then he left and went back down the Madawaska . . . and he stayed there two or three years and then he got married. And then they said, no, he wasn't happy down here and he was going back where he came from, and went back onto the old property again, and that's where my mother was born . . . She married my father from there . . .

Hemon Townes said that he saw the work of Joe Mufferaw and he said they had huge pine that deep, that would be a good four feet across the stump, you know, and that four or five bangs of Joe Mufferaw's double-bitted axe he said would do more than what two men could do with a cross-cut saw in half an hour . . .

I asked Mrs. Parcher if she remembered the earliest time she heard Joe Mufferaw stories from her family: perhaps when she was a little girl?

Oh, yes. I couldn't have been more than seven years old when I can truly and deeply remember my grandfather, and that's where the stories come from. I never heard them from my father because he was one of the ones that came up from Arnprior and then they went across the Kamaniskeg, the other side. So they were too far from the water to get mixed up with a man that worked along the rivers and lakes as much as Joe Mufferaw done, because he never went inland much . . .

Joe Mufferaw's Giant Heel

I asked about Joe Mufferaw's giant heel and what year Mrs. Parcher found it, as it was the most enormous heel I had ever seen.

It must have been in 1964 or '65. It's just terrific! You know a lot of people wouldn't believe it. They said it was just a chunk of rubber, and my daughter said fiddlesticks on that! It's a real heel. If you ever seen a rubber heel on anyone else's rubbers, you know very well how they fit on—how they fit right on to a boot. You see every nail that went in there [she shows the heel]. Well, it was certainly nailed on. Well, that was enormous! Now you just take my heel and put it alongside that—no comparison. No wonder he wore a number twenty-one size boot!

Mrs. Parcher, have you compared this to a man's size boot?

Oh, yes! Now my nephew on the hill, he takes a twelve, and his heels are just like a kitten alongside of that . . .

Did you immediately think it was Joe Mufferaw's heel when you saw that?

That was my daughter's thought, when I told her. I phoned her and she wanted to know the whole thing . . . I told her it was huge. "Would you measure it for me?" she asked. And I have measured it and I forget whether it is fifteen, but I think it is fifteen inches around here [around the outside of the rubber heel]; and she said, "It couldn't be that size." And I said, "Well, it is, and that's the size of it." And then right off she said, "That certainly must belong to Joe Mufferaw. He just had to be right around here." And I said, "Well, he followed where the pine was, and this was all heavy, heavy pine long time ago, and there is still lots of pine." "Well," she said, "he was there, that's all there was to it. Nobody in this whole Canada could have any bigger foot than Joe Mufferaw." Well, there it is to show it.

How did you find it?

I planted flowers down alongside of the house there. I was planting dahlias. And of course you have to dig a trench and you have to dig them quite deep and put some fertilizer and manure, and this is when I hoed up to this [the heel]. And you see, I hoed the end and it wouldn't come. It would fly back, and then I hoed it again, and so much it would fly back, and I knew I had ahold of something. But I thought it was an old piece of tube, is what I thought it was, and I didn't want it there as it would interfere with the roots, you know. So I had to dig it up.

Well, then when I first saw the thickness of the thing coming up, I dug a little more careful, but I do believe that I . . . ripped that likely with the hoe, and then I seen the thickness I knew that it wasn't a tube . . . So I dug more careful, and when I got it partly out then I could see these nails; then I knew what it was right off the bat. So then I dug more careful and took it right out of the ground just the way it was. Now you know that is just as big as a horseshoe. It's about the size of a number five horseshoe . . .

Mrs. Parcher keeps it in a jar of purified water — captured rain water.

B. Told by Jean Richter

Joe Mufferaw's Cord
When Fred [Fred Parcher, Jean Richter's brother] drove up the road [Chippewa Road] towards Haskins cottage with the tractor in the wintertime, this is when he came across this, you know, cord stretched across the road; and it was ordinary cord, and he

got out to see where it came from and how it got there. So he said it was from one tree to another right across the road. So he waded through the snow, and it was up the tree, and it went right to the tree-tops up in those big maple, beech, and oak and elm. You know they are tall trees, and the string went right up to the top, and it followed the tops of the trees. So when I went over home [to Mrs. Simon Parcher's home, Chippewa Road, Barry's Bay], I took the skidoo and I followed the road and I followed the string; followed the tops of those trees almost into the cottages. And there it stopped, you know, all of a sudden, and this I sent in to the Ottawa *Journal*. First I phoned it in. I phoned it in to the police station, and I said, "Where on earth, have you any idea where something like this could come from? It had come from somewhere and we can't figure it out. It had to come from Joe Mufferaw because nobody else could reach the tree-tops, you know, only Joe Mufferaw." So they said it could have come off of a plane. Maybe somebody had left a roll of cord laying on the wing of a plane or someplace, and it gradually unwound, you know, and it would naturally lay on the tree-tops. But it was just like a telephone line runs up that road on the very tops of those trees, and you know yourself how tall those trees are. Well, Fred just cut the cord that was across the road and left the other there . . . .

Joe Mufferaw's Raspberries
That was in the winter, and then in the spring, in raspberry time . . . a way up on a limb of a pine tree, so far you would have to get a ladder to get up there, there was a raspberry plant growing out of the pine tree with raspberries on it. So Fred said Joe Mufferaw had to plant that raspberry. How else would it get there, and it was there for everybody to see? You know, of course, it could have been a squirrel that took seeds up; there may have been a bird's nest there, or some earth grooving; but he said that Joe Mufferaw must have planted it.

Joe Mufferaw's Tree-House
Ever since that happened, you know, anything that's big or we don't know how to explain, well, Joe Mufferaw, you know! Mom and I have often intended to go down into the bush, because one time she said there was a tree-house down in the bush below our place. She doesn't know if it's still down there or if it's blown down with the wind or something, but this darn tree-house was away up, and you know how big the pines are over home, white pines, really huge! It was away to heck up [in the

tree], but it belonged to somebody else's land and at the time we didn't want to go down there, while they were there. We never did get together to go down there to see if it's still there. I was going to go down and take pictures of a tree-house away up in the trees that high. Who else put it there but Joe Mufferaw? Who else, you know?

Joe Mufferaw's Knife

Some years ago my father Simon and brother Fred were cutting wood up in your cottage area [Barry's Bay, northern Ontario], and about fifteen feet off the ground they found the end of a hunting knife about three inches long, broken off and embedded in the middle of a tree sixteen inches thick! Who else but Joe could drive a knife that far into a solid hardwood tree, and fifteen feet off the ground? It's always been a mystery. Mom had the piece of hunting knife for years but she can't find it; maybe Daddy threw it away in later years.

25. HUMOROUS STORIES FROM AROUND CHAPEAU, QUEBEC

While tall tales and ethnic jokes are the most common types in the category of "Jokes and Anecdotes," these stories illustrate a third type: stories about local characters, usually attributing to them certain familiar jokes or exaggerating their perceived characteristics. As Margaret Bennett-Knight notes: "Every community has its anecdotes about well-known local characters who have gained a reputation for their wit, their foolishness, their eventful lives, or for some particular eccentric trait. These individuals are usually held in affection and even esteem by their neighbours. Even when storytellers seem to be making fun of them, it is obvious that no malice is intended."

In Alberta Herbert Halpert found many jokes about Dave McDougall; in New Brunswick Carole Spray recorded a group of Miramichi stories about an old trapper named Geordie Brown; in Nova Scotia Arthur Huff Fauset found jokes about Jim Grey; and in the Eastern Townships of Quebec Margaret Bennett-Knight heard anecdotes about the outlaw Donald Morrison and also about other local characters.

Sheldon Posen, a Canadian folklorist who spent some time collecting folklore in the Ottawa Valley around Chapeau, heard these amusing stories while he was researching local songs for his doctoral dissertation. He has changed some of the names to avoid embarrassing the persons involved.

Humorous Stories from around Chapeau, Quebec

A. Local

Experienced Hand

Told by O'Kane Payne

Dan Couvrette went upriver to hire on for the drive. There were a couple of young lads ahead of him in line. The first went in and the clerk asked him, "How much experience have you had on the drive?" The young lad answered, "I never drove before." The clerk said, "Well, you can't get on here. It takes men with big experience. No, no, you can't get a job here at all." So out he went. Next fellow went in. "How long have you been driving?" He said, "I've been driving for one year." "No good," said the clerk. "No good, you have to be on the drive for a *long* time to get a job here." So Dan went in. The clerk asked him the same question as the others: "How long have you been driving?" He says, "Oh, I've been driving a *long* time." The clerk says, "Well, I have to put something more than that down in my report here. Tell me, how long have you been driving?" Dan says, "Did you ever hear of the time the Lord walked on water?" "Yeah," he says. "Well," Dan says, "I was tight to His arse on a spruce!"

Not Responsible

Told by Loy Gavan

Felix Vaillancourt was pressing hay around home, staying at different people's houses. He went into Chapeau one night for a drink or two, and when he came back to where he was staying he found that the people of the house were all in bed. So he went into the barn and climbed up in the hay mow to sleep. Not long after, a young couple crept into the barn and they had a time together. Afterwards, the girl said to the fella, "If anything happens to me, what am I going to do?" The young fella said, "Never mind. We'll leave it to The Man above." Felix shouted, "Don't leave nothing to me. I've got to leave early in the morning."

Careful Spitting

Told by Loy Gavan

Jim Michaud went to visit Eddy Sullivan's one time. Mrs. Sullivan was a wonderful housekeeper, but Jim used to spit his tobacco juice right on the floor. He was doing it that night, so Mrs. Sullivan went and got the spittoon and moved it close to Jim. Well, he spit to one side of it. So she moved it again, closer to him. And Jim said, "If you don't move that thing away, I'm going to spit right into it."

Fast Driver

Told by John Berrigan

Well, Donald Retty was an awful man to drive a car. Clemmie Hayes once got on with him at the hotel in Sheen and asked for a lift home. Joe Slattery asked her afterwards whether she'd had a good ride. "Well," she said, "he drove so fast I stuck out my hand to wave at Devine Morris and Angie Chartrand waved back!" Devine and Angie lived two miles apart.

Growing Up Poor

Told by Tom and Viola Kennedy

Pat Couvrette liked to embarrass his sister when he went to visit her in Sudbury by telling stories of how poor they had been growing up. "Our family ate so much wild meat," he would say, "that whenever we heard a dog bark we tried to jump the fence. For supper, Mother would hang a piece of pork over the table, and the rest of us would point our potatoes at it. One night, there was an extra pork chop. Father said he'd turn out the lights, and the person who needed it the most could take it. The lights went out, and when they came on again, there were eight forks in the old man's paw." All his sister could say was, "Oh, Pat!"

The Mutual Suit

Told by Lennox Gavin

Percy and Mervyn Slattery were twins who lived around Sheenboro. One time there was a dance at Sheen, and somebody asked Mervyn where Percy was. "At home," he replied. "He's not coming to the dance?" they asked. He said, "No, it's my turn to wear the suit!"

The Sitting Disease

Told by Geordie Brunette

Poor old Paddy Berrigan was too lazy to yawn. You couldn't get him to work. So one weekend we'd been down home, and my mother's hens were sick. I was telling Tom Berrigan — we were having dinner at his house, I guess, and Paddy was at the other end of the table — that I didn't know what the hell was wrong with the chickens. "I don't know," I said. "Mother's hens just sit like that and then," I said, "they die." "Oh," Tom said, "that's the 'sitting disease,' " he said. "Paddy has that!"

B. Stories of the Couvrettes

Retold by I. Sheldon Posen

The Couvrettes were a family who lived at Chichester, a settlement near Chapeau, Quebec, about 120 miles northwest of Ottawa. Stories about them still circulate in the area, all featuring the elements most prized in local humour: smart answers or remarks that neatly summarize a situation.

Impolite Cows
Paddy Couvrette once took a neighbour, Clare Gavan, to a dance at Malone's — one of the farmers near them. Of course, everyone walked everywhere then. Anyway, they decided to take a shortcut through a cow pasture, and they found it pretty rough going, stepping over and around the cowpies. Paddy took Clare by the hand, stepping first this way, then that, and he said, "My goodness, Clare," he said, "I like butter and milk, but do I ever hate those impolite cows!"

A Fight at the Fair
One time, Paddy Couvrette went to the Chapeau Fair and got into a fight. Those times, the fair was held the second week in September. So we were digging potatoes when he came by, looking awful, and Father said to him, "What happened, Paddy?" "Oh," he said, "Martin and I got into a fight." And Father said, "How's the other lad?" Paddy said, "You should see the son of a bitch! There's not a mark on him!"

Revenge on the Warden
Paddy's brother Tommy made money by catching foxes and keeping them in cages until their fur was prime. This was illegal, of course, and someone informed the game warden who came to the farm one day and made Tommy set them all free. Well, the warden had come back so often that he got to know Tommy's sister, Annette, and he finally married her. Paddy, who had been threatening to shoot the warden each time he came, was asked

how he could have allowed this to happen. "Well," he said, "I couldn't shoot him, and we knew the son of a bitch was no good, so for spite we gave him Annette!"

Stolen Chickens

One night the Couvrettes decided to have a gambling and a bouillon — invite the neighbours to play cards for chickens and have chicken stew afterwards. Only they didn't have any chickens. So they invited old cross-eyed Mrs. Murphy who lived on a farm nearby to come especially early, and went and stole her chickens. All night she was playing for her own chickens. She put the ones she had won in a potato sack to carry home, only stopping at the end of the night to ask where they had got them. "Mother went out and bought some today," Pat told her — this when his mother was so frail she could hardly walk across the kitchen floor. Anyhow, Mrs. Murphy went home and never noticed anything until morning when she found the tags from the chickens' legs on the ground in the back of her house. She stormed down the road and accused Pat of stealing her chickens. "Those aren't your chickens," he told her. "Oh, yes they are," she insisted. "I saw the marks on their legs." Looking at her crossed eyes, Pat retorted, "You couldn't see nothing. Jesus Christ, your eyes are so crooked you'd have to lie on your back to look down a well!" Oh, he was quite the lad.

Clever Potato Bugs

One of Jack Couvrette's stories concerned old Mrs. MacFarland who was a great woman to pray. One year, he says, she forgot to spray her potatoes and was having a terrible time with potato bugs. So she went to the priest who gave her some holy water and a crucifix. She put them on the gate post leading to her field, but the potato bugs fooled her, says Jack: they went round and came in the gap by Giroux's!

A Simple Trick

They were on the drive one spring, Jack Couvrette and Eddie Gagnon. They had a bag of bread and the meat that they carried along with them: meal-time come, they just sat down and they ate. Well, one day Eddie was on one side of the river, and Jack was on the other, and it was coming near dinner-time. So Jack calls to Eddie. "Eddie," he says, "can you come across the logs there with the bag of bread?" "Oh, by ginger," said Eddie, "that's a simple trick!" So he starts across, running on the logs with the bag of bread, and in he goes, bag of bread and all. Jack

Couvrette says: "Oh, oh, black Jesus! 'Simple trick!' He's in the water with the bag of bread!" That was his word — "black Jesus"!

26. *JOKES ABOUT RELIGIONS*
Jokes about religions are somewhat similar to ethnic jokes in that they make fun of an identifiable group, but they differ in that ethnic jokes are transferable from one group to another: Polish jokes become Newfie or Ukie or Paki jokes by the simple change of name. However, most of these religious jokes cannot be transferred: Anglican jokes are distinct from Catholic, and Presbyterian from Jewish. There are a few exceptions: the Catholic joke about the steak that becomes a fish has a counterpart in which Jewish dietary laws are broken, and the one about the golf-playing rabbi could be told of a minister, but in general these jokes play on the differences between religions.

Alice Kane's phenomenal memory and storytelling ability were demonstrated in her book, *Songs and Sayings of an Ulster Childhood*. Since then, she has continued to come up with interesting items of folklore, including this large assortment of religious jokes. A few are memories from her childhood, others she heard from friends, and the origins of some she can't identify.

Jokes about Religions

Told by Alice Kane

Anglicans
Pisky, Pisky up an' doon,
Cross yourself and turn aroon'.
(Glasgow children's rhyme. For Pisky read Episcopalian.)

Sergeant at British Army church parade (circa World War I): "Church of England on the right, Roman Catholics on the left, all fancy religions — fall out."

Tactful Anglican cleric at ecumenical service: "There's no need for us to be at odds, no need at all! Why, we all worship the same God, you in *your* way, we in *His*."

There was a young curate of Salisbury
Who was such a halisbury-scalisbury
    He wandered through Hampshire
    In bright purple pampshire
Till his bishop forbade him to Walisbury.
(For Salisbury read Sarum; for Hampshire read Hants.)

The new arrivals in heaven were being shown around by a friendly angel. He led them down the main street: "Here is our bank — very prosperous. The Presbyterians run it." And to the riverside: "The Jordan," he told them, "the Baptists use it *and* the Holy Rollers." And across to a large meadow: "That large tent is for the Methodist camp meetings." Then he led them to the solid brick building of the Four Square Gospel, and the onion domes of the Russians. Two women asked, in great distress: "But *where* are the Anglicans? You can't tell us there are none here?"

"Oh, the Anglicans," said the angel. "Of course there are Anglicans." And he led them to the top of a high cliff and, laying his finger to his lips and saying, "Shsh — hush, please," he pointed to a broad ledge down below. There they were, lots and lots of them, neat and orderly and liturgically correct, divided tidily into High and Low. "There they are," said the angel, "safe and sound. But *quiet* please — they like to think there is no one here but themselves."

An Anglo-Catholic friend used to tell of his early days at St. Thomas Church, where the High and Low factions warred over carrying the cross in procession. The Low group won temporarily, and the Highs sang: "Onward, Christian soldiers, marching as to war,/With the Cross of Jesus behind the vestry door."

And then there was the little girl who called her teddy bear "Gladly" because he was cross-eyed: "Gladly my cross I'd bear." And the one who loved the hymn about the little girl bear: "Can a mother's tender care/Cease toward the child she bear."

The Presbyterians

Question one from *The Shorter Catechism of the Westminster Assembly of Divines*: What is the chief end of Man? Answer: Man's chief end is to glorify God and to enjoy Him for ever. Glasgow children chant: "Presby, Presby, never bend./Sit ye doon on man's Chief End."

The squire was a hearty man fond of a good joke. The parson was a timid one, but fond of a quiet nip now and again, if the parish didn't know.

One day Squire said, "Parson, I've got a fine big bottle of excellent cherry brandy. I'll send it to you if you promise to acknowledge it in the parish magazine."

Parson, after a moment's thought, agreed, and the brandy was sent and enjoyed. The next issue of the parish magazine carried the following announcement: "Parson wishes to thank

Squire for his kind gift of fruit, and even more for the spirit in which it was sent."

In my mother's day (she was born in 1880), Presbyterian churches were debating fiercely the singing of hymns and paraphrases and the use of organs. The precentor, with a tuning fork, was the only aid to music. In the days of illiterate congregations he also read the words:

Precentor: My eyes are dim, I cannot see,
Congregation: My eyes are dim, I cannot see.
Precentor: I have not brought my specs with me,
Congregation: I have not brought my specs with me.
Precentor: I merely said my eyes were dim,
Congregation: I merely said my eyes were dim.
Precentor: I did not mean to sing a hymn.
Congregation: I did not . . .

A group of Ulster Presbyterian ministers were in a pub. They were well-educated, travelled men, and they were discussing the Pope: his scholarship, his courtesy, and so on. A little country clergyman (my father always said from Annalong in the Mourne Mountains) finally burst out: "He may be all you say, gentlemen, he may be all you say — but he's got a bad name in Portadown."

Constabulary officer (to farmer): "You must have your name on your truck — one foot high or more in clear Roman capitals."
Farmer: I will *not* then. I'll have nothing Roman on my truck no matter what you say!"

There is a story about a stout Presbyterian in a small town in Ontario in the nineteenth century. He fought and fought against an organ, and when it came he left and joined the Methodists. Some months later a friend met him and asked how he liked the Methodist Church. "Oh, it's fine," he said. "Just fine."

"But," protested the friend, "there's an organ in the Methodist Church."

"I know," he said, "I know. I've nae objection tae organs, except in the House of God."

There was a poor Catholic farmer in New Brunswick who sold his horse to the Presbyterian minister. After some time they met one day and the farmer asked how the horse was doing.

"Oh, very well, very well indeed," replied the minister. "I'm making a good Presbyterian out of him."

"Well," said the farmer, scratching his head, "it's a good religion. For a horse."

Catholics

A Protestant from Northern Ireland moved to a village in the South. He established a successful business and became a respected citizen. Then he wanted a wife. He sought out a farmer with three lovely daughters, but none of them would marry a Protestant, so he agreed, finally, to turn Catholic. But it was hard—it went against the grain, so the priest taught him to repeat over and over: "I'm a Catholic, not a Protestant. I'm a Catholic, not a Protestant."

So they were married, and the wife reported to the priest that all was going well except that her husband could not get used to fish on Friday. The priest urged him to keep repeating: "I'm a Catholic, not a Protestant; I'm a Catholic, not a Protestant."

One day the priest passed the newlyweds' house and smelt a lovely smell of cooking steak. "But it's Friday," he thought. He knocked on the door.

"Oh, Father," said the wife. "I cooked fish—but go and look in the kitchen."

In the kitchen stood the husband turning a big steak in the pan and repeating firmly: "I'm a Catholic, not a Protestant. I'm a Catholic, not a Protestant. You're a fish, not a steak. You're a fish, not a steak . . ."

(from Joe Heaney)

The market gardeners in a little French village came to the *curé*. "Father," they said. "Our vegetables are dying on the stalk — we've had a drought now for weeks. Please, will you pray for rain?"

"Of course," replied the *curé*. "Of course. But first you must all decide what day you want it to rain. *I*, for one, don't want it on Sunday for it would spoil the Corpus Christi procession."

So the gardeners went to the people. "Rain of course," said the housewives, "but not on Monday. That is wash day and we need the sun to dry it."

"Not Tuesday," said the farmers. "Our hay won't be all in, and if the hay is ruined we are ruined."

"Oh, and not Wednesday," cried the schoolmaster, "for that is our Sports Day."

"Any day but Thursday," said the shopkeepers. "That is early closing and our only day to be out."

"Friday would be bad for us all," said the villagers, "for that is market day."

"Oh, *please*, not Saturday!" cried the children.

"I think," said the *curé*, "we had better leave it to the good Lord to decide."

A sex therapist moved into a little town in the mountains and proved very successful in increasing the sexual activity [of the town]. Most of those who consulted him showed great improvement and satisfaction, but one middle-aged man seemed to improve very slowly.

"You know," said the therapist, "you may think you're doing very well; but three times a month is hardly a record to crow about."

"You don't think so?" said the patient. "Me, I think it's not bad for a Catholic priest."

A stranger was watching a religious procession. "Who is that man," he asked, "with the kind face, who is riding on the little donkey?"

"Oh, that," they told him, "is the Lord of Earth and Heaven."

"And who," asked the stranger, "is this, in the golden chair with the jewelled crown and the servants to carry him?"

"That," he was told, "is the Vicar on Earth of the Lord of Earth and Heaven."

It happened at an Irish border crossing. All seemed quiet as three illicit immigrants approached. Just as they thought they were safe the sentry raised himself and shouted: "Who goes there?"

The woman gasped and crossed herself. "Jesus, Mary, Joseph!" she exclaimed.

"Pass, Holy Family," said the sentry.

(from Professor Nevil Norton Evans, my first-year chemistry professor at McGill)

The customs officer boarded the boat train from France. People opened bags and parcels and two little girls, demure in convent uniforms, clutched tightly a bottle each. The customs man nodded at the bottles: "What's in those?"

"Holy water," said the mother. "Just holy water from Lourdes!"

The officer twisted a cap and sniffed. "It's French brandy," he said.

The mother rolled her eyes to heaven and cried: "Glory be to God, a miracle!"

The Protestant Boys

An American visitor arrived in Belfast on a bright July day. He found arches and banners and bonfires everywhere, and fife and drum bands (*and* the Lambeg drums) on every street.

"What is it?" he asked. "What's the celebration?"

"It's the *Twelfth*, man."

"The twelfth — the twelfth what?"
"The Twelfth of July."
"What's the Twelfth of July?"
"Oh, for God's sake, man, go home and read your Bible!"

Sign on wall (very usual): NO POPE HERE
Sign underneath (less usual): LUCKY OLD POPE

Mrs. Paisley was getting into bed one night when she hit her toe on a box. "Oh, God," she moaned.
  "There now, dear," said the Reverend Ian. "You don't have to call me that when we're alone."

A stout brave Orangeman was walking down a Belfast street when he looked in the window of a wee shop. It was just crammed with clay statues of saints and rosary beads and crucifixes and such. The Orangeman saw his duty plain. He found a fine brick and heaved it clear through the shop window. "I *hate* bigotry," he said.

It was wee Jimmy's bedtime but he didn't want to leave. Daddy had a roomful of guests and it was lively and exciting. He sidled up to his father and said, "To hell wi' the Pope, Daddy."
  "Go on now, Jimmy, away to bed with ye — you know you can't say your prayers here."

Wee Jimmy was dyin', no doubt of it.
  "Is there anything you want, Jimmy?"
  "Aye," he said. "Bring me my wee orange sash."
  So they brought him his wee orange sash.
  "Bring me my wee orange drum."
  So they brought him his wee orange drum.
  And wearin' his wee orange sash and beatin' his wee orange drum and shoutin', "To hell wi' the Pope!" wee Jimmy fell asleep in the sweet arms o' Jesus.
(from Hugh and Rose Ferguson of an old Toronto Catholic family)

Jews

The Italian obstetrician at St. Michael's Hospital had just delivered a sickly-looking baby. He looked at it in distress, quickly took a jar of water and baptized the child: "I baptize you Joseph in the name of the Father, the Son, and the Holy Spirit."
  "Well," he said, mopping his brow, "I hope the parents think the name is all right."
  The nurse looked up and smiled. "The baby's name is Cohen, doctor."

The young rabbi had two loves: his synagogue and golf. But he seldom got to play golf, for the synagogue kept him so busy. But one Sabbath morning, a crisp sunny day, everything was over nice and early. No Sisterhood meeting to address, no calls of condolence.

He looked at the sky, he sniffed the air, he remembered the months since he had been on a golf course. And then (sin no. 1) he went and got his golf clubs and carried them to the car. Then (sin no. 2) he drove thirty miles to the golf course. And then he started to play.

Up above him, in the skies, Moses looked down. He saw the orthodox rabbi about to make his first shot.

"God!" cried Moses. "Look!"

"Yes, I see," said God calmly.

"Look again," Moses begged. "It's the orthodox rabbi and it's the Sabbath."

"I know," said God. "I'll take care of him."

The rabbi drove. The ball sailed into the air, clearing the bushes, clearing the stream, and it fell on the green. Then it rolled, gently, directly, right into the first hole.

"Did you see *that*?" asked Moses bitterly of God. "You call *that* taking care of him?"

"Oh, yes," God said. "I've punished him. It's the best shot of his life — but who can he tell about it?"

(from Wilma Paskus)

27. JEWISH JOKES FROM TORONTO

These jokes illustrate still another type: the esoteric jokes that are told within a folk group, and are inspired by the real or supposed characteristics of that group. They differ from the usual ethnic jokes told by the majority group about a minority to make fun of that minority. As already mentioned, those *"blasons populaires"* are easily transferred from one group to another; the esoteric jokes, like the preceding religious jokes, are more specifically related to one group. However, they differ from the religious jokes in that they are told within the group they satirize, while the religious jokes are more apt to be told by persons outside the group.

These examples form part of Barbara Kirshenblatt-Gimblett's Ph.D. dissertation, "Traditional Story-Telling in the Toronto Jewish Community: A Study in Performance and Creativity in an Immigrant Culture." Dr. Kirshenblatt-Gimblett now heads the

Department of Performance Studies at the Tisch School of the Arts, New York University.

Introducing the first joke, she notes that in the Old World, the social position with the highest prestige was that of rabbi, but in the New World rabbis earned less than doctors and lawyers, so the most prestigious careers were in the medical and legal professions rather than the religious.

She uses the second joke to illustrate the speech variety available to a multilingual immigrant, saying that Martin uses five different dialects: English and Yiddish, imitations of Jewish immigrant English, imitations of Texas English, and technical "Astronaut English." She also calls attention to the way in which he switches from one type of language to another, thus heightening the humour.

Jewish Jokes from Toronto

The Singing Dog

Told by Shelly Weiss

A man went back to the synagogue where he was bar mitzvahed, and as he walked up the walk, you know, he gets a very warm feeling in his heart. He puts his hand on the knob. He can feel his hands shaking. He starts to go inside and the *shames* [beadle] meets him at the door.

He says, "Mister, you got a ticket?" He says, "No, as a matter of fact I don't." He says, "Well, you know, it's the high holidays. You got to have a ticket." He says, "Well, you know I was bar mitzvahed in this synagogue." He says, "Yes, but the seats are full. You got to have a ticket. If not you can't come in." He says, "Well, you know, I was considering making a donation to the synagogue. Perhaps a thousand dollars." "A thousand dollars? We make some kind of arrangement," he says.

So he leads the guy inside. And, no, the guy first goes out to the car and he brings with him a French poodle. The *shames* takes a look. "A French poodle *brengsti du aran in di shil* [you bring in here in the synagogue], you know. All right. A thousand dollars." He closes his eyes. He brings him into the synagogue. And the rabbi sees what's going on and he says to the *shames*, "What's he doing here?" "He's donating a thousand dollars." "A thousand dollars? All right."

They seat him down, you know, *mit di hint* [with the dog] and they're about to open the services with opening chants of the hymns, you know, et cetera, and the man stands up and he starts to sing along with the *khazn* [cantor]. The poodle sees what his master's doing. The poodle stands up on his back two legs and he opens his mouth and he sings. And such beautiful notes of music you never heard before from a dog or from any person [laughter]. The rabbi can't believe his eyes. The rabbi can't believe his eyes! The congregation is completely astounded. Such beautiful notes of music and from a dog.

Well, after the synagogue services were over, the rabbi comes down from the platform, from the *bime* [platform in the synagogue from which the Torah is read] there, and he shakes hands with the man and he says, "It's a pleasure having you here in our synagogue." And the man said, "Well, you know, I was bar mitzvahed in this synagogue."

"Yes, yes," he says. "And your dog. He was fantastic," he says. "We never heard such beautiful sounds coming from a dog," he says. "He should become a cantor, he should become."

The man looks at the rabbi. He says, "Talk to him, rabbi. He wants to become a doctor."

The Jewish Astronaut

Told by Martin Sokolov

The President of the United States was going for re-election, and [an adviser] told him that he was going to lose the Jewish vote, and Lyndon Johnson says, "Whadda you mean, ahm gonna lose da Jewish vote? Wha?"

He says, "Because you're discriminating." He says, "Have you ever had a Jewish astronaut?"

He thought about it. He says, "No, we nevah have." He says, "Well, get me a Jewish astronaut," he says. "But don't get me one of these ringers. You go to the *Yeshive*[1] in New York, and you pick up a real genuayne Jewish astronaut."

So they get a guy in New York with the sombrero, and the ten-gallon hat with the *peyes* [sidelocks] and the *gartl* [belt] and the *mantl* [coat], and they take him to Cape Kennedy and they give him a crash course on astronauting and he is ready to go up in the cone of the rocket. And the Commander comes up and he says, "Astronaut Hymie Berkowits, Astronaut Hymie Berkowits. This is control tower. In honour of your faith we are going to take the countdown in Jewish. Remember?" So he goes, "*Tsen, nayn, akht, zibn,* and holding, *zeks, finf, fir, dray,* and holding,

---

1. An institution of higher talmudic learning; Orthodox Jewish all-day school.

tsvey, eyns un avek [ten, nine, eight, seven and holding, six, five, four, three, and holding, two, one and away]."

And away goes Astronaut Hymie Berkowits into the clouds. And he's going for about five minutes and the control tower calls him and says, "Control tower to Astronaut Hymie Berkowits, control tower to Astronaut Hymie Berkowits. Are you ready to push phase five to start operation twelve?" "Oy, I'll tell you da truth. I got no time."

So this goes on three, four times. Finally the General comes into the control tower and he calls up and he says, "Astronaut Hymie Berkowits, this is control tower, General speaking. What is this business, we keep calling you and you keep saying you got no time? What's going on there?"

He says, "Vell, you see General, it's like dis. I'm goink around de vorld very, very fest; around and around from light to dark and from dark to light. In between putting on de *Tfiln* [phylacteries], taking off de *tfiln; minkhe, mayrev* [the Jewish afternoon prayer, the Jewish evening prayer], I got no time!"

28. THE LOBSTER SALAD: A RECITATION

Although we usually think of folktales as prose narratives told orally, the stories in ballads and poems also serve as folktales when they are sung or recited. Traditional prose tales and ballads have long been studied, but only recently have folklorists turned their attention to recitations or, as they are perhaps more properly termed, monologues. In 1976 Kenneth S. Goldstein and Robert D. Bethke edited a double issue of the *Southern Folklore Quarterly* devoted to "Monologues and Folk Recitations," and since then other folklorists have become increasingly interested in this genre.

In Canada, recitations commonly formed part of school and church concerts, and have frequently been performed at parties. Lately they have been revived at some folk clubs, folk festivals, and storytelling sessions. They seem to have been more popular in Newfoundland than elsewhere: they shared with singing, storytelling, and dancing at the traditional Newfoundland "times."

Wilfred Wareham, a professor in Memorial University's Folklore Department, writes of "The Monologue in Newfoundland" in *The Blasty Bough*, noting that it "may be defined as a solo, stylized, theatrically mannered, oral performance from memory of a self-contained dramatic narrative, in either poetic or prose form." He lists the most common themes as "history, local disaster, politics, religion, and bawdy scenes," and includes some samples. He says that "The Lobster Salad," which he recorded from his brother Baxter, is probably the most widely known of the group, and that it is sometimes called "Kelly's Dream," "Burke's Dream," or "Kelly and the Wren Beer."

The Lobster Salad

Recited by Baxter Wareham

Last Saturday night I was invited by an old time friend of mine
To eat his lobster salad and drink his beer and wine.
We drank a toast unto each other until the hour of two;
Me head felt kind of shaky and me legs was shaky too.

But anyhow I staggered home and I think my prayers I said.
But anyway I was paralyzed when I got in the bed.
I dreamt I died and went to heaven and met St. Peter at the Gate,
And I found repentance for me was just a bit too late.

"You go out," St. Peter said. "You know you can't come in.
You know you have to pay for your awful gluttonous sin."
Slowly then I turned away, tied by grief and shame,
And I saw St. Peter's clerk close by; he wrote "lost" above me name.

Next there comes was a Hebrew, a friend that I knew well,
And I listened to the story that he had to tell.
"Oh, goodly Father Peter, I come to you at last,
And one request I ask of you if you would let me pass.

"On earth I had a clothin' store and me clothes was good and strong,
And to show you this nice little overcoat I'll fetch it along."
"You go out," St. Peter said. "For very well you know
That you'll have no place for overcoats in the place where you got to go."

Next there come was an Italian, one on earth that I knew well,
So I stepped aside and I listened to the story he did tell.
He said, "Oh, goodly Father Peter, I come to you at last,
My peanut days are over, my banana days are past.

"While on earth I treated my neighbour like myself—no beg, no rob, no steal,
And never on the sidewalk did I throw banana peel."

"You go out," St. Peter said. "Your gains are all ill-gotten.
Your peanut shells were empty, your bananas ofttimes rotten."

Next there come was an old maid and she was bound to have her
    say,
And she addressed St. Peter in a pure sort of way.
"Oh, goodly Father Peter, I come to you at last,
And one request I ask of you if you would let me pass.

"Oh, holy Father Peter, oh won't you let me in,
And give me a nice little place to meself away from those naughty
    men?"
"You go out," St. Peter said. "No angels have grey hairs.
You have no sons or daughters, so you cannot come in here."

Slowly the old maid turned away forever to repine;
Like me and all the rest of us she entered in the line.
Next there come was a German and he was paralyzed with fear,
And while on earth he often paralyzed his customers with beer.

He said, "Oh, goodly Father Peter, I come to you at last,
And one request I ask of you if you would let me pass."
He said, "The wife she ran away from me and to hide me shame I
    tried,
So I went down by the river and committed suicide."

"You go out," St. Peter said, "and suffer your disgrace.
You come before we sent for you; now we can't find your
    place."
Slowly the German turned away forever to repine;
He came and stood beside us with a teardrop in his eye.

Now, next there come was Paddy, yes, a son of old Erin's Isle,
And he addressed St. Peter with a loving, gracious smile.
"Ah, 'tis yerself, St. Peter, you're lookin' so nice and sweet,
Open the door, boy, and let me in and show me to me seat."

"You go out," St. Peter said. "Your case like the rest must be
    tried.
You have to show a pass for it before you get inside."
"Ah, hurry up, St. Peter, or for supper I'll be late."
He then took off his old slouch hat and hove it inside the gate.

"Go and get that hat," St. Peter said. "You sacrilegious slouch."
Pat ran in, closed the door, and he barred St. Peter out.
Then through the keyhole Paddy cried, "I'm skipper now you
    see,

And I'll give up the crown and keys to heaven if you'll set old
   Ireland free.''

Now when I awoke me head was jammed between the bedpost
   and the wall.
Mc lcgs was tangled in the sheets; 'twas them lobsters done it all.

VI. Formula Tales

MOST TALES ARE interesting because of their characters or plots, but there is a small group in which the form is more important than anything else. The most common formula tales are cumulative: the type of "The House That Jack Built" or songs like "Alouette," which keep getting longer as new elements are added and the whole rigmarole is repeated. Others are endless or circular: an action must be repeated an infinite number of times, or the story reaches a point where it starts over and repeats again and again. Some, known as jump or catch tales, have startling, ridiculous, or impossible endings.

Formula tales are usually told to children, and sometimes they serve a particular function: for example, cumulative stories can take on the aspect of a game, circular stories may be used to discourage youngsters who are too persistent in demanding "another story," and endless stories may help to put children to sleep.

29. THE OLD WOMAN AND HER PIG: A CUMULATIVE TALE
The largest group of formula tales are cumulative, based on interlocking chains in which each incident is linked to the next, and the phrases are repeated over and over as something new is added each time. These are longer and more complicated than the other formula tales, and part of their charm is the successful manipulation of the ever-lengthening chain. "The Old Woman and Her Pig" is the most popular and most widespread of all the

formula tales: it has been told on every continent and in practically every country of the world. In England it became a song.

Mrs. Bigrow was a good folksinger who also told stories. Her fine version of Child 215, "Willie Drowned in Ero," has been taken up by several contemporary singers. When she begins this story she is a little confused, starting with the stick instead of the dog, but she quickly recovers the thread and proceeds smoothly to the climax, delighting in rhyming off the rigmarole at a good pace. Some versions end with the cow giving the milk, lacking her final step where the woman has to bring it hay first.

Among the other cumulative tales told in Canada are the Icelandic *pular*, of which Magnus Einarrson collected two that resemble "The Old Woman and Her Pig" and "The Twelve Days of Christmas."

The Old Woman and her Pig

Told by Eva Bigrow

A woman was sweeping out her kitchen and she found an old crooked sixpence. So she said, "What'll I do with this sixpence? I think I'll go to the market and I'll buy a little pig." So she went to the market and bought a little pig. But on the way home she met a stile and she says, "Well, how'll I get over the stile?" So she looked around and she saw a stick. So she said, "Stick, stick, beat pig. Pig won't get over the stile and I can't get home tonight." So the stick wouldn't.

So she looked around again and she saw a . . . dog. So she said, "Stick, stick, beat dog. Dog won't bite pig, pig won't get over the stile and I won't get home tonight." But the stick wouldn't.

So she looked around again and she saw a fire. She said, "Fire, fire, burn stick. Stick won't beat dog, dog won't bite pig, piggy won't get over the stile and I can't get home tonight." But the fire wouldn't.

So she looked around and she seen some water. She said, "Water, water, quench fire. Fire won't burn stick, stick won't beat dog, dog won't bite pig, pig won't get over the stile and I can't get home tonight." But the water wouldn't.

So then she looked around and she seen an ox so she said, "Ox, ox, drink water. Water won't quench fire, fire won't burn stick, stick won't beat dog, dog won't bite pig, pig won't get over the stile and I shan't get home tonight." But the ox wouldn't.

So she looked around again and she seen a butcher. She said, "Butcher, butcher, kill ox. Ox won't drink water, water won't quench fire, fire won't burn stick, stick won't beat dog, dog won't bite pig, pig won't get over the stile and I shan't get home tonight." But the butcher wouldn't.

So then she looked around again and she seen a rope. She said, "Rope, rope, kill butcher. Butcher won't kill ox, ox won't drink water, water won't quench fire, fire won't burn stick, stick won't beat dog, dog won't bite pig, piggy won't get over the stile and I shan't get home tonight." But the rope wouldn't.

So she looked around and she seen a rat. She said, "Rat, rat, gnaw rope. Rope won't hang butcher, butcher won't kill ox, ox won't drink water, water won't quench fire, fire won't burn stick, stick won't beat dog, dog won't bite pig, piggy won't get over the stile and I shan't get home tonight." But the rat wouldn't.

Then she seen a cat. She says, "Cat, cat, kill rat. Rat won't gnaw rope, rope won't hang butcher, butcher won't kill ox, ox won't drink water, water won't quench fire, fire won't burn stick, stick won't beat dog, dog won't bite pig, piggy won't get over the stile and I shan't get home tonight." So the cat said to the old lady, "If you'll go over to the cow and get some milk, I'll kill the rat."

So the old lady went over to the cow and said, "Cow, cow, give milk. Cat won't kill rat, rat won't gnaw rope, rope won't hang butcher, butcher won't kill ox, ox won't drink water, water won't quench fire, fire won't burn stick, stick won't beat dog, dog won't bite pig, piggy won't get over the stile and I shan't get home tonight." So the cow said, "You go over to the farmer and get some hay, and I'll give you some milk."

So the old lady went to the farmer and got some hay. So the cow began to give the milk, the cat began to kill the rat, the rat began to gnaw the rope, the rope began to hang the butcher, the butcher began to kill the ox, the ox began to drink the water, the water began to quench the fire, the fire began to burn the stick, the stick began to beat the dog, the dog began to bite the pig, and the pig went over the stile and the woman got home.

30. A CATCH TALE

Perhaps the most interesting of the formula tales are the catches, in which the storyteller tricks the listener. The most common form is a story involving contradictions that force the listener to ask a particular question, to which the teller gives a ridiculous answer.

Tales like Charlie Slane's that involve contradictions or impossibilities are sometimes told simply as tall tales. This one has turned up in Indiana, Missouri, and Ohio, and somewhat similar yarns about mixed weather were told in Alberta and Ontario. Carole Spray heard this version in New Brunswick.

A Catch Tale

Told by Charlie Slane

You don't see bears around as often as you used to. But I remember seeing one once when I was out picking raspberries. It was the end of August and it was hot. It was a real scorcher! And there I was, down on my knees making my way around the raspberry canes. Suddenly, I came nose to nose with this great, black bear.

He was doing the same thing, of course. He was eating the raspberries, stripping them off with his big paw and stuffing them in his mouth. He was surprised and annoyed that I was picking his berries, because he growled and got up on his hind legs. Well, I didn't hang around.

I took off down the old woods road, and when I looked back he was coming along after me on all fours. Bears can run pretty fast. I can run pretty fast, too. I was running the mile in about two minutes, at least. But so was the bear and he was right behind me.

I ran and ran and ran. It was awful hot. The sweat was just pouring off me. I'd look back every once in a while, and the bear seemed to be getting a little closer. So I put on a little more effort and I ran for an awful long time. I was getting tired, too. But the bear was still coming on. He wasn't getting any farther away. In fact, he was just as close as he could be.

So I ran and ran and ran. I ran for an awful long time. And just when I thought I couldn't run another step, I came to this lake. It was frozen over a little bit. There was just an inch of ice over it, and I knew that it would hold me if I ran over it real fast, and I knew if the bear followed me, it wouldn't hold him.

So I ran out onto the ice, and I stopped in the middle. And there came the bear, charging after me. He paused for a minute when he saw me out there, then he ran right out on the ice. He got just about halfways when the ice cracked and gave way and down he went and drowned. That was the end of him.

"Hey! That can't be true. You said it was summertime and awful hot. There couldn't be any ice on the lake then!"

Yup, it's true all right. It was summertime when I started running. But like I said, I ran for an awful long time.

VII. Legends

WHILE THE SUPERNATURAL and romantic tales and the jokes and anecdotes are recognized as fictional, legends are, or have been, regarded as true by the people who tell them, and hence are sometimes called belief tales. These are akin to the myths, which also are believed; but where the myths deal with supernatural beings, other worlds, and prehistoric times, legends usually involve natural beings and this world, although supernatural figures like the devil, fairies, ghosts, or witches may appear in them.

Some of the most common legends deal with miracles, ghosts, vampires, werewolves, or buried treasure; others explain physical features or weather, or describe strange occurrences, strange creatures, or strange persons. A popular kind today is the urban belief tale which is usually rather gruesome or embarrassing, and spreads mainly among teenagers.

Many have counterparts in other countries, but the versions told are usually more definitely linked to a particular place or group than are the ordinary folktales, and hence are more distinctively Canadian than most other types. While the first two legends came here from the Old World, most of the others relate to Canada.

31. THE SEAL-WOMAN: A SHETLANDIC LEGEND
The folklore of all northern peoples in Europe is rich in tales of the seal-folk, commonly known as "silkies." A widespread belief

was that they could come up on land, doff their seal-skins, and take on human form. This belief, found in folktales like the following, also forms the basis for one of the most beautiful ancient ballads, "The Great Silkie of Sule Skerry." Some northern families are said to believe that they are descended from silkies, and hence eating seal meat is tabu among them. Another belief, illustrated in this tale, was that the silkies must have their skins to return to the sea: if a human captured the skin, the silkie was trapped on land.

Tales of the seal-folk are particularly popular in Scotland's Shetland, Orkney, and Hebridean islands, so it is not surprising that folk from the Shetlands brought some of them to Canada. J. A. Teit heard this and many other stories from Shetlanders who had settled in British Columbia early in the present century.

The Seal-Woman

Once an unmarried man went to a place where the flat rocks on the shore were a haunt for seals. As he wanted to see the seals in their human form, he hid himself and waited until evening, when he saw a number of seals come ashore, throw off their seal coverings, and play and dance in human form.

A pretty young woman disrobed near his hiding-place and left her skin nearby, neatly folded up. He managed to seize the skin unobserved by any of the seal-people, and sat down on it. The woman danced with a young seal-man who, he thought, must be her lover.

At daybreak a great clamour of gulls alarmed the seals, who ran for their skins and made for the sea. The young woman, unable to find her skin and return to the sea with her friends, began to cry bitterly. A single seal, no doubt the lover with whom she had danced, remained near the shore in the sea, waiting for her after all the others had disappeared.

Soon the man came up and tried to comfort her, saying that she would be better off on the land, and in him would find a better lover than she could find in the sea. Seeing that he had possession of her skin, she begged him to give it back to her, offering to do anything for him in return. He refused, and went off carrying the skin. She followed him, and at last had to consent to remain with him as his wife. He kept her seal-skin in his trunk, and always concealed the key or carried it on his person. When he was absent, she often looked for the skin, but could never find it.

Many years she lived with him, and bore a number of children. Often her lover, the lone seal, came to the shore looking for her, and the woman was seen going there and talking with him. Some neighbours reported this to her husband. One day the man went fishing and forgot the key to his trunk. The woman noticed this, and opened the trunk. There she found the skin; and when the man came home, his wife was gone.

He went down to the shore and found her in the water, with a seal at her side. She called to him, "Goodbye!" and told him to look well after the children. She also asked him not to kill any seals, because by doing so he might kill her, her seal-husband, or her seal-children. If he heeded not this request, he would have bad luck. After she had departed in seal-form with her companion, he saw her no more.

32. ONE OF THE THIRTY-SIX JUST MEN:
A JEWISH LEGEND

This tale of a *lamedvovnik* is one of many that the Jewish people have been telling for centuries in both Hebrew and Yiddish. The widespread belief in the "thirty-six hidden saints" is based on a passage in the Talmud where Rabbi Abaye, a Babylonian teacher of the fourth century, wrote: "There are in the world not less than thirty-six righteous persons in every generation upon whom the *Shekhina* [God's radiance] rests." There had been earlier proverbs and tales about just men, but he was the first to introduce the number thirty-six. In *The Messianic Idea in Judaism*, Gershom Scholem discusses the background of the legend and indicates various numerological and astrological theories said to have inspired the number.

Legends about these "righteous" or "just" men circulated among the sixteenth- and seventeenth-century cabalists, and then in the eighteenth century among the *Hasidim* of Eastern Europe. It was a fundamental part of the belief that a *lamedvovnik* could never let his identity be known, and that he would die if it was discovered.

Barbara Kirshenblatt-Gimblett (who contributed the "Jewish Jokes from Toronto" in a previous section) collected this story when she was studying folklore at Indiana University. She notes that Jack Starkman, who was born in Poland in 1914, was apprenticed to an old furrier named Fishl, in Lodz, from 1929 to 1934. Fishl used to sing and tell tales by the hour, and in 1929, when Jack was fourteen years old, Fishl told him this legend. Jack came to Canada in 1935, and Barbara recorded this from him in Toronto in 1972.

One of the Thirty-Six Just Men

Told by Jack Starkman

I'll tell you one story that he told me, Barbara, and it's priceless. He told me about a *lamedvovnik*. You know what a *lamedvovnik* is? It's one of the thirty-six that . . . the sages say there have to be in order that the world should exist. If there was one less then the world cannot exist: thirty-six just men. Now the essence of the *lamedvovnik* is that no one should discover that he is one of those *lamedvovniks*. In the minute they discover, he has to die. And he can be in various forms. He can be a *holtsheker* [woodcutter], you know, a water carrier. He can be rich. He can be poor. But he's got to be one of those.

So this same Fishl told me a story that he heard from his rabbi. Who knows if it's true or not? That in this particular city, you know, not a small, a middle-sized city, there was one man that lived there that everybody used to hate. Everything that he did, he did for some remuneration.

There used to be an *agine* in the city. You know what an *agine* is? An *agine* is a woman, her husband disappeared. He left her and she had no way of supporting herself. So he found out that she's an *agine*. All of a sudden, he [the unpopular man] went away to another city. He came back and he says to her, "I met your husband and I told him that you're suffering. Anyway, he sends you some money. But in order for me to transfer the money to you, I want half of it." So he gave her twenty rubles a week and he says, "The twenty rubles I keep for myself, for my doing this."

The city found out, you know, and they were so mad at him, they wanted to kill him. His name was Moyshe. Moyshe, Moyshe. They wouldn't call him up to the *seyfer* [religious book], to read a passage from the liturgy. They gave him a seat, you know, at the very end. And they were talking to him, when he's going to die, they're never going to bury him. They're going to bury him inside the [plot], you know . . . near the fence. "How can you take twenty rubles away?" He says, "Otherwise I'm not doing your chores." She had no other alternatives so she accepted.

Another man, also a very, very poor man, he told the man that he received a letter from America from a daughter of his, and he [Moyshe] wrote a letter and he was instrumental that she should send him [the poor man] some money. But for his work, he [Moyshe] again wanted half. So the city got so mad at him, you know. They wanted to kill him. But he wouldn't budge. "I don't do anything for free,'' he says. So the city got more and more mad. All of a sudden he did this to a few people, and every time he took a heavy share for himself.

One day this Moyshe died and the city said this is the time to get even with him. They made him a funeral like for the worst pauper in the city, you know. They carried him to the *besoylem* [cemetery] at night. Nobody knew about it. They buried him without the *takhrikhim* [shrouds]. They just threw him in, in the grave, and they put a marker and on the marker they put down *Poynitmin* [Here lies] *Moyshe Goy*, *Moyshe Goy* [Moses Gentile]. See.

All of a sudden, a certain time passed, and this *agine* stopped receiving money altogether. This poor man stopped receiving money from his daughter. These other *vaser treygers* [water carriers] and the *holtshekers* [woodcutters], everybody, they stopped receiving money. So when they start finding out, investigating, they saw there was never actually . . . the *agine*'s husband was never found. The daughter was never found. So it all boiled down that he actually was the sole supporter of these people, but in order to keep his identity, his *lamedvovnik* identity hidden, he purposely made it sound so vicious that they could never know that he did it.

So the city started to sit *shiva* [the seven days of mourning after a close relative], and cry over this saint who departed in such an obnoxious way, as far as they were concerned. And they went to the rabbi and they asked what to do about it. Anyway, they exhumed his body. They covered it. They gave him a real fancy funeral. And on the marker that they put on *Moyshe Goy* [Moses Gentile], the rabbi said: ''Leave this. Only add one word. After the *Goy* [Gentile], *kadosh* [holy].''

So *goy kadosh* has two meanings. *Moyshe Goy* by itself means Moses Gentile. You know, he was a *goy*. But *Moyshe goy kadosh* means Moyshe the holy man from his nation. *Goy* means nation.

So this is the story that I remember from Fishl.

But don't you think his *geshikhte* [story], his story about the *lamedvovnik* is a, is . . . it's a terrific climax there.

And why did he tell me? I still remember why he told me. They used to show a picture in those days in Lodz and it was called *The Lamedvovnik* with Yonas Turkof. Did you see this? So we were talking about this *lamedvovnik*. How true is it? Is it false? Is it true? And he says, ''Well, I'll tell you a story that my parents used to attest that this is a true story about this particular man in his city who undoubtedly was a *lamedvovnik*. Otherwise he would never done these things, you know.''

33. THE WRONG CHILL WINDIGO: A CREE LEGEND

Stories about monsters in one form or another are popular
throughout the world, but Canada seems to have more indige-
nous monsters than most countries. Tales of the Windigo,
D'Sonoqua, loup-garou, Ogopogo, and Sasquatch are all part of
our folk tradition. Perhaps their popularity results from the fear
of the unknown that is part of the Canadian "garrison mentality" that Northrop Frye postulates.

The Windigo, the most feared supernatural creature in Indian
folklore, is sometimes a demon and sometimes a man who has
"gone Windigo" — become crazed by hunger and turned canni-
bal. Tales of the Windigo recur throughout Canadian literature, from the early reports of missionaries and explorers like
Paul Le Jeune and Samuel Hearne, to more recent accounts of
anthropologists and Indians, like Diamond Jenness and Norval
Morrisseau. John Robert Colombo has collected some forty-four
narratives dating from 1636 to 1976 in *Windigo. An Anthology
of Fact and Fantastic Fiction.*

"The Wrong Chill Windigo" is from a collection of thirty-
one such tales that Howard Norman collected and published in a
volume titled *Where the Chill Came From: Cree Windigo Tales
and Journeys.* He heard them from members of the Swampy
Cree who lived in the subarctic forests and swamplands west of
Hudson Bay.

The Windigo has many names and takes on many different
forms. Among the Cree the most common nonhuman form is a
wandering giant with a heart of ice, as in the tale that follows. All
the tales in *Where the Chill Came From* emphasize the combination of hunger and cold characteristic of most Windigo legends,
and create a vivid impression of the hardships that the Cree
suffered during the long icy winters. Most of the tales end with
the Windigo's death, thus giving heart to the Cree who were
constantly threatened with starvation.

This particular tale features a magic owl that talks and can
perform supernatural feats. It also illustrates one interesting dif-
ference between Indian and white folklore. Among whites, three is
the magic number — everything occurs in threes — while among
the Indians four is the magic number. Here the man has to suffer
three wrong chills until the fourth one brings the owl to his
rescue.

Howard Norman is a folklorist and naturalist who has travelled extensively among the Cree of northern Manitoba. In his
introduction he notes:

*In most instances, the Windigo tales collected here were part
of "announced" performances. People gathered into the tents
of the various storytellers and heard all sorts of things, sometimes Windigo-related anecdotes, sometimes formal Windigo
narratives. Such performances are traditionally audience-
participation events; sometimes, for instance, children sat
in totally rapt attention, while at other times an ongoing
dialogue between narrator and audience prevailed, making the performance a collaborative telling. A good storyteller can be prolific in gestures and voices, an entertainer
as well as an educator.*

The Wrong Chill Windigo

Told by Andrew Nikumoon

In a village lived a man named Upichisik (Teal Duck). There was
much illness from hunger in his village at that time. Many fevers,
in children and others. Upichisik went out hunting to try to find
food to eat. He went out by himself. It was when the first ice was
breaking up on streams and lakes. "Maybe some ducks will arrive
soon," Upichisik said. It had been a hard winter, with little food.

Some days before, Upichisik had found a wide stream that
was mostly clear of ice. He set out for that stream. It wasn't too
far from his village. But when he arrived, the stream was frozen
over again! Just then Upichisik saw an owl fly down. "Why did
you freeze this stream back up?" Upichisik called at the owl.

"Get out on the ice and shiver, then I'll thaw this stream
open again!" answered the owl.

With that, Upichisik walked out on the stream. He sat down
on the ice. He held himself tightly with his arms. Then he began
shivering.

But the owl said, "No! That's the wrong kind of shivering!
You've got the wrong chill in you! That's a chill from a childhood fever!" Then the owl flew away.

Upichisik stood up. That's when he heard, in the distance,
another ice breakup! He said out loud, "Maybe that's where the
ducks are!" Upichisik walked toward that sound. When he arrived
at the distant stream, he saw that it too had frozen over! Again
Upichisik saw the owl! The owl was sitting in a tree. Upichisik
shouted, "Why are you doing this to me?" Again the owl said,
"Get out on that ice!" Upichisik, further away from his village
now, and starving, walked out on the ice. He sat down. He
shivered.

But the owl said, "No, that's not it! That's the shivering from a nightmare dream, when it sits you up in fear, awake. That's the wrong chill. That's the wrong shivering." Then the owl flew away.

So Upichisik had shivered up the memory of a childhood fever, and he had shivered up that other thing . . . a nightmare. "That is enough for one day!" he called out at the flying owl. But just then ice was cracking in the distance, further yet from his village.

Again Upichisik walked in hunger toward cracking ice. Again he arrived at a frozen stream! Again, the owl was there! The owl said, "The right chill will thaw this ice for ducks to arrive. Then you can get food. Then you won't starve!"

So Upichisik went out on the ice to shiver. He sat down. With his fever he sat. With his nightmare he sat. Upichisik shivered. He shivered past those two things . . . past those days. He was very hungry.

Then a Windigo arrived.

Upichisik knew where the chill came from. The Windigo sent the chill into him. The Windigo did that.

Upichisik called at the owl, "You've been working for this Windigo. Now you'll do so for me!" With that, Upichiski conjured all the fevers from his village into that owl! The owl began burning up! Then Upichisik shouted, "Strike your talons into it!" The owl did so. The owl struck its talons into the Windigo's chest. That melted its heart. The Windigo was dying. It howled loud in a tremendously fearful way. Then it died.

That howl brought the others all the way from Upichisik's village. They arrived. Upichisik said to them, "As the owl is now working for me, I'll make it thaw more ice!" Upichisik said, "Owl, get to work!"

With that, the owl thawed more ice open. It had such powers. It cracked open the ice on many lakes and streams. Upichisik and the others could hear the owl on the ice in the distance, thawing it. The owl, full of those fevers that Upichisik had conjured into it, was hissing in the water.

So that is what happened.

After that, there were ducks to eat.

34. STEER NORTH AND NORTH EAST

The strange events in this legend of the sea do not seem to correspond to the magic occurrences documented in other tales of the supernatural. There are innumerable stories of ghosts who appear to warn or to help mortals, but here it is a living man who appears somewhere that he could not be, and his object is not to warn others but to procure help for his own ship.

This narrative comes from a collection of Gaelic material that Seumas Eoghainn collected and donated to Calum MacLeod, who lists it as "The James Hugh MS." In introducing this legend he notes: "The following words are written at the end of the story: 'Narrated by Clark, the skipper of a ship called *Julia*. This man and a fellow called Bruce were sailing together in the year 1837. Clark got the story from Bruce eight years after that extraordinary event took place. Bruce continued sailing out of New Brunswick, and he was the skipper on a ship called the *Comet*, but she was lost.' "

Steer North and North East

Told by Captain Clark

Once upon a time Big John was a mate on a handsome barque that left from Glasgow, in the Old Country, and that set course for New Brunswick, a province that is west from us in the Island of Cape Breton. When the ship was near the headlands of Newfoundland, the skipper and the mate were up on the bridge taking the bearings of the sun, at twelve o'clock noon, as usual. Having taken the bearings they descended, each man to his own cabin, to work on the sailing-charts.

When the mate was ready, he went into the skipper's cabin to show him what he thought was the position of the ship. The skipper was sitting at the desk writing on the slate; and without even raising his eyes from the sailing-chart that was in his own hand, he asked him where he thought their present position was. When the skipper did not reply the mate went nearer to him, and he asked the same question again. In spite of this the man who was at the desk did not reply, but he turned his head, and then the mate noticed that it was not the skipper at all, but a man he had never seen before.

Without further delay, the mate lifted the soles of his feet out of the cabin, and he ran up the stairs to the ship's bridge. The skipper was there walking up and down without a care on earth, but when he saw that the mate had a frightened look, he asked him what was wrong. "Who," said the mate, "is sitting at the desk in your cabin?" "I am not aware," said the skipper, "that there is anybody else in my cabin." The skipper started to pull his leg, saying that he was half asleep and dreaming, and that it must have been some other member of the crew that he had seen. "That may be," said the mate, "but it was no person belonging to the ship that I saw sitting at the desk. I never eyed him before, and I saw him clearly writing on your slate."

The final result was that they went down together to the skipper's cabin, but when they opened the door there was nobody inside. The skipper lifted the slate, and here are the words that were written on it: "Steer North and North East." "Was it you," said he to the mate, "who wrote this on the slate?" "Indeed, it was not me," said the mate. The skipper made the mate write the same words on the other side of the slate, but even a one-eyed person could see that the two handwritings were not at all similar.

Although the skipper interrogated nearly everyone on board he never found a solution to the mystery, and he tried to block out the affair from his mind; but the more he tried to forget it, the stronger the words were winding around his heart: "Steer North and North East." At last he gave an order to alter the ship's course, and to "Steer North and North East." He kept the barque on that course for five hours. At the end of that time the man on the look-out mast shouted that there was an iceberg straight ahead of them. When they came alongside they saw a large ship stuck in the iceberg, and people on her deck trying to give signals that they were in danger. The ship's lifeboats were lowered, and in the space of three hours everybody on board her was saved.

When the passengers on one of the lifeboats were approaching the side of the ship, and the mate [was] helping them to climb on board, he stared hard at one of the men, and he said to the skipper, "That is the man I saw writing on the slate at the desk."

When the work of mercy was completed, the skipper sent for this man, and he asked him if he would be good enough to write the words, "Steer North and North East," on the slate. The man did as he was told, and then the skipper turned the slate, and he said to him without telling him that he turned it, "Do you recognize this handwriting?" The skipper's question made the man wonder. "How," he said, "would I not recognize my own handwriting? That is what I wrote a minute ago." Then the skipper let him see that the words were written on the two sides of the slate. "I only wrote what is on the one side," said the man, "but it is my handwriting that is on the other side, without any doubt."

35. THE GHOSTLY SAILORS: A BALLAD

This is an unusual Canadian ballad that is very well known along our east coast. It was inspired by a real sea tragedy which is linked with a sailors' legend, and is one of the very few native North American ballads that has a supernatural theme.

Harry L. Marcy composed the original text which appeared in 1874 in *Fishermen's Ballads and Songs of the Sea*. First used as a recitation, it soon acquired a tune and became, in Doerflinger's words, "A favorite of fishermen from Cape Ann to Cape Race." However, all reported versions are from Canada: more than a dozen have turned up in the Maritime Provinces and Newfoundland. Kenneth Peacock collected the one that follows from Alan MacArthur of Upper Ferry, Newfoundland, in 1959.

In *Bluenose Ghosts*, Dr. Creighton gives an account of the tragedy that inspired the ballad as it was described in the *Boston Globe*. The *Charles Haskell* from Boston was anchored on George's Bank on March 7, 1866, when another ship got adrift and hurtled directly towards it. To save themselves the crew cut the *Haskell*'s rope, and then she was driven upon another ship, the *Andrew Jackson* of Salem, and cut it in two. It sank with all hands. The next time the *Haskell* returned to the same fishing grounds the crew testified that sailors of the *Andrew Jackson* came up over the sides in their oilskins and manned the *Haskell*. After that the *Haskell* became known as a ghost vessel, and the owners could not get anyone to work on it. Dr. Creighton concludes: "I have talked to men who had heard the story personally from the crew, and I too heard it confirmed from one who saw it happen, Captain Ammon Zinck of Lunenburg."

Elisabeth Greenleaf, who collected a version from Uncle Dan Endicott, noted that James Gillespie of Fortune Harbour said he had seen the ship that the ghostly seamen boarded: "They have the sails off her and let her rot at the wharf in St. John's harbour because they could never get a crew to sign on her, after the trip when the spirits was seen." She goes on to compare the ballad to Coleridge's poem "The Ancient Mariner," quoting Wordsworth's account of its planning, in which he says that he suggested "the navigation of the ship by the dead men," an indication that he had come across the tradition.

Many sailors firmly believe the tale of the ghostly fishermen, which is based on the old sea superstition that the spirits of men lost from a vessel will board that vessel when it appears again at the spot where the tragedy occurred. There is a similar story about the 1914 sealing disaster when the *Newfoundland* lost seventy-seven men out of a crew of two hundred. On the Folkways record *Songs from the Outports of Newfoundland*, Pat Maher of Pouch Cove tells how he sailed on the *Newfoundland* when it had been renamed the *Blanford*, and, on the anniversary

of the tragedy, sailors swore that they saw ghostly figures walk
up the side of the ship and into the boat. He concludes, "I think
that brings the tradition true that men do come home."

The Ghostly Sailors

Sung by Alan MacArthur

Smile if you have a mind to, but perhaps you'll lend an ear.
For boy and man together nigh on for forty years
I sailed upon the water to the Western Banks and Grand,
And in some herring vessels that went to Newfoundland.

Oh, I've seen storms, I tell you, when things looked rather blue,
But somehow I was lucky and always have got through.
Now I'll not brag, however, and won't say much, but then
I'm not much easier frightened than most of other men.

'Twas one drear night I speak of, we were off the shore a way;
I never shall forget it in all my mortal days
'Twas in the dim dark watches I felt a chilling dread;
It bowled me down as if I heard one calling from the dead.

Then on the deck there clambered all silent one by one
A dozen dripping sailors — just wait till I have done.
Right on the deck they clambered, yet not a voice we heard.
They moved about together and never spoke a word.

Their faces pale and sea-wet shone ghostly through the night.
Each took his place as freely as if he had a right,
And they all worked the vessel, the land being just in sight,
Or rather I should say, sir, the lighthouse tower's light.

And then those clambering sailors moved to the rail again
And vanished in the deep ere sun could shine on them.
I know not any reason in truth why they should come
And navigate the vessel till just in sight of home.

It was the same poor fellows — I pray God rest their souls —
That our old craft ran under one night near George's shoals.
So now you have my story; it was just the way I say,
And I've believed in spirits since that time, anyway.

36. THE WALKER OF THE SNOW/THE HAUNTED HUNTER: A BALLAD

This poem by a nineteenth-century Canadian poet, Charles Dawson Shanly (1811–1875) used to appear in school readers and

was occasionally used as a recitation. At some point it also acquired a tune, passed into oral tradition, and was carried down to the United States where Austin Fife, the noted Mormon folklorist, collected a Utah version as "The Haunted Hunter." The story is typical of the many legends about encounters with ghosts that cause a person's hair to turn white.

Rosalie Sorrels, a folksinger from Utah, recorded it from the Fife collection, and Billie Maxwell recorded it commercially in 1929. As Maxwell's record came out before Fife collected the song, you might suppose that his informant had learned it from the record. However, a comparison of the two versions indicates that both were probably traditional: hardly two lines are exactly the same, and both show many minor changes from the original poem. Below both Shanly's text and the Fife version sung by Rosalie Sorrels appear, illustrating the kind of changes that take place when a printed text passes into the oral tradition.

The Walker of the Snow

By C. D. Shanly

Speed on, speed on, good Master!
　　The camp lies far away;
We must cross the haunted valley
　　Before the close of day.

How the snow-blight came upon me
　　I will tell you as we go,
The blight of the Shadow Hunter
　　Who walks the midnight snow.

To the cold December heaven
　　Came the pale moon and the stars
As the yellow sun was sinking
　　Behind the purple bars.

The snow was deeply drifted
　　Upon the ridges drear
That lay for miles between me
　　And the camp for which we steer.

'Twas silent on the hillside
　　And by the sombre wood.
No sound of life or motion
　　To break the solitude,

Save the wailing of the moose-bird
    With a plaintive note and low,
And the skating of the red leaf
    Upon the frozen snow.

And I said, "Though dark is falling,
    And far the camp must be,
Yet my heart it would be lightsome
    If I had but company."

And then I sang and shouted,
    Keeping measure as I sped
To the harp-twang of the snowshoe
    As it sprang beneath my tread.

Nor far into the valley
    Had I dipped upon my way
When a dusky figure joined me
    In a capuchon of grey,

Bending upon the snowshoes
    With a long and limber stride,
And I hailed the dusky stranger
    As we travelled side by side.

But no token of communion
    Gave he by word or look,
And the fear-chill fell upon me
    At the crossing of the brook,

For I saw by the sickly moonlight
    As I followed, bending low,
That the walking of the stranger
    Left no footmarks on the snow.

Then the fear-chill gathered o'er me
    Like a shroud around me cast,
And I sank upon the snowdrift
    Where the Shadow Hunter passed.

And the otter-trappers found me
    Before the break of day,
With my dark hair blanched and whitened
    As the snow in which I lay.

But they spoke not as they raised me,
    For they knew that in the night
I had seen the Shadow Hunter
    And had withered in his blight.

Sancta Maria speed us!
    The sun is falling low.
Before us lies the valley
    Of the Walker of the Snow!

The Haunted Hunter

Sung by Mrs. Gwen Meador

Speed on, speed on, good comrades; our camps lie far away.
We must cross the haunted valley before the break of day.
How I became snow-blighted I will tell you as we go
By the blight of the Haunted Hunter that walks the midnight
    snow.

Through the cold December heavens came the pale moon and
    the stars;
The yellow sun was sinking fast behind the purple bars.
The snow it lay drifted all along the ridges drear
For miles and miles between me and that camp for which we
    steer.

Said I, "The dark 'tis coming and far our camp must be,
But my heart it would be lightsome if I had but company."
So I sang and I shouted, keeping measure as I sped
To the sharp twang of my snowshoes as they sprang beneath my
    tread.

There was silence on the hillside and by the solemn wood;
No sound of life or motion for to break the solitude
Save the wailing of the moosebird in his plaintive note so low,
And the skating of the red leaf upon the frozen snow.

Not far into the valley had I gone upon my way
When a dusky figure joined me in a caprochone of grey,
Bending on his snowshoes with a long and a limber stride.
I hailed the dusky stranger as we travelled side by side.

No token of communion gave he by word or look
When a fear chill fell upon me at the crossing of the brook,
For I saw by the sickly moonlight as I followed bending low
That the walking of the stranger left no footprints in the snow.

Then a fear chill fell upon me like a shadow round me passed
As I fell upon a snowbank as the Haunted Hunter passed.
There the other trappers found me just at the break of day,
With my black hair white and blanchened as the snow on which
    I lay.

They spoke not as they raised me, for they knew that in the night
I had seen the Haunted Hunter and had withered in his blight.
Saint Maria speed us, for the sun is sinking low
And before us lies the valley of the Walker in the Snow.

37. THE DEVIL'S POTATO FIELD

This little legend is similar to many that purport to explain local
phenomena. It is easy to see how some farmer, working end-
lessly to remove stones from his land, might conceive this story
of the devil cursing a field. Eva Bigrow, who told the story, had
worked in northern Ontario and Quebec where the land is
notoriously rocky for farming, and hence likely to inspire such
a legend.

The Devil's Potato Field

Told by Eva Bigrow

There was a farmer that was digging his potatoes on Sunday, and
he said neither God nor the Devil would stop him. So he worked
all forenoon — and when he went back to his work after dinner
all the potatoes had turned to stones. And ever since that, that
field has been known as the Devil's potato field. They take thousands and thousands of loads of stones from that field every year
for construction, but the stones are always there.

38. A MIRACLE IN MONTREAL

Miracles, or events regarded as miracles, naturally attract attention and form the basis for many tales. In Canada the most
important source of such stories is the shrine at Ste. Anne de
Beaupré in Quebec, which is visited by thousands of pilgrims
every year and hailed as the font of many cures. Other individual
stories are more varied.

André E. Elbaz, who collected this account from the Reverend Salomon Amzallag in Montreal, notes that he "presents it as
an actual experience of the heroine which she had recently
recounted to his wife." The Rabbi Haim Pinto mentioned is the

hero of countless legends among Sephardim of Moroccan origin, and the Nessim Pinto of this story is a descendant of Haim Pinto.

A Miracle in Montreal

Told by Rev. Salomon Amzallag

This event happened recently in Montreal. Mrs. L. and her husband had always had great veneration for the Saint Rabbi Haim Pinto. In Morocco, they never missed an opportunity of showing their devotion to Rabbi Haim by pilgrimages, alms, se'udot [traditional meals honoring saints].

One day Mrs. L. happened to be at Mrs. Nessim Pinto's, here in Montreal. They were in the kitchen, gossiping at leisure, when Mrs. Pinto placed a saucepan of boiling oil, which she was holding, on top of the refrigerator. She made a clumsy movement and spilled the saucepan on Mrs. L. The contents poured over Mrs. L.'s face, arms, and clothing.

Mrs. Pinto, distracted, rushed up to her: "My poor friend, you are hurt! You must be scalded all over! I'll call the doctor."

"Not at all, don't worry about it," replied Mrs. L. "It's not hurting at all. It's funny, but it feels like cold water has been poured over me."

Mrs. L.'s dress had not even been stained by the oil. What is more, Mrs. L., who until then had been suffering from acute rheumatism in her arm, was completely cured as a result of this miracle. That night she felt a tingling in the affected arm, but in the morning she found it completely healed. There was no burn of any kind and, better still, no more rheumatism!

I know Mrs. L. well. It was she who told this story to my wife. Just imagine! Right here in Montreal!

39. THE POT OF GOLD

Legends about buried treasure abound in most countries, and Canada has a good stock of them. Some of the most famous stem from the belief that Captain Kidd buried his fabulous treasure in Nova Scotia: there have been scores of attempts to locate it at various places, of which Oak Island is the most famous. In *Bluenose Ghosts* Helen Creighton notes many Nova Scotia tales in a chapter titled "Ghosts Guard Buried Treasure," emphasizing the belief that pirates were in the habit of killing one of their members and burying him on top of the treasure to guard it. Arthur Huff Fauset also noted a number of Nova Scotia tales of treasure, and Joyce Coldwell made a more extensive study of treasure stories in Atlantic Canada for her doctoral dissertation.

Scottish settlers in the Eastern Townships of Quebec also tell many tales of buried treasure, and "The Pot of Gold" is one of the most popular. It stems not from pirates but from the American Civil War. Here the ghost is a Civil War soldier who was thought to have been killed in battle. Another version from Donald MacLennan told what happened when anyone who dug down hit the pot of gold with a pick-axe or bar: "When the bar hit the thing there was supposed to have been the awfulest racket — cannons going off, and everything, and the regular battles of the Civil War was started all over again."

The Pot of Gold

Told by Bill Young

Up in Milan, or near Milan, during the Civil War, there was a man who was supposed to have recruited young fellows up there to go and work in the woods in the United States. You heard that one? In return he was getting ten or twenty dollars per man. And, of course, money in those days was either in silver or gold, eh, there was no paper. So these fellows were got together and sent down to the States, supposedly to work in the woods, because the Americans were serving in the army. Once they got down here, they were drafted into the American army, and sent south to fight.

So this man made a considerable amount of money. And one night him and his wife were sitting in the house, and they had this money spread out on the table in the kitchen, and they were counting it. And he happened to look up, and out in the — outside the window, there was a man standing in the uniform of a Civil War soldier. And he looked at him so hard that this fellow and his wife took fright, and she swept all the money into her apron and she run and dumped it into a pot — an iron pot that was there. And the next morning, he took this iron pot full of money into the woods and buried it.

And according to the story, it's still there today. And there have been people go to find this; but when they're finally getting close to where this pot is buried they're seized with such a fright that they couldn't go on. One man, apparently, was picked up by an unseen force and thrown twenty feet through the air or something, and broke a leg! Now, that's an old one. I think everyone's told that story.

40. YOUNG LAD: A SANDY LAKE CREE LEGEND

Wiskehneegee, Young Lad, is a legendary hero of the Cree. He is thought to have been a hunter in the Crane Clan of Indians along the Severn or Bay River. Journal references indicate that there was probably a human original who inspired the legendary figure. In the tales Young Lad is not young: in fact, he is referred to by the contradictory title of "old Young Lad." As Chief Thomas Fiddler explains, Young Lad was said to have been over two hundred years old and was called Young Lad because he hadn't aged although he was so old.

Chief Thomas Fiddler is the hereditary leader of the Sucker Clan at Big Sandy Lake on the Upper Severn River in Ontario. Both his father and his grandfather were leaders before him, and the tales he tells — which include stories of the trickster hero Weesakayjac, and of clashes with neighbouring clans, as well as several about the legendary hero Young Lad — are traditional in his tribe.

James R. Stevens, who previously published *Sacred Legends of the Sandy Lake Cree*, edited *Legends from the Forest* from which this story comes, and another book, *Killing the Shamen*, in which Chief Thomas Fiddler tells how the North West Mounted Police prosecuted his grandfather and other members of his clan for shamanistic activities back in 1907.

Young Lad

Told by Thomas Fiddler

This man, Young Lad, lived for about two hundred years. His limbs never got old. When he was living he always looked the same. For this reason they called him Wiskehneegee — Young Lad. He never seemed to age.

I will tell you a story about him. This happened in the time they used the Yorkboats to get supplies from the James Bay area. At this time, they used to haul lots of fire-water. They used to haul barrel containers and they weighed about four hundred pounds. They did not pick up those barrels or haul them on their backs; they usually rolled them.

Young Lad and other Indians had plenty of whisky at this time. These Indians tried to get Young Lad drunk so they could stab him with their daggers. They drank lots of whisky and the other men on the Yorkboat got very drunk, but Young Lad stayed sober. When they attacked Young Lad with their daggers it didn't even bother him.

I heard people tried to do many bad things to Young Lad. They were jealous because they could not do anything to him. People even tried to kill his children to make Young Lad suffer. But Young Lad did not get into fights or things like that first.

41. THE VANISHING HITCHHIKER
42. THE BLUE CARDIGAN
43. THE PINK SHAWL
These three tales are typical of the migratory "urban legends," sometimes known as belief tales, that circulate among teenagers and spread quickly from one region to another. A number of Canadian tales of this kind, including a version of "The Vanishing Hitchhiker," appear in Susan Smith's collection of "Urban Legends" in *Folklore of Canada*. Two other varied collections are Jan Brunvand's *The Vanishing Hitchhiker* from the United States, and Paul Smith's *The Book of Nasty Legends* from England.

"The Vanishing Hitchhiker" is older than most of the other belief legends and is very common throughout Europe and North America. Gillian Bennett traces its background and gives numerous references in an article in *Perspectives on Contemporary Legend*.

The other two are related to a very old international tale. It has also circulated as a ballad known in English as "The Suffolk Miracle," versions of which have turned up in Nova Scotia. The ballad tells of a girl sent away from her lover, who then dies. A month later the lover calls for his sweetheart and carries her to her home on horseback. On the way he complains of a headache and she ties her handkerchief around his head. When they reach her home he goes to put the horse in the stable. When they look for him, the horse is there but he is not. They then open his grave and find his corpse with the handkerchief around his head. These children's tales simplify the story and substitute a blue cardigan and a pink shawl for the handkerchief, but the parallel is clear.

Students at St. Francis Xavier Public School in North York told these tales as part of a storytelling festival, January 22, 1985. This was the climax of a project initiated by Alice Kane of the Storytellers School of Toronto. She began by telling the students stories, then encouraged them to tell some themselves. From those sessions came the festival at which these and many other tales were told or dramatized, and then taped by Judy Smith, the school librarian.

The Vanishing Hitchhiker

Told by Pauline Caughtry and Cyndi Burns

Joel Harris was driving home one night from a business trip, and as he was driving it began to rain. To make matters worse he was very tired, and as he was driving along he noticed a flash of white, and as he got closer he realized that it was a young girl in a white party dress. She was wet and she was crying so he stopped to ask her [if she wanted] a ride, and when he did she said thank you, she'd love one, so she got in the back seat. He offered her his jacket because she was shivering; and when he got to the place where she had told him to stop at, he turned around to ask if this was the right place, and she was gone.

He realized that she must of jumped out of the car when he got to the house, and ran in. So he went up to the door and knocked on it. An old lady answered the door and asked what he wanted. Joel asked, "Do you have a daughter named Linda?" The lady answered, "Yes, but she died ten years ago in a car accident on her way home from a party." So Joel told her the story of how he picked Linda up on the freeway and drove her home. He expected the lady to call him crazy or mad, but instead she just said: "I know, it happened many times before. It seems she is trying to get home. Her grave is in Oakville Cemetery a couple of miles up the road." So Joel got into his car and went down to the cemetery. When he looked around he finally found Linda's tombstone, and lying neatly folded on top of her tombstone was Joel's jacket.

The Blue Cardigan

Told by Walter Scodeller and Joe Dominelli

One day there lived a man named Antoine. He was a carpenter in the town of Bordeaux, France. Although he was very handsome and very gentleman-like, he was still a bachelor at age twenty-seven.

He had dated many young girls in his life, but none did he love until he met Katrine. He met Katrine outside of town in a hall. Katrine was a beautiful, well-mannered young lady. The problem was Katrine never allowed Antoine to drive her to the hall or drive her home from the hall.

One day Antoine decided to follow Katrine home so he could think up a little plan which would make him return the next day. The next day when they met, Antoine was trying to find out a plan to get to her house. It just happened that that day Katrine had the shivers so Antoine thought that if he would give her his blue cardigan he would be able to retrieve it the next morning at her home. So Antoine gave Katrine his blue cardigan. At twelve midnight, like every other night, Katrine left—but this night she said something very unusual. She said, "Antoine, thank you for everything, but it is now my time to go." And they both departed.

Early next morning Antoine arrived at Katrine's home very early. He knocked on the door. An old lady answered. He asked, "Is Katrine in?" The old lady looked bewildered and said, "Katrine, she was my daughter. Today is the tenth anniversary of her death."

Antoine was astounded. He answered, "How can that be? I met her last night at a dance just out of town in a hall, and the day before that. She was wearing a bright red dress." The mother was also amazed when he said a bright red dress. She said, "That was Katrine's favourite dress, but I can tell you it is still untouched in her closet." The mother decided to check, and to her amazement the red dress was missing. They decided to investigate at the grave which was just outside the gates of the home.

They broke down a fort that Katrine's father had built for her around the grave, and began to dig. They both dug until they reached the coffin, and there, nicely laid over it, was a blue cardigan.

The Pink Shawl

Told by Rosemary Tatangelo

This story that I am going to tell you is from a lady named Mrs. Vigilanti. Many years ago it was about her brother and his army crewmates. They arranged this dance in this restaurant and there was these beautiful girls in the restaurant. The army crewmates sat at the table, and this one army crewmate saw this lady at the bar. He liked her so he went up to her and asked her to dance. She said, "Okay, I'll dance with you, [but] I have to be home by twelve o'clock."

So that night the army crewmate and the girl danced all night and had a great time together until the clock struck twelve. She asked him to bring her home and he said, "Okay." That night it was really dark so he didn't know exactly where he was going. So she told him to stop the car. He dropped her off at this place, but he didn't know exactly where it was. So he said goodnight. He asked her if he could walk her to the door and she said no. So they said goodnight.

The army crewmate went back to the restaurant and he saw

that the lady had left her shawl. The next day he went back to the place where he had dropped her off. He didn't see any houses, but he only saw this cemetery. So he asked the landlord if he saw this beautiful girl last night who was wearing this beautiful pink gown, and he said no. So he had the shawl in his hand and he was explaining the story to the landlord until this lady overheard the story. She asked him where he got the shawl, and he said he had gotten it from this lady last night that was at the bar. And she said that the shawl belonged to her daughter who had been dead for many years. Ever since that day the man has been in shock.

44. OLD MAN GIMLI: A CAMP LEGEND

This is typical of the scary stories that circulate in summer camps. Each region seems to develop its own tale which spreads from one camp to another, acquiring many variations. In Ontario the featured character is Anson Minor; in Manitoba it is Old Man Gimli. The stories, told by the camp counsellors, are usually fairly gruesome, designed to prevent the campers wandering abroad at night. They are akin to the urban legends or belief stories popular among teenagers, except that those tend to be international while the camp legends are usually peculiar to a particular region. Also, the urban legends usually circulate among teenagers, while the camp legends usually originate with the counsellors.

Marlies Suderman collected this and other stories at Camp Robertson just outside Gimli, a small town about forty-five miles north of Winnipeg that was settled by Icelandic fishermen. She notes that the stories were encouraged, if not inspired, by the large statue of a Viking in the town of Gimli, and quotes another counsellor's answer to the question of who Old Man Gimli was:

> *Well, nobody really knows who he was. Some people say he was an Icelandic fisherman, a really big guy, about eight feet tall, who used to fish around here. He drowned on the lake. People say that after he died, Old Man Gimli's ghost used to come out at night and roam around here. People say that he could still drive his old car around, and that every few weeks, if you were out on your front porch in Gimli late at night, and if you saw an old red-brown car without a driver roll by, that it was him. But one night Old Man Gimli drove down the beach and went off the side. He crashed into the big rocks and the wreck of the car has been there ever since.*

The collector goes on to say that the stories proved so popular with the girls that they wouldn't go to sleep without hearing one, and that the counsellor who told them was a very effective narrator: "Hearing the stories told in his low, spooky voice in the dark cabin was kind of scary, even for me. One story which he told is a combination of the Old Man Gimli tradition with a ghost story I heard outside of camp. This was the one about the bloody axe."

Old Man Gimli

Told by Marlies Suderman

One night this family was going down the highway that goes north of Gimli up to Hecla Island, and it was a really stormy night in the fall. It was really blowing and raining, and sure enough, what should happen, but they ran out of gas. Well! They didn't know what to do. They decided that they should spend the night at this farmhouse they had seen by the road just before they had to stop, and in the morning they would borrow some gas and go on. So they all walked over to the farmhouse.

Now, they hadn't realized this before, but there was no one living in this farmhouse. It was kind of a spooky old deserted place. But they figured it was so miserable out, it would have to do. So they bedded down for the night. Just when they all got to sleep, there was a tremendous chopping noise coming from the front yard of the farm. Now the storm had gone down a bit and they could hear really clearly that somebody was chopping on wood in the front yard. Now they figured it was just funny noises and they tried to go back to sleep, but soon they began to hear terrible shrieks, like somebody was in real agony.

Now the father figured that nobody was going to get any sleep until he found out what this noise was. By this time everyone was quite scared. I guess anybody would be. So the father, who was a pretty tough guy, went out the front door with a flashlight. But as soon as he opened the front door the noise stopped, just like that. And he couldn't see anything in the yard. All he could see was a chopping block with an old axe in it. So he went back inside, but in a little while the chopping and screaming started up again and the father went out again—and again he didn't see anybody at all, and again the chopping stopped just as he opened the front door. Now this kept up most of the night, almost until dawn, with the father going out and the chopping starting when he came back in. And the screams kept up, too. And the whole family thought that the screaming voice sounded like a little child. So when it got light outside and the screams and other noises finally stopped, everyone was pretty glad. The family got ready to go and went outside. And the first thing they saw when they got outside was the chopping block all covered with blood, with five little fingers lying beside the axe. Well, you can guess they were pretty fast getting out of there.

When they finally got someone driving on the highway to lend them some gas, and they got into the next town, they told some people in the town what had happened, and those people told them that a long time ago there had been a terrible happening. The people said that the house used to belong to Old Man Gimli before he drowned, and that his ghost had come back to bother people that lived there because he was jealous that they were still alive and living in his house. Apparently he had chopped off the fingers of the little son of the family while the boy was playing outside. And now whenever people stayed overnight in the farmhouse, the chopping axe and the bloody fingers reappeared.

VIII. Personal Experience Narratives

AMONG THE MOST common tales told in Canada are the personal experience narratives. These are often stories told in families where things that happened to parents or grandparents are repeatedly related to the children until they become part of the family tradition. They also include dramatic events that are described by the people involved, reminiscences about pioneer life, and accounts of rituals and local incidents: the kind of stories that are recorded as oral history and reflect the folklife of a particular group.

It is sometimes difficult to decide whether certain stories belong with the legends or should be considered as personal experience narratives. Some reports of the Sasquatch or of UFOs might be classified either way. As the examples of these two phenomena chosen for this collection are straightforward accounts of things seen, they appear in the following section of personal experiences, although such phenomena often have legendary characteristics. Other narratives include a prairie pioneer story, a first-person account of a famous disaster, a grandson's recollection of his grandfather's stories, and a reminiscence about a special community festival.

45. A SASQUATCH SIGHTING

The Sasquatch, a name anglicized from a Coast Salish word meaning "wild man of the woods," has its counterpart in the United States where it is called Bigfoot, in India where it is known as the Yeti or Abominable Snowman, and in Russia where it is the Almas. While other Canadian monsters like the Windigo, D'Sonoqua, and loup-garou are conceived of as supernatural, the Sasquatch is considered to be natural, but there is no agreement on whether it is human or animal.

More than three hundred witnesses in western Canada and California have reported seeing a monster who conforms to the Sasquatch concept, and numerous books and innumerable magazine and newspaper articles have featured these reports, many of which are very convincing. Photographs and models of enormous footprints have become common, and there is even a film that apparently shows the monster running away. Scientists have investigated the phenomena, but so far have come to no agreement. Some ridicule the idea that a Neanderthal man could exist today, while others are convinced that the Sasquatch is real. Those who doubt will not be convinced until someone manages to produce either a live or a dead Sasquatch. Because of this doubt, tales of the Sasquatch may be considered legendary, but as the one that follows is an eye-witness account sworn to by its author, it is presented as a personal experience narrative.

The most prolific Canadian writer on this subject is John Green, whose books such as *On the Track of the Sasquatch* include many first-hand accounts of sightings. In another extensive book, *Sasquatch*, Don Hunter collaborates with a devoted Sasquatch hunter, René Dahinden, to trace the stories and summarize the opinions and research of scientists. In *Manlike Monsters on Trial*, Marjorie Halpin and Michael M. Ames have gathered a number of reports and scientific analyses of various monsters, including the Sasquatch.

Both Green and Hunter quote the following account by William Roe which is one of the most detailed and convincing. Mr. Roe supported his story by making a sworn declaration of its truth before a commissioner for oaths in Edmonton in 1957.

A Sasquatch Sighting

Told by William Roe

I had been working on the highway near Tête Jaune Caché for about two years. In October 1955, I decided to climb five miles up Mica Mountain to an old deserted mine, just for something to do. I came in sight of the mine about three o'clock in the afternoon after an easy climb. I had just come out of a patch of low brush into a clearing, when I saw what I thought was a grizzly bear in the brush on the other side. I had shot a grizzly bear near that spot the year before. This one was only about seventy-five yards away, but I didn't want to shoot it, for I had no way of getting it out. So I sat down on a small rock and watched, my rifle in my hands. I could just see part of the animal's head and the top of one shoulder. A moment later it raised up and stepped out into the opening. Then I saw it was not a bear.

This, to the best of my recollection, is what the creature looked like and how it acted as it came across the clearing directly towards me. My first impression was of a huge man, about six feet tall, almost three feet wide, and probably weighing somewhere near three hundred pounds. It was covered from head to foot with dark-brown silver-tipped hair. But as it came closer I saw by its breasts that it was female.

And yet its torso was not curved like a female's. Its broad frame was straight from shoulder to hip. Its arms were much thicker than a man's arms, and longer, reaching almost to its knees. Its feet were broader proportionately than a man's, about five inches wide at the front and tapering to much thinner heels. When it walked it placed the heel of its foot down first, and I could see the grey-brown skin or hide on the soles of its feet.

It came to the edge of the brush I was hiding in, within twenty feet of me, and squatted down on its haunches. Reaching out its hands it pulled the branches of bushes toward it and stripped the leaves with its teeth. Its lips curled flexibly around the leaves as it ate. I was close enough to see that its teeth were white and even.

The shape of this creature's head somewhat resembled a Negro's. The head was higher at the back than at the front. The nose was broad and flat. The lips and chin protruded farther than its nose. But the hair that covered it, leaving bare only the parts of its face around the mouth, nose, and ears, made it resemble an animal as much as a human. None of this hair, even on the back of its head, was longer than an inch, and that on its face much shorter. Its ears were shaped like a human's ears. But its eyes were small and black like a bear's. And its neck also was unhuman. Thicker and shorter than any man's I had ever seen.

As I watched this creature, I wondered if some movie company was making a film at this place and that what I saw was an actor, made up to look partly human and partly animal. But as I observed it more, I decided it would be impossible to fake such a specimen. Anyway, I learned later there was no such company near that area. Nor, in fact, did anyone live up Mica Mountain, according to the people who lived in Tête Jaune Caché.

Finally, the wild thing must have got my scent, for it looked directly at me through an opening in the brush. A look of amaze-ment crossed its face. It looked so comical at the moment I had to grin. Still in a crouched position it backed up three or four short steps, then straightened up to its full height and started to walk rapidly back the way it had come. For a moment it watched me over its shoulder as it went, not exactly afraid, but as though it wanted no contact with anything strange.

The thought came to me that if I shot it, I would possibly have a specimen of great interest to scientists the world over. I had heard stories about the Sasquatch, the giant hairy Indians that live in the legends of British Columbia Indians, and [which], many claim, are still in fact alive today. Maybe this was a Sas-quatch, I told myself.

I levelled my rifle. The creature was still walking rapidly away, again turning its head to look in my direction. I lowered the rifle. Although I have called the creature "it," I felt now that it was a human being and I knew I would never forgive myself if I killed it.

Just as it came to the other patch of brush it threw its head back and made a peculiar noise that seemed to be half-laugh and half-language, and which I can only describe as a kind of a whinny. Then it walked from the small brush into a stand of lodge-pole pine.

I stepped out into the opening and looked across a small ridge just beyond the pine to see if I could see it again. It came out on the ridge a couple of hundred yards away from me, tipped its head back again, and again emitted the only sound I had heard it make, but what this half-laugh, half-language was meant to convey, I do not know. It disappeared then, and I never saw it again.

I wanted to find out if it lived on vegetation entirely or ate meat as well, so I went down and looked for signs. I found it in five different places, and though I examined it thoroughly, I could find no hair or shells of bugs or insects. I believe it was strictly a vegetarian.

I found one place where it slept for a couple of nights under a tree. Now the nights were cool up the mountain, at this time of year especially, yet it had not used a fire. I found no sign that it possessed even the simplest of tools. Nor a single companion while in this place.

Whether this creature was a Sasquatch I do not know. It will always remain a mystery to me, unless another is found.

I hereby declare the above statement to be in every part true, to the best of my powers of observation and recollection.

46. *HOW I LEARNED TO MAKE BREAD*

Among the most common personal experience narratives in Canada are biographical accounts by immigrants and pioneers. Many early books are first-person stories of the activities of homesteaders, ranchers, or lumbermen. In recent years oral historians have been collecting such tales on tape and publishing their transcripts. Two of the most prolific workers in this field are Barry Broadfoot, who has produced many books including *Ten Lost Years*, *The Six War Years*, and *The Pioneer Years* (from which this item comes), and Bill McNeil, who introduces his tapes on the CBC's Sunday morning "Fresh Air" program as "Voice of the Pioneer" and has published two books of his interviews.

In a letter Barry Broadfoot describes the value of these stories: "From the first I considered my oral histories as an enrichment of Canadian history, adding flesh and blood and facial expressions and depth and vigor to the skeleton of history taught in our schools."

Stories by and about newcomers to Canada are an important element in our literature. In the West, jokes about remittance men and greenhorns are common, and the difficulties faced by English brides are likewise frequently described. Several of our most famous nineteenth-century books have detailed the experiences of English emigrants, including Susanna Moodie's *Roughing It in the Bush* and Catharine Parr Traill's *The Backwoods of Canada*. This story of an English girl who marries a Canadian and comes to live on the prairies reflects the attitude of such English brides, and shows how an initial unfavourable impression can be modified by contact with the neighbours.

Mr. Broadfoot notes of "Mary Watson" (a pseudonym because she did not want her name published) that when he interviewed her she was a very old lady living by herself in a highrise in Calgary. Her daughter had come in from Drumheller to see that her mother didn't say anything to disgrace the family. He comments: "She was rather frail although I remember she made very good cookies which we ate with tea at her tiny kitchen table while her daughter sat in the livingroom ten feet away with ears wide open."

How I Learned to Make Bread

Told by Mary Watson

Oh, I'll never forget that first year. I made a perfect fool of myself. A perfect fool.

Bread. My husband said a family needed bread, and I had a

recipe book my mother had given me and it told how to make bread. But I just couldn't do it. I tried and tried but it wouldn't rise or it was sour or like lead or [had] big air holes in it. Always something wrong. Well, my husband said, "Why can't you make the barmy stuff?" And I said I had never been taught. After all, in the town I had lived in, the baker came around with his wagon and his hot box every morning and you just went out to the lane and chose bread and scones and whatever you wanted. Well, Weyburn certainly wasn't England. I'll say that again. My husband told me to ask the neighbours and I said I didn't like the neighbour women. And I didn't. They were coarse. I wasn't putting myself on a pedestal. These women were coarse gossips. Almost strumpets. Some of them, anyway. We got this farm paper and there was a column that gave advice and it was printed by a woman called Millicent Miller. I'm sure that was the name. You wrote her a question and she'd answer it, so I wrote this woman — which wasn't her real name, I found out after — and lo and behold in about three weeks the paper came back and there was my letter printed, and with my name on it. Well, you can imagine how I felt. Other letters she printed had initials, like G.T. or B.R. I thought she'd do it with me, but there was Mary Watson, Weyburn, large as life. But there was a recipe to make bread, which as far as I could see was the same as the one in my book. So I just forgot about it that day. I didn't tell my husband, that's for certain.

Next morning there is a knock on the door and I look out and there's a Mrs. Ratigan on the stoop. I knew her. She was one of the coarse ones. Irish. A big woman and even though I didn't have much to do with her on our street I believed her to be capable. She just looked like she was. In the store she was always wiping some child's nose or slapping another, but they obeyed her and that was something. Children were as much ruffians in those days as they are now.

When I opened the door she just barged in and said, "Mary Watson. Weyburn. Bread. I read it," and she sat down. Then she said, "Nobody ever learned to make bread out of a book. It takes a mother to teach her daughter. Where's your mother?" I said in Guildford in England, and she said, "Fine. Leave her there. I'll be your mother this morning and we'll make bread."

And we did. She stood beside me and told me how to mix and how to pour and how to get the heat up and how to punch and poke. When it was rising we sat around and drank tea and I even thought of giving her something in her tea out of my husband's cabinet, but I decided I wouldn't. Then she said, "The good Lord never said that a person always has to have Irish coffee. There's Irish tea, too, you know, dear." I laughed and got up and got the brandy. I was getting to like her and when I came back with the bottle she poured a great whack in it, smiled, and said, "If you weren't Anglican I would have said you were one of the true faith."

She left about three in the afternoon. There wasn't much left in my husband's bottle but I didn't care. He'd forget about that when he saw that I'd learned to bake bread and buns. There were four nice loaves and some buns waiting for him under clean washcloths on the kitchen table when he came home from the store. I was that proud.

He never knew about the little ad I'd put in Millicent Miller's column in the paper. He only found out about it years later and he said that half the town must have been laughing at me. I said no, I didn't guess so. I got some very nice smiles when I went shopping after that; people talked to me and I met some nice ladies. And besides, Mrs. Ratigan told me that day if anybody laughed at me for what I'd done, she said she'd conk them on the snoot.

47. THE FRANK SLIDE DISASTER

Disasters, whether shipwrecks, fires, explosions, or mining cave-ins, are nearly always memorialized in personal narratives or ballads. Famous Canadian disasters like the Miramichi fire of 1825, the Halifax explosion of 1917, the *Southern Cross* tragedy of 1914, and the various Springhill mine disasters have all inspired songs.

Mining disasters have been a tragic part of our history, and the avalanche that almost wiped out the little Alberta town of Frank in 1903 is one of the most famous. No one is certain what caused that great rock slide. A minor earthquake two years earlier may have loosened the rock, or the large chambers opened up in the mine underground may have weakened the mountain's foundation. As Turtle Mountain is a peculiar structure of limestone overthrust upon shale sandstone and coal beds, it forms an unusually weak mass.

This account, which Barry Broadfoot recorded from a man who was present at the time, is doubly interesting because it not only gives a vivid eye-witness description of a dramatic event but also throws light on a widespread legend: that the only survivor was a baby girl. Robert Gard, an American folklorist who spent some years in Alberta collecting stories, used that legend as the basis of his "Ballad of the Frank Slide," which achieved some popularity in the folk clubs of the nineteen-sixties.

The narrator, a Scotsman, was born near Kingston and went west in 1903. Mr. Broadfoot remembers him as:

> ... *a tall and very thin and fragile old man, living in an apartment in the west end, one of those dark old apartments of pre-first world war vintage with long narrow and dark halls with a lot of turns in them ... This was a big event in his life — as it was with so many of the old-timers I interviewed. They were usually so alone and neglected. Before I started taping he brought out a mickey of Scotch. It was as if he was making a party of it. Anyway, we drank the bottle. In fact, as I remember, I drank about four ounces and he knocked off the rest.*

The Frank Slide Disaster

I had a brother Charlie doing some subcontracting in the coal mine at Frank in Alberta, so I figured I'd ride out and see him. I arrived on a Sunday, 10:20 A.M., and on Monday afternoon I went to work in the mine at three dollars for eight hours.

Well, Frank was quite a town then. I guess there were about eight hundred to a thousand men working there. I arrived there on April nineteenth. In ten days, on the twenty-ninth of April, at five minutes after four in the morning, Turtle Mountain took a notion to tumble down and bury the valley. It was one of the worst disasters up to that time in Canadian history, let me tell you, and don't just believe the newspapers. Listen to me, I was there. Eighty-seven people killed and about fifty injured.

Well, my brother and I were sleeping in the Union Hotel, just across the street from the Crows Nest Pass main line. Well, just about that time a freight train used to go through, and I used to wake up. This time I thought to myself that that was an awful long and loud freight train. So I woke up Charlie, who was sleeping with me, and he said, "Hell, that ain't no freight train."

And just then the building began to shake and the roar got louder and I said, "I guess it's an earthquake." But a blacksmith with a nice name, Dick Slugg, came running down the hall yelling, "Everybody out, the mine has blown up, the mine has blown up!" I threw up the window curtain and there was a half an inch of frost on the window, just like there is in cold wintertimes, and when we got outside all the puddles that had been wet and muddy the night before was suddenly frozen hard. We couldn't figure it out, but it had something to do with Turtle Mountain coming down into the valley and forcing all the warm air out, the cold air from way up in the mountains pouring in in an instant and freezing everything. At least that's the theory: the change of air from 3,500 feet up coming down.

We groped our way around in the dark and went down the street, and there was this huge company bunkhouse, maybe a hundred men sleeping in it, and just beyond it, not thirty feet away, was this huge wall of rock of dark limestone and that building, so close, and not even one pane of glass broken. It took quite a bit of time for us to get it through our heads that everything and everybody beyond that point, where the wall of rock began, was dead. Was blank.

Oh, I could tell you much more, but what did we do? We went over to where some miners' cottages had been hit by a small slide coming off the big slide, and we found dead people in some of the cottages, but we rescued some. This is where the legend of the Frank Slide Baby began, that out of that whole town there was just one survivor and that was a baby. I still see it in newspapers, in articles in magazines and books about the Frank Slide, and they all say that there was only one survivor, a baby. I know about the baby. It was the baby belonging to a Mr. and Mrs. Frank Leech and it was saved. But remember, Frank was a fairly big town and there were hundreds of miners, and only those at one end of the town, the fringe, eighty-seven people, were killed. But to this day, to this very day, people are still writing about the Frank Slide and the only survivor, a baby, which was the Leech baby, which was rescued when I was there. In fact, it wasn't rescued. Its mother put it on a bale of hay that had rolled down from the livery barn and when we came along, all us rescuers, there was the baby outside in its blanket, safe and sound. Its mother went back in the house and was killed by some more rock and mud. Its father, Frank Leech, died too, and two boys did; but two girls, teenagers, in that house, we got them out. They went to hospital and was okay after a while. So there were hundreds safe in the town and not just one baby. That was in 1903 and seventy-three years later they're still talking about that one baby.

Eighteen men were trapped in the mine, the night shift, and when the slide came it blocked the river and a lake began to form. But the railroad construction crews knew powder and they got to work and blew out a path, and the water began to go down after it had crept up to the knees, the thighs, and then the waists of the eighteen men trapped in the mine. They got themselves out by digging a raise forty-five feet and coming out higher up the mountain. The first one out was a little fellow named Shorty Dawson, who wriggled through the hole they'd made further up and yelled "Help" to us who were working in gangs trying to get in to them from below. We got all eighteen out then, and the only one who was injured was a fellow named Warrington, who'd hurt his leg. It was after five o'clock in the afternoon when we took them up through town to the hospital and it was like a parade, miners and townspeople carrying these miners who had dug themselves out. Yes, it was like a parade.

That's a very short telling of how it actually was. It would take a whole book to tell of how they were trapped in there, how the explosions blew in the doors and the air shut off and the water coming up. But they got out because they kept their heads and figured out what was to be done and did it. There were some very experienced miners on the night shift and they led them out, out through that raise, but they was lucky, too.

The people killed, all but a few of the eighty-seven, are still under all that rock in the valley. That was their graveyard. Whole families, single men, townspeople, Canadians, Welshmen.

But there's one story I want to tell you. Thirty-one days after the Frank Slide disaster, the first men went back into that mine to look at the damage. My brother was one of them. In there with safety lamps, half a candle-flame, and they don't know what they'll find and they're groping their way in and they hear chains rattling. Well, chains can only mean ghosts and spirits. There is nothing alive in that mine. Remember, it's thirty-one days. So grown men that they were, they turned turtle and got out of there. But then they stopped and said, "We can't do this. This sort of thing isn't done. We've got a job to do." So they went back in again past where they'd been, and they saw two round eyes reflecting in their lamps and they found this horse, they called him Big Charlie. One of the miners on the night shift had taken him in the night of the slide to do some particular work. This horse was still alive, lying with his head towards the ditch where he could lap the mine water.

Well, sir, they hugged him, they cried over him, they sent out for a veterinary and they did everything to comfort that animal. And the mine manager offered a reward of a thousand dollars if the vet could save him. Well, they tried, but next morning he died because his stomach was so full of wood which he had gnawed off the wooden side of the mine cars, gnawed the wood off the sides of those cars in that mine in pitch darkness trying to keep alive. Thirty-one days. Well, that's the story of Big

Charlie. He was the last casualty of the Frank Slide Disaster, as they call it now.

48. MY GRANDFATHER'S WAR

The following anecdotes are typical of the stories that soldiers remember and relate to their families long after the wars are over. Jack Henderson, the grandfather of this item, was an excellent raconteur who frequently told stories of his many adventures to his five grandchildren.

Jack Henderson's peripatetic early life naturally inspired many stories. He was born in Newcastle, England, in 1880, became a steam engineer, worked on the Cape-to-Cairo Railway, and fought in the Boer War. He also worked in Pennsylvania before emigrating to Canada in 1907 and settling in Vancouver. As the following stories indicate, he served with the Canadian Engineers (Third Army Troop Company) in World War I. Shortly afterwards, he worked on railway construction in Russia and the Rockies. Later he was very active in various public organizations in Vancouver, becoming well known for his long and devoted service as a school trustee. Mr. Henderson died in 1968.

In 1978 Norman W. Moss of Kamloops, British Columbia, first recorded these stories and then wrote them down for his cousin, Carole Henderson Carpenter, as part of an extensive family folklore project on-going since 1976. Dr. Carpenter notes that her grandfather's stories were an important influence in leading her to become a folklorist. She is now an Associate Professor in the Humanities Division of York University.

Many Canadians have recorded their war experiences, most notably of World War II. Barry Broadfoot presents numerous reminiscences in *The Six War Years*, and Farley Mowat gives a vivid and moving account of his war experiences in *And No Birds Sang*.

My Grandfather's War

Told by Norman W. Moss

In the First World War my grandfather was in Canada, and conscription hadn't come along, and the First World War force was a volunteer force, and he volunteered, but there are a number of stories that came around the volunteering. One was [about] the Sergeant-Major who was stationed at Victory Square (which is in Vancouver) and had a recruiting booth, and a man walking down the street [who was] obviously of the age for military conscription. And he called him over and said, ah, was he a soldier? And the man replied he wasn't. He [the Sergeant-Major] said didn't he think it was about time he signed up, and the man looked rather astonished and he said, "What, didn't you see my leg? Didn't you see me, the way I walk?" And the Sergeant-Major said, "No, I didn't." He said, "Well, I'll walk. Watch me." And he proceeded to walk down the street and kept going.

Before going to Europe in the First World War the Canadian troops left Vancouver and arrived at Val-Cartier, Quebec, which was sort of a training, jumping-off point before going across overseas. And one of the stories my grandfather recalls was that they had a large parade square on the Plains of Abraham overlooking the St. Lawrence River — the large cliff and a drop-off. And he recalls the story of a Regimental Sergeant-Major who was training his Sergeant to drill squads of men to get the proper order and discipline from them. And one of these squads of about thirty or forty men was parading in different directions and the recruit was calling out the various orders under the watchful eye of the Regimental Sergeant-Major. And the men were moving in different directions and he was calling out "Forward" and "About turn" and so on. And the squad at this time was continually moving across the parade square, and the new man couldn't recall the order for stop. And he tried a number of commands without any effect at all, and the men were continually moving towards the end, the end of the parade square which dropped over a cliff. And the man was perspiring quite freely now because he didn't know what to do. And finally in desperation he turned to the Regimental Sergeant-Major and said, "What do I say? What's the command? What'll I say?" And the Regimental Sergeant-Major, who obviously had a sense of humour, said, "Well, son, you better say something even if it's only goodbye."

At the time, too, there were many men who had come into the army for the first time and some of them had very, very bad personal habits. One of these men wouldn't wash, and after asking him several times my grandfather and several men grabbed him [and threw him] in a bucket of water or a horse-trough, and took corn brooms to him. Needless to say, he wasn't needing any convincing in the future to wash.

When they did arrive in Europe, the stories seemed to stem in large part around Vimy Ridge where he was stationed, and Vimy

Ridge and Petit Vimy, were sort of small hills that were constantly under bombardment, and the lines changed back and forth and there was a lot of mining and drilling underneath. And part of his job was to lay mines under the ground. If the lines were retaken by the Germans, these lines were blown up from underneath. This was trench warfare and the men were in constant mud [and water], and a number of debilitating physical diseases and whatnot would come on these men, such as trench-foot and, of course, lice. He tells us about the washing of the men's clothes in machines that resembled cement mixers, and having to shovel the lice out with shovels.

Another story he tells is of the men going "over the top" on a raid at night, and falling back into the shell-holes with full gear on, and being weighed down and drowning in these shell-holes full of water. The officers in many cases would sound a whistle when the men went over the top and often they would stay back, because many of them were shot when they were leading their troops. [They] weren't well received, especially on suicide missions.

He recalls one particular story of a Guard Regiment — that's the Grenadier Guards near him on the front. And they were apparently to lead a charge on a German bunker that was certain suicide, but the command had come down. And while they were getting ready in the early morning — the signals were to go up at six or seven in the morning, and they were to charge across a front of a hundred yards — the batman for the Regimental Sergeant-Major produced several boxes, and in these boxes were stainless white dress gloves, and each member of the regiment put these on. When the whistle came they charged over against the German machine-guns and were all killed, but their idea was to go out as they were, as British gentlemen.

The fighting the first year of the war, 1914, wasn't quite as vicious as later on, and the Christmas of the first year my grandfather recalls singing in the German trenches, and on [one] occasion something landing near their men in the trench, and thinking it was a bomb they ran to grab it and throw it out quickly, and they found it was an orange, and they threw an orange or something back. And eventually the Germans and the British were throwing presents and fruit and candies and so on back and forth. But he said by the second war year so many had been killed and bitterness was so engrained that this, of course, didn't happen.

He also mentioned the story of the YMCA truck which had Christmas goodies loaded in it, mainly for British officers, and the kids in the French town that they had taken over were starving and had never seen anything, and so his men decided to give some of these kids some fruit. So they hijacked the YMCA truck and turned it over to the town.

As an engineer at the time, my grandfather was involved in digging bunkers fifty feet deep for officers four or five miles behind the lines, which he thought were rather amusing in contrast to the troops' [bunkers] that were only six feet below the ground's surface. Apparently from the air [over] the battlefield you couldn't see the troops at all, they were all in either bunkers or trenches and would come out only on raids.

One of the problems, as I mentioned, was cleanliness, and what they used to do to gather water they would [put] canvas down in these shell-holes, and the water from rain would collect in there. And then they would drain it off for drinking and washing. It so happened that in this area was a lot of coal, so my grandfather got two fifty-gallon drums and some coal — and the water, of course — and rigged up a small furnace-heating system, and the men had hot showers. Now some of the officers, hearing of this, came by and asked if they could use it, and of course they were willing to give ration coupons for food, blankets, and whatever, and by the end of that winter my grandfather had enough to outfit a good portion of the men that were working with him.

49. ST. PETER'S DAY

The Doukhobor culture springs from a social movement that began over two centuries ago in southern Russia. Its members reject formal religion and militarism, arguing that authority lies in the individual heart guided by love, nonviolence, and universal brotherhood. In 1895 many thousand Doukhobors in Tsarist Russia burnt their firearms to proclaim that wars and militarism must end. That led to harsh punishment and exile, with some 7,500 emigrating to Canada where they were guaranteed exemption from military service.

Canadian Doukhobor settlements annually commemorate the burning of the firearms on St. Peter's Day, June 29, and for many years this was their main community celebration. In 1923 a group at Blaine Lake, Saskatchewan, re-enacted the burning of the guns, an event that a janitor in Vancouver recalls as a significant part of his childhood. Koozma J. Tarasoff, a leading Doukhobor scholar, recorded his account in *Traditional Doukhobor Folkways*.

Many Canadians have similar memories of childhood events. Various towns used to have a school holiday to celebrate Queen Victoria's birthday (May 24), or George V's birthday (June 3), or Canada Day (July 1), with parades, picnics, and sports competitions. St. Peter's Day was distinctive because of its emphasis on peace, but the description of it is fairly typical of stories Canadians tell about their own special local celebrations.

St. Peter's Day

When we grew up as young boys, it was nothing to go out on a Sunday with .22 rifles and shoot rabbits or ducks or something. It wasn't considered extreme. It was a common practice. Until about the early 1920s, however, when there was a sort of religious revival in the Blaine Lake District and they re-enacted the burning of firearms at the traditional place near Blaine Lake where they celebrated St. Peter's Day. And all the Doukhobors came to that meeting, that special celebration, and everybody brought their guns (about a hundred of them) and they re-enacted the burning of the firearms. They actually burnt their guns. It was quite a sensation, a news story — because a lot of non-Doukhobors heard about it and they came and they watched this strange scene. They couldn't understand it and remarked about it. And a lot of them came and tried to recognize the kinds of guns, the molten pieces without the other, for the wood was burnt off. They were all lovers of guns. They were kind of more interested to know who possessed what kind of gun. But that's as far as it went; it didn't have any other meaning.

Besides the re-enactment, in which hundreds of Doukhobors participated, there was the usual program of the singing of psalms and speeches by some people. A noonday picnic lunch with their *pirogi*, watermelon, and the like. As a young boy the celebrations didn't mean much to me except as a holiday. But as I grew older I found the significance of it. There were also a number of visitors, including the local Baptists around the place. Also, Doukhobors from the Langham District came out. Each district usually brought along a choir. Only a few cars came out at that time. I can't recall youths playing games there at the time, most people started out early on their wagons over roads that were pretty dusty ... We never minded that; we were always looking forward to something great. As for participation, I think about 90 percent came out; I think very few people remained at home. At this time, it was the height of St. Peter's Day because you had nothing else to look forward to throughout the whole year.

50. UFO STORIES

Strange sights in the sky have been the stuff of innumerable legends and superstitions, as witness the star that guided the wise men to Bethlehem, and Calpurnia's comment that, "The heavens themselves blaze forth the death of princes." In modern times when stars and comets have yielded much of their mystery to science, those looking for mystery see in the skies the outriders of distant worlds.

UFOs — Unidentified Flying Objects — are undoubtedly among the most frequently reported phenomena of the mid- and late-twentieth century. Scientists have studied them, books have recorded and analyzed them, motion pictures have glamorized them, and folk continue to relate their personal experiences with them.

In *The UFO Handbook*, Allan Hendry analyzes 1,300 UFO reports with the help of J. Allen Hynek, Director of the Center for UFO Studies, and finds that about nine out of ten can be identified by experts as stars, advertising planes, aircraft, meteors, weather balloons, and the like. However, some cannot be ascribed to conventional objects or effects, and remain unidentified.

Chris Rutkowski, who supplied the following accounts, reports that in the 1970s in the southern Manitoba town of Carman, "the tale of Charlie Redstar began, a tale that saw literally thousands of people giving eye-witness testimony to the flight of Charlie Redstar, the visitor from outer space." A mysterious nocturnal red light attracted the attention of television film crews and photographers, and their films showing a strange light gave Charlie Redstar his name.

These sightings are typical: Hendry found that nocturnal lights accounted for nearly 90 per cent of the UFO reports that he analyzed. The men who gave these accounts did not wish to be identified, but Mr. Rutkowski notes that they are in their late twenties, with families, and that they are both custodians at the University of Manitoba.

UFO Stories

First Report, May 13, 1975
Well, we were sitting two miles north of Carman, about a quarter mile from Highway 13, facing west. We were sitting for a good hour, I'm sure, and we noticed to the west of us this . . . object: a large red light. It seemed to be bouncing up and down in the sky from occasion to occasion.

What I saw was — it seemed to me — it would start off as a white light that would rise up; it would glow — grow in intensity to a brilliant white and then turn red as it seemed to get either closer or stronger. It went through this in a short time; oh, maybe five to seven seconds ... and it would be floating up, hovering above the road, I would say at least seven to eight miles — at least that — to the west. That would be how I would approximate the distance. We would watch it and we would notice a car coming either from the north or from the south along Highway 13, and as soon as it approached, the light would seem to be frightened of the approaching car, almost as if it was aware.

[Later] we then proceeded about three miles west with our lights on. We dimmed off our lights to just parking lights, drove another two miles west, and we watched — couldn't see a thing. We went on farther west. We noticed this large red light up in the sky, about fifty feet up in the air. Now, we knew it wasn't Haywood tower because we could see Haywood tower.

As we saw it, I saw it take off just straight up and disappear in a matter of a second and a half. It just, just ... zot! And it was gone. It was just a fraction of a moment and there was no trace of it at all.

Second Report, July 10, 1976
As I turned the corner without my lights, Little Charlie could be seen at his regular spot. I drove three miles south without lights.

On the way down the road Little Charlie went from the brilliant white to a very intense orange, and when we stopped to view with the binoculars we would plainly see what appeared to be one sitting on top of another ... For the next half hour we waited for him to do something. He seemed very inactive and did not respond to the flashlight or the car lights [flashed at "him" in code]. Suddenly at about 1:45 [A.M.] he started to flare up and move to the right ... He had turned brilliant white with a slight yellowish-orange tinge around his edges. Rather than being a ball, he now gave the appearance of a small domed saucer.

[Later] I drove to the mile cross-over and turned east to look back down the road. There, in the middle of the road, was a bright flaring light. We stopped and turned out our lights to see what it was. I told John that it looked now like a car, and he said, "That's no damn car!" Then in my rear-view mirror the object suddenly flared up and went down to nothing. It flared up again. Time after time it would flare up to a brilliant orangeish light, then disappear. We decided to move back down the road. As I crossed the bridge I looked in the rear-view mirror and saw him start to flare. "Here he comes, John!" There was little doubt that he was following us down the road and was closing the distance between us. From mile to mile down the road we watched as he followed us back. At the two farms one mile up the road I turned west, as Little Charlie never follows us any further than that point.

Sources and References

THE FOLLOWING NOTES on the individual tales give the source of each tale, list the relevant tale types and motifs, give a few comparative references (particularly to other Canadian versions), and details of any items mentioned in the introductory notes. Most references are cited by the author's name, with an abbreviated title where necessary; the full listings appear in the bibliography.

I. MYTHS

1. Old-One

"Okanagan Tales," collected by James A. Teit. In *Folk-Tales of Salishan and Sahaptin Tribes*, edited by Franz Boas (Lancaster, PA & New York: American Folk-Lore Society, 1917), pp. 80–81.
Motifs: A401, Mother Earth; A1241, Man made from clay; A830, Creation of earth by creator; A831, Earth from body of person; A1714.3, Animals created from earth.

2. Crow Makes the World

Tagish Tlaagu: Tagish Stories by Mrs. Angela Sidney, recorded by Julie Cruikshank (Whitehorse: Council for Yukon Indians and the Goverment of Yukon, 1982), pp. 12–15.
Cf. Thompson, *North American Indians*, 22–24, references, 281.
Motifs: A522.2, Bird as culture hero; A511.1.3.3, Immaculate conception of culture hero; T512.3, Conception by drinking water; A511.1, Birth of the culture hero; A721.1, Theft of sun; A1411.2, Theft of light by being swallowed and reborn; A1412.3, Acquisition of daylight by culture hero; A814.2, Earth from sand strewn on primeval water; A1252, Creation of man from wood.

3. The Moon
Traditions of the Thompson River Indians of British Columbia, collected by James A. Teit (Boston and New York: American Folk-Lore Society, 1898), p. 91.
Motifs: A753, Moon as person; A753.2, Moon has house; A751.8, Woman in moon.

4. The Mosquito and the Thunder
Traditions of the Thompson River Indians of British Columbia, collected by James A. Teit (Boston and New York: American Folk-Lore Society, 1898), p. 56.
Motif: A1132, Origin of thunderbolt.

II. ANIMAL TALES

5. A Wolf, a Fox, and a Lion
Carla Bianco Collection, CCFCS Archives, tape 28, #419. Told in Italian by Antonio Carofano, Toronto, 1967. Translated by Carla Bianco.
Motif: K961.1.1, Tit for tat.

6. The Race Between Turtle and Frog
"Sanpoil Tales," collected by Marian K. Gould. In *Folktales of Salishan and Sahaptin Tribes*, edited by Franz Boas (Lancaster, PA and New York: American Folk-Lore Society, 1917), p. 111.
Cf. Thompson, *North American Indians*, 258–59; Fauset, 45–52; Briggs, A:1, 108.
Type AT 1074: Race Won by Deception: Relative Helpers (K11.1).
Motif: K1840, Deception by substitution.

7. How the Agouti Lost Its Tail
Rita Cox wrote this down as she tells it, Toronto, November, 1985.
Motifs: A2493.01, Former friendships between domestic and wild animals; A2216, Animal characteristics: members bitten or cut off; A2494, Why certain animals are enemies; A2513, Why certain animals serve man.

III. SUPERNATURAL TALES

8. Once Upon a Time There Was a Shepherd
Carla Bianco Collection, CCFCS Archives, tape 33–34, #470. Told in Italian by Antonio Carofano, Toronto, 1968. Translated by Carla Bianco.
Motifs: F341.1, Fairies give three gifts; D813, Magic object received from fairy; D1451, Inexhaustible purse furnishes money; D1470.1, Magic wishing object; D1472.1.8, Magic tablecloth supplies food and drink; D832, Magic objects acquired by acting as umpire for fighting heirs; D1012.1, Magic legs of animal; B505, Magic object received from animal; D1440, Magic object gives power over animals; D684, Transformation by helpful animals; D1021, Magic feather; D1022.3, Magic hair of lion's tail; K452, Unjust umpire misappropriates disputed goods; D1361.12,

Magic cloak of invisibility; K532, Escape under mantle of invisibility; D1520.10, Magic transportation by shoes.

9. *The Talking Nightingale*

Folktales of the Canadian Sephardim, collected and translated by André E. Elbaz (Toronto: Fitzhenry & Whiteside, 1982), pp. 94–97. Told by Jacques Cohen, Montreal, in French and Judeo-Arabic.
Type AT 707: The Three Golden Sons.
Motifs: C664, Injunction to marry first woman met; K2115, Animal birth slander; K512, Compassionate executioner; B535, Animal nurse; R131.3.1, Shepherd rescues abandoned child; H1154.7, Task: capturing bird; G270, Witch overcome or escaped; Q40, Kindness rewarded; D1076, Magic ring; B211.3, Speaking bird; B451.2, Helpful nightingale; B131.2, Bird reveals treachery; N731.3, Father unexpectedly meets abandoned son and reinstates him; S451, Outcast wife at last united with husband and children; Q42, Generosity rewarded; Q261, Treachery punished.

10. *The White Bear*

Folktales from Western Newfoundland, told by Angela Kerfont, collected and edited by Marie Annick Desplanques (Mont Saint Aignan: Université de Rouen, 1985), pp. 23–25.
For the domestic tradition, see Ives, "Lumbercamp Singing and the Two Traditions."
Motifs: S12, Cruel mother; R131, Exposed or abandoned child rescued; D435.4, Helpful bear, B535, Animal nurse; B535.03, Goat as nurse for child; B540, Animal rescuer; D766, Disenchantment by liquid, E80, Resuscitation by water, B211.3, Helpful bird; B143.1, Bird gives warning; B521.1, Animal warns against poison; Q411, Death as punishment.

11. *The Magic Chest*

Folk Narrative Among Ukrainian-Canadians in Western Canada, by Robert B. Klymasz (Ottawa: National Museum of Man, CCFCS Mercury Series 4, 1973), pp. 39–44. Recorded in Dauphin, Manitoba, July 23, 1963. Archival finding No. KLY 38, c-19a, item 13.
Motifs: L143, Poor man surpasses rich; K890.1, Poor man deceives rich man, plays trick on him, causes his death; J514, One should not be too greedy; K1840, Deception by substitution; B505, Magic object received from animal; F360, Malevolent or destructive fairies; D1470.2.2, Supplies received from magic box.

12. *The Blacksmith and Beelzebub's Imps*

Folk-Lore of Waterloo County, Ontario, by W.J. Wintemberg (Ottawa: National Museum, Bulletin 116, 1950), p. 63.
Cf. Fauset, 45–52; Briggs, A:1, 493–44.
Type AT 330A: The Smith and the Devil.
Motifs: G303, Devil; M211, Man sells soul to devil; D1721.1, Magic power from devil; D1413.1.2, Pear tree from which one cannot descend; D1413.6, Chair to which person sticks; D1413.9, Sack holds person who puts his hand into it; K210, Devil cheated of his promised soul.

13. The Fox Wife

Paper Stays Put: A Collection of Inuit Writing, edited by Robin Gedalof (Edmonton: Hurtig, 1980), pp. 160–61. Recorded by Leah Tataniq at Frobisher Bay, 1966, transcribed in Inuktitut by Joanasie Salomonie, and published in *Inuktitut*, Summer 1967.
Cf. Thompson, *Tales of the North American Indians*, 161–62, references, 342.
Motifs: D313.1, Transformation: fox to person; C963.1, Person returns to original animal form when tabu is broken.

14. The Two Brothers

The Greeks of Vancouver: A Study in the Preservation of Ethnicity, by G. James Patterson (Ottawa: National Museum, CCFCS Mercury Series 18, 1976), pp. 73–75.
Cf. Fauset, 25.
Type AT 676: Open Sesame.
Motifs: N455.3, Secret formula for opening treasure mountain overheard from robbers; F721.4, Underground treasure chambers; D1552.2, Mountains of rocks open and close; N512, Treasure in underground chamber; N471, Foolish attempt of second man to overhear secrets.

15. The Green Flag and the Devil's Head

Archives de Folklore, Université Laval, collection Luc Lacourcière, No. 1334. Recorded by Luc Lacourcière (and Felix-Antoine Savard), July, 1954, from Johnny Larocque, aged 67, of Saint-Raphael-sur-Mer, Ile Shippagan, Gloucester county, New Brunswick. Translated by Margaret Low. Luc Lacourcière discusses the 43 French-Canadian versions in *"Le ruban qui rend fort."*
Types: AT 590: The Prince and the Arm Bands. Cf. AT 507A: The Monster's Bride.
Motifs: D840, Magic object found; D1335, Object gives magic strength; H1333.3.1.5, Quest for healing apple; H933, Princess sets hero tasks; N825, Old person as helper; D1361.14, Magic hat renders invisible; H971, Task performed with help of old person; G303, Devil; L161, Lowly hero marries princess; D861, Magic object stolen; S165, Mutilation: putting out eyes; H94.5, Identification through broken ring; D1505.5.4, Holy spring restores sight; V256, Miraculous healing by Virgin Mary; T96, Lovers reunited after many adventures.

16. The Shoemaker in Heaven

Prairie Folklore, edited by Kay Stone (Winnipeg: University of Winnipeg, 1976), pp. 195–96. Collected by Kay Stone from a Polish-born Canadian woman in her early twenties. Dr. Stone discusses the storyteller in "I Won't Tell These Stories to My Kids."
Type AT 800: The Tailor in Heaven (P441.1).
Motifs: A661.0.1.2, Saint Peter as porter of heaven; F1037.1, Footstool thrown from heaven.

17. Mac Crùslain

Luirgean Eachainn Nill: Folktales from Cape Breton, transcribed and translated from the original Gaelic by Margaret MacDonell and John Shaw (Stornoway: Acair, 1981), pp. 2–10. Told by Hector Campbell, Hillsdale, Inverness County, Nova Scotia. The editors list several other Cape Breton versions.
Types: AT 1049, The Heavy Axe (K1741.1); AT 1063A, Throwing Contest: Trickster Shouts (K18.1); AT 1088, Eating Contest (K81.1).
Motif: K525, Escape by use of substituted object.

IV. ROMANTIC TALES

18. There was a Lord in Edinburgh

Sung by LaRena Clark. Collected by Edith Fowke and issued on *Canadian Garland*, Topic 12T140, 1965.
Cf. Child #221, IV, 216; Bronson III, 352; Coffin and Renwick, 132, 261.

19. The Scotchman who Loved an Irish Girl

Folklore from Nova Scotia, by Arthur Huff Fauset (New York: American Folklore Society, 1931), pp. 124–25. Told by Mrs. Caroline Reddick, aged 87, New Glasgow, Nova Scotia.
Type AT 974: The Homecoming Husband (N681).

20. The Love Story of Laing Sanbo and Zhu Yingtai

Collected by Ban Seng Hoe from Mrs. G. Chan in Montreal, 1976.
Cf. "Faithful Even in Death," Eberhard, #15.
Motifs: K1837, Disguise of woman in man's clothes; T81, Death from love; T86, Lovers buried in same grave.

V. JOKES AND ANECDOTES

21. Little Claus and Big Claus

Folklore of Lunenburg County, Nova Scotia, by Helen Creighton (Ottawa: National Museum Bulletin 117, 1950), pp. 140–45. Told by Edward Collicutt.
Type AT 1535: The Rich and Poor Peasant.
Motifs: K1571.1, Trickster discovers adultery: food goes to husband instead of paramour; K443.1, Hidden paramour buys freedom from discoverer; K114.1.1, Alleged oracular horse-hide sold; K941.1, Cows killed for their hides when large price is reported by trickster; K940.2, Man betrayed into killing his wife or grandmother; K842, Dupe persuaded to take prisoner's place in a sack: killed; K890.1, Poor man deceives rich man, plays tricks on him, causes his death.

22. Dickie Melbourne

Tradition: Songs, Stories and Tunes from Newfoundland & Labrador, Pigeon Inlet PIP 3717. Told by Leo O'Brien. Recorded by Kelly Russell. "Our Goodman" is Child 274. Cf. Briggs A:2, 154; Creighton Collection, CCFCS Archives, tape 174A.
Type AT 1360C: Old Hildebrand (K1556).

23. Tall Tales from Northern Ontario
Told by Forrest Eugene Sandberg, Fort Francis, Ontario. Collected by Lily Nattel, for an English 430 project, 1978. York Archives Group 6C — Acc. 2, August 1978.
Cf. Halpert, "Tall Tales," #28, #29, #30; Taft, #16, #17, #80, #81.
Types: AT 1889F, Frozen Words Thaw (X1623.2.1); AT 1960M, The Great Insect (X1286.1).
Motifs: X1237.2.1, Remarkable colour of ox; X1286.2, Lies about ferocious mosquitoes.

24. On the Trail of Joe Mufferaw
Told by Mrs. Simon Parcher, Chippewa Road, Barry's Bay, and Mrs. Jean Richter, Purdy, Ontario. Collected by Jeanne L. Pattison, for an English 430 project, York University, 1974. York Archives, Group 6C — Acc. 2, August 1978.
Paul Bunyan tales: Fowke, "In Defence of Paul Bunyan."
Motifs: X920, Lie: large man; X986, Lie: skilful axe-man; X987, Lie: remarkable logger; X1022, Lie: other extraordinary personal effects of remarkable person; X1081, Lie: remarkable logging operations; Z230, Remarkable exploits of hero.

25. Humorous Stories from around Chapeau, Quebec
Collected by I. Sheldon Posen.
Cf. Dave McDougall: Halpert, "Tall Tales," #1–#13; Donald Morrison: Bennett-Knight, 94–99, local characters, 114–26; Geordie Brown: Spray, 116–22; Jim Grey, Fauset, 106–8.

26. Jokes about Religions
Told by Alice Kane. *Joe Heaney*, Philo 2004, 1975: "I'm a Catholic, not a Protestant."
Motifs: X410, Jokes on parsons; X610, Jokes concerning Jews.

27. Jewish Jokes from Toronto
"Traditional Story-telling in the Toronto Jewish Community: A Study in Performance and Creativity in an Immigrant Culture." Barbara Kirshenblatt-Gimblett, Ph.D. dissertation, Indiana University, 1972, pp. 300–1, 375–76.
For esoteric jokes, see Wm. Hugh Jansen, "The Esoteric-Exoteric Factor in Folklore."
Motif: X610, Jokes concerning Jews.

28. The Lobster Salad
Collected by Wilfred Wareham from his brother Baxter Wareham. Published in *The Blasty Bough*, ed. Clyde Rose.
Recitations: Spray, 123–29.

VI. FORMULA TALES

29. The Old Woman and Her Pig
Fowke Collection, York Archives, tape FO 35. Told by Mrs. Eva Bigrow, Calumet, Quebec, 1964.
"Willie Drowned in Ero" (Child #215), Leader 4057: *Far Canadian Fields*. Cf. Fauset, 28–32; Wintemberg, "Grey County," 117–19; Briggs A:2, 551. Palmer, #14 (song).
Type AT 2030: The Old Woman and Her Pig (Z41).

30. A Catch Tale
Will o' the Wisp: Folk Tales and Legends of New Brunswick, by Carole Spray (Fredericton: Brunswick Press, 1979), pp. 100–1. Told by Charlie Slane.
Cf. Halpert, "Tall Tales," #10; Thibadeau, #6.
Type: AT 2200, Catch Tales.
Motifs: X1133.2, Man escapes bear by running for a long time from summer to winter; X1605, Mixed weather.

VII. LEGENDS

31. The Seal-Woman
"Water-Beings in Shetlandic Folk Lore, As Remembered by Shetlanders in British Columbia," by J.A. Teit, *The Journal of American Folk-Lore*, 31(1918), pp. 191–92.
"The Great Silkie of Sule Skerry," Child #113. Cf. Briggs B:1, p. 258.
Motifs: D327.2, Transformation: seal to person; B651.8, Marriage to seal in human form; cf. D361.1.1, Swan maiden finds her hidden wings and resumes her form.

32. One of the Thirty-Six Just Men
Told by Jack Starkman. Collected by Barbara Kirshenblatt-Gimblett, Toronto, Spring 1972. Barbara notes another of Jack's stories in her article on "A Parable in Context," pp. 315–17.
Motifs: V410, Charity rewarded; V417, Charity given secretly; V433, Charity of saint; C436, Tabu: disclosing own identity; N848, Saint (pious man) as helper; J903.1, Humility of saints; K2110, Slanders.

33. The Wrong Chill Windigo
Where the Chill Came From: Cree Windigo Tales and Journeys, gathered and translated by Howard Norman (San Francisco: North Point Press, 1982), pp. 91–93. Narrated by Andrew Nikumoon, near Cormorant, Manitoba.
Northrop Frye discusses the garrison mentality in *The Literary History of Canada*, pp. 821–49.
Motifs: B211.3, Speaking bird; B450, Helpful bird.

34. Steer North and North East

Stories from Nova Scotia, collected and translated by Calum I.N. Mac-Leod (Antigonish: Formac, 1974), pp. 64–67. From the James Hugh MS. MacLeod describes it as "An unpublished MS. of Gaelic stories, songs, periodicals, personal correspondence, and local historical articles collected and compiled by Seumas Eoghainn." (This material was donated to Calum MacLeod by Vincent MacLean and is now housed at 12 Fairview Street, Antigonish, Nova Scotia.)

Motif: D1825.7, Magic sight of incident before it actually happens.

35. The Ghostly Sailors

Songs from the Newfoundland Outports, by Kenneth Peacock (Ottawa: National Museum, 1965), pp. 873–74.

References: Laws D16, 168; Doerflinger, 80; Creighton, *Bluenose Ghosts*, 128–29; Greenleaf, 227. Additional references: Fowke, *Sea Songs*, 96–99. The *Newfoundland* disaster, *Songs from the Outports of Newfoundland*, Folkways 4075.

Motifs: E510, Phantom sailors; E271.4*, Ghosts of dead sailors go aboard ship passing their burial spot, take stations as crew.

36. The Walker of the Snow/The Haunted Hunter

The Walker of the Snow: By C.D. Shanly. *A Victorian Anthology 1837–1895* (Boston and New York: Houghton Mifflin, 1895), ed. Edward C. Stedman, p. 634.

The Haunted Hunter: Sung by Mrs. Gwen Meador, Moab, Utah. Collected by Austin Fife in August, 1953. (Fife Mormon Collection I-998; Fife Mormon Recordings 506-A, tape 17:129.) The Fifes also found a version in the John Lomax papers at the Texas Historical Society that came from an old cowpuncher, R.C. Blasingame of Pierce, Idaho, and was said to have been "sung long ago around the camp fires of the round-ups and the long drive up from Texas." It had some minor differences from the Meador text, and retained a title close to the original: "The Walker in the Snow." (John Lomax Papers 265.) Records: Rosalie Sorrels, *Rosalie's Songbag*, Prestige International 13025; Billie Maxwell, 78 rpm, Victor V-4024, 1929; reissued on *Authentic Cowboys and Their Western Songs*, RCA Victor LPV 522.

Motifs: E332.2, Person meets ghost on road; E421.2.1, Ghost leaves no footprints; F1041.7, Hair turns grey from terror.

37. The Devil's Potato Field

Fowke Collection, York Archives, FO 35. Told by Mrs. Eva Bigrow, Calumet, Quebec, 1964.

Motif: A977.4, The devil turns object or animal to stone which is still seen.

38. A Miracle in Montreal

Folktales of the Canadian Sephardim, collected and translated by André E. Elbaz (Don Mills: Fitzhenry & Whiteside, 1982), p. 54. Told by the

Reverend Salomon Amzallag who got it from a Montreal woman who told it to his wife.
Motifs: Q28, Reward for religious pilgrimage; V221, Miraculous healing by saints.

39. *The Pot of Gold*
"Folkways and Religion of the Hebridean Scots in the Eastern Townships," by Margaret Bennett-Knight, in *Cultural Retention and Demographic Change: Studies of the Hebridean Scots in the Eastern Townships of Quebec*, edited by Laurel Doucette (Ottawa: National Museum, CCFCS Mercury Series 34, 1980), p. 111. Told by Bill Young (BEK 5:A). Afterword by Donald MacLennan (BEK 5:A).
Cf. Creighton, *Bluenose Ghosts*, pp. 42–68; Fauset, pp. 88–93.
Motifs: N511, Treasure in ground, N576, Ghosts prevent men from raising treasure.

40. *Young Lad*
Legends from the Forest, told by Chief Thomas Fiddler, edited by James R. Stevens (Moonbeam, Ontario: Penumbra, 1985), pp. 71–72.

41. *The Vanishing Hitchhiker*
Told by Pauline Caughtry and Cyndi Burns, aged 12, St. Francis Xavier School, Toronto, March, 1985. Recorded by Judy Smith.
References: Susan Smith, 265; Dorson, *American Folklore*, 250, 299; Gillian Bennett, 45–63.
Motifs: E332.3.3.1, The vanishing hitchhiker; E425.1, Revenant as woman, E585.4, Revenant visits earth yearly; E599.8, Ghost vanishes when taken home.

42. *The Blue Cardigan*
Told by Walter Scodeller (who learned it from his uncle in 1980) and Joe Dominelli, aged 13, St. Francis Xavier School, Toronto, March, 1985. Recorded by Judy Smith.
Cf. "The Suffolk Miracle," Child #272; Creighton and Senior, pp. 88–90; Peacock, pp. 407–8.
Motif: E425.1, Revenant as woman.

43. *The Pink Shawl*
Told by Rosemary Tatangelo, aged 13, St. Francis Xavier School, Toronto, March 1985. Recorded by Judy Smith.
Motif: E425.1, Revenant as woman.

44. *Old Man Gimli*
Prairie Folklore, edited by Kay Stone, University of Winnipeg, pp. 79–81. Collected by Marlies Suderman at Camp Robertson, near Gimli.
Cf. Fowke, "The Tale of Anson Minor."
Motifs: E225, Ghost of murdered child; E279.2, Ghost disturbs sleeping person; E281, Ghosts haunt house; E299, Miscellaneous acts of malevolent ghosts; E402.1.1.3, Ghost cries and screams; E402.1.8, Miscellaneous sounds made by ghost of human being.

VIII. PERSONAL EXPERIENCE NARRATIVES

45. A Sasquatch Sighting

Affidavit by William Roe, cited in *On the Track of the Sasquatch*, by John Green, and in *Sasquatch*, by Don Hunter with René Dahinden.

M. Carole Henderson [Carpenter] discusses "Monsters of the West: The Sasquatch and the Ogopogo" in Fowke, *Folklore of Canada*, pp. 251–62.

Motifs: B29.9, Man-ape; F521.1, Man covered with hair like an animal; F531.1.6.3, Giants with shaggy hair on their bodies.

46. How I Learned to Make Bread

The Pioneer Years, by Barry Broadfoot (Toronto: Doubleday Canada, 1976), pp. 200–2. Broadfoot quotations, letter, Dec. 2, 1985.

47. The Frank Slide Disaster

The Pioneer Years, by Barry Broadfoot (Toronto: Doubleday Canada 1976), pp. 374–77. "Ballad of the Frank Slide," Fowke and Mills, 192. Broadfoot quotations, letter, Dec. 2, 1985.

Disaster ballads, Creighton, *Maritime Folk Songs*, 185, 201, 208; Peacock, pp. 903–84.

48. St. Peter's Day

Traditional Doukhobor Folkways, by Koozma J. Tarasoff (Ottawa: National Museum of Man, CCFCS Mercury Series No. 20, 1977), pp. 93–94.

49. My Grandfather's War

Recorded September 1978 and written down November 1978 by Norman W. Moss of Kamloops, British Columbia, for his cousin Carole H. Carpenter.

50. UFO Stories

Collected by Chris Rutkowski in Winnipeg, 1984.

Tale Types and Motifs

THE TYPE NUMBERS are from *The Types of the Folktale* by Antti
Aarne and Stith Thompson (Folklore Fellows Communications
1984, Helsinki, 1961). Motif numbers are from Stith Thompson:
Motif-Index of Folk Literature, 6 vols. (Bloomington: University
of Indiana Press, 1955–58).

Index of Types

Type No.		Tale No.
330A	The Smith Outwits the Devil.	12
507A	The Monster's Bride.	15
590	The Prince and the Arm Bands.	15
676	Open Sesame.	14
707	The Three Golden Sons.	9
800	The Tailor in Heaven.	16
974	The Homecoming Husband.	18, 19
1049	The Heavy Axe.	17
1063A	Throwing Contest: Trickster Shouts	17
1074	Race Won by Deception: Relative Helpers.	6
1088	Eating Contest.	17
1360C	Old Hildebrand.	22
1535	The Rich and Poor Peasant.	21
1889F	Frozen Words (Music) Thaw.	23
1960M	The Great Insect.	23
2030	The Old Woman and Her Pig.	29
2200	Catch Tales.	30

Index of Motifs

A. Mythological Motifs

Motif No.		Tale No.
A401	Mother Earth.	1
A511.1	Birth of the culture hero.	2
A511.1.3.3	Immaculate conception of culture hero.	2
A522.2	Bird as culture hero.	2
A661.0.1.2	Saint Peter as porter of heaven.	16
A721.1	Theft of sun.	2
A751.8	Woman in moon.	3
A753	Moon as person.	3
A753.2	Moon has house.	3
A810	Primeval water.	2
A814.2	Earth from sand strewn on primeval water.	2
A830	Creation of earth by creator.	1
A831	Earth from body of person.	1
A977.4	The devil turns object or animal to stone which is still seen.	37
A1142.01	Origin of thunderbolt.	4
A1210	Creation of man by creator.	1
A1241	Man made from clay.	1
A1252	Creation of man from wood.	2
A1411.2	Theft of light by being swallowed and reborn.	2
A1412.3	Acquisition of daylight by culture hero.	2
A1714.3	Animals created from earth.	1
A2216	Animal characteristics: members bitten or cut off.	7
A2493.0.1	Former friendship between domestic and wild animals.	7
A2494	Why certain animals are enemies	7
A25213	Why certain animals serve man.	7

B. Animals

B29.9	Man-ape.	45
B131.2	Bird reveals treachery.	9
B143.1	Bird gives warning.	10
B211.3	Speaking bird.	9, 10, 33
B435.4	Helpful bear.	10
B450	Helpful bird.	10, 33
B451.2	Helpful nightingale.	9
B505	Magic object received from animal.	8, 10
B521.1	Animal warns against poison.	10
B535	Animal nurse.	9
B535.0.3	Goat as nurse for child.	10
B540	Animal rescuer.	10
B651.8	Marriage to seal in human form.	31

C. Tabu

C410	Tabu: asking questions.	13
C436	Tabu: disclosing own identity.	32
C664	Injunction to marry first woman met.	9
C963.1	Person returns to original animal form when tabu is broken.	13

D. Magic

D313.1	Transformation: fox to person.	13
D327.2	Transformation: seal to person.	31
D361.1.1	Swan maiden finds her hidden wings and resumes her form.	31
D684	Transformation by helpful animals.	8
D766	Disenchantment by liquid.	10
D813	Magic object received from fairy.	8
D832	Magic objects acquired by acting as umpire for fighting heirs.	8
D840	Magic object found.	15
D861	Magic object stolen.	15
D1012.1	Magic legs of animal.	8
D1013	Magic bone of animal.	8
D1021	Magic feather.	8
D1022.3	Magic hair of lion's tail.	8
D1076	Magic ring.	9
D1335	Object gives magic strength.	15
D1361.12	Magic cloak of invisibility.	8
D1361.14	Magic hat renders invisible.	15
D1413.1.2	Pear tree from which one cannot descend.	12
D1413.6	Chair to which person sticks.	12
D1413.9	Sack holds person who puts his hand into it.	12
D1440	Magic object gives power over animals.	8
D1451	Inexhaustible purse furnishes money.	8
D1470.1	Magic wishing object.	8
D1470.2.2	Supplies received from magic box.	8, 10
D1472.1.8	Magic table-cloth supplies food and drink.	8
D1505.5.4	Holy spring restores sight.	15
D1520.10	Magic transportation by shoes.	8
D1552.2	Mountains or rocks open and close.	14
D1721.1	Magic power from devil.	12
D1813	Magic knowledge of events in distant place.	31
D1825.7	Magic sight of incident before it actually happens.	34

E. The Dead

E80	Resuscitation by water.	10
E225	Ghost of murdered child.	44
E271.4*	Ghosts of dead sailors go aboard ship passing their burial spot, take stations as crew.	35
E279.2	Ghost disturbs sleeping person.	44
E281	Ghosts haunt house.	44
E299	Miscellaneous acts of malevolent ghosts.	44
E332.2	Person meets ghost on road.	36
E332.3.3.1	The vanishing hitchhiker.	41
E402.1.1.3	Ghost cries and screams.	44
E402.1.8	Miscellaneous sounds made by ghost of human being.	44
E421.2.1	Ghost leaves no footprints.	36
E425.1	Revenant as woman.	41, 42, 43
E510	Phantom sailors.	35
E585.4	Ghost visits earth yearly.	41
E599.8	Ghost vanishes when taken home.	41, 42, 43

F. Marvels

F341.1	Fairies give three gifts.	8
F360	Malevolent or destructive fairies.	11
F521.1	Man covered with hair like an animal.	45
F531.1.6.3	Giants with shaggy hair on their bodies.	45
F721.4	Underground treasure chambers.	14
F1037.1	Footstool thrown from heaven.	16
F1041.7	Hair turns grey from terror.	36

G. Ogres

G303	Devil.	12, 15
G270	Witch overcome or escaped.	9

H. Tests

H94.5	Identification through broken ring.	15
H1154.7	Task: capturing bird.	9
H933	Princess sets hero tasks.	15
H971	Task performed with help of old person.	15
H1333.3.1.5	Quest for healing apple.	15

J. The Wise and the Foolish

J514	One should not be too greedy.	11
J903.1	Humility of saints.	32

K. Deceptions

K11.1	Race won by deception: relative helpers.	6
K18.1	Throwing contest: trickster shouts.	17
K81.1	Deceptive eating contest: hole in bag.	17
K114.1.1	Alleged oracular horse-hide sold.	21

K210	Devil cheated of his promised soul.	12
K443.1	Hidden paramour buys freedom from discoverer.	21
K452	Unjust umpire misappropriates disputed goods.	8
K512	Compassionate executioner.	10
K525	Escape by use of substituted object.	17
K532	Escape under mantle of invisibility.	8
K842	Dupe persuaded to take prisoner's place in a sack: killed.	21
K890.1	Poor man deceives rich man, plays trick on him, causes his death.	11, 21
K940.2	Man betrayed into killing his wife or grandmother.	21
K941.1	Cows killed for their hides when large price is reported by trickster.	21
K961.1.1	Tit for tat.	5
K1556	Old Hildebrand.	22
K1571	Trickster discovers adulterer: food goes to husband instead of paramour.	21
K1741.1	Felling the whole forest.	17
K1741.3	Bringing the whole well.	17
K1837	Disguise of woman in man's clothes.	20
K1840	Deception by substitution.	6, 11
K2110	Slanders.	9
K2115	Animal-birth slander.	9

L. Reversal of Fortune

L143	Poor man surpasses rich.	11
L161	Lowly hero marries princess.	15

M. Ordaining the Future

M211	Man sells soul to devil.	12

N. Chance and Fortune

N455.3	Secret formula for opening treasure mountain overheard from robbers.	14
N471	Foolish attempt of second man to overhear secrets.	14
N511	Treasure in ground.	39
N512	Treasure in underground chamber.	14
N576	Ghosts prevent man from raising treasure.	39
N681	Husband (lover) arrives home just as wife (mistress) is to marry another.	18, 19
N731.3	Father unexpectedly meets abandoned son and reinstates him.	9
N825	Old person as helper.	15
N848	Saint (pious man) as helper.	32

P. Society
P441.1   Tailor occupies God's throne for a day.   17

Q. Rewards and Punishments
Q28   Reward for religious pilgrimage.   38
Q40   Kindness rewarded.   9
Q42   Generosity rewarded.   9
Q261   Treachery punished.   9
Q411   Death as punishment.   10

R. Captive and Fugitive
R131   Exposed or abandoned child rescued.   10
R131.3.1   Shepherd rescues abandoned child.   10

S. Unnatural Cruelty
S12   Cruel mother.   10
S165   Mutilation: putting out eyes.   15
S451   Outcast wife at last united with husband
and children.   9

T. Sex
T81   Death from love.   20
T86   Lovers buried in same grave.   20
T96   Lovers reunited after many adventures.   15
T512.3   Conception by drinking water.   2

V. Religion
V221   Miraculous healing by saints.   38
V256   Miraculous healing by Virgin Mary.   15
V410   Charity rewarded.   32
V417   Charity given secretly.   32
V433   Charity of saints.   32

X. Humour
X410   Jokes on parsons.   26
X610   Jokes concerning Jews.   27
X920   Lie: the large man.   24
X941   Lie: remarkable lifter.   24
X986   Lie: skilful axe-man.   24
X987   Lie: remarkable logger.   24
X1022   Lie: other extraordinary personal effects
of remarkable person.   24
X1081   Lie: remarkable logging operations.   24
X1133.2   Man escapes from bear by running for a
long time from summer to winter.   30
X1237.2.1   Remarkable colour of ox.   23
X1286.1   Lie: the large mosquito.   23
X1286.2   Lies about ferocious mosquitoes.   23

X1605   Mixed weather.   30
X1623.2.1   Lie: frozen words thaw out in the spring.   23

Z. Miscellaneous

Z41   The old woman and her pig.   29
Z230   Remarkable exploits of hero.   24

Bibliography

THIS BIBLIOGRAPHY INCLUDES most items of traditional Canadian folktales published in English with the exception of native collections. It also lists items that classify, discuss, or analyze Canadian tales, and any other books or articles cited in the notes or references. Asterisks indicate the sources of tales in this collection. The few abbreviations used are:

CCFCS: The Canadian Centre for Folk Culture Studies.

Explorations: Explorations in Canadian Folklore. Ed. Edith Fowke and Carole H. Carpenter. Toronto: McClelland & Stewart, 1985.

JAF: Journal of American Folklore.

Aarne, Antti, and Stith Thompson. *The Types of the Folktale*. Helsinki: Academia Scientiarum Fennica, 1961.

Ardus, Jane Catherine (Dunsinger). "A Comparative Study of Narrative Accounts of Visits Home Drawn from the Immigrant Ethnic Community in St. John's." M.A. Thesis, Memorial University, 1983.

Augimeri, Maria C. *Calabrese Folklore*. Ottawa: National Museum, CCFCS Mercury Series 56, 1985, pp. 189–242.

Baughman, Ernest W. *Type and Motif Index of the Folktales of England and North America*. The Hague: Mouton, 1966.

Bauman, Richard. "The LaHave General Store: Sociability and Verbal Arts in a Nova Scotia Community." *JAF*, 85(1972), pp. 330–41.

Bedore, B.V. *Tall Tales of Joe Mufferaw*. Arnprior, Ontario: Mufferaw, 1966.

Bemer, John W. "Nineteenth Century French-Canadian Folk Tales." *Journal of Canadian Fiction*, 2:3(1973), pp. 69–74.

Bennett, Gillian. "The Phantom Hitchhiker: Neither Modern, Urban nor Legend?" In *Perspectives on Contemporary Legend*. Ed. Paul Smith. Sheffield: University of Sheffield, 1984, pp. 45–63.

*Bennett-Knight, Margaret. "Folkways and Religion of the Hebridean Scots in the Eastern Townships." In *Cultural Retention and Demographic Change: Studies of the Hebridean Scots in the Eastern Townships of Quebec*. Ed. Laurel Doucette. Ottawa: National Museum of Man, CCFCS Mercury Series 34, 1980, pp. 91–126.

Bettelheim, Bruno. *The Uses of Enchantment: The Meaning and Importance of Fairy Tales*. New York: Knopf, 1976.

*Boas, Franz, ed. *Folk-Tales of Salishan and Sahaptin Tribes*. Lancaster, PA & New York: American Folk-Lore Society, 1917.

Briggs, Katharine M. *A Dictionary of British Folk-Tales in the English Language*. 4 vols. London: Routledge & Kegan Paul, 1970–71.

*Broadfoot, Barry. *The Pioneer Years 1895–1914: Memories of Settlers Who Opened the West*. Toronto: Doubleday Canada, 1976.

Broadfoot, Barry. *The Six War Years 1939–1945*. Toronto: Doubleday Canada, 1974.

Bronson, Bertrand H. *The Traditional Tunes of the Child Ballads*. 4 vols. Princeton, NJ: Princeton University Press, 1959–72.

Brunvand, Jan Harold. *Norwegian Settlers in Alberta*. Ottawa: National Museum, CCFCS Mercury Series 8, 1974, pp. 25–37.

Brunvand, Jan Harold. *The Vanishing Hitchhiker: American Urban Legends and Their Meanings*. New York: Norton, 1981.

Burke, J.C. *A Treasury of Newfoundland Humour and Wit*. St. John's: Breakwater, 1985.

Burmeister, Klaus. "Folklore in the Intercultural Context: Legends of the Calling River." In *Ethnic Canadians: Culture and Education*. Ed. Martin L. Kovacs. Regina: Canadian Plains Research Center, University of Regina, 1978, pp. 43–52.

Bydanavicius, Vytautas. "The Canadian French Tale and Its Analysis." *Cultural Wellsprings of Folktales*. Part I, Chapter 5. New York: Manyland Books, 1970.

Calder, James G. "Humor and Misunderstanding in Newfoundland Culture." *Culture and Tradition*, 4(1979), pp. 49–66.

Child, Francis James. *The English and Scottish Popular Ballads.* 5 vols. Boston and New York: Houghton, Mifflin, 1882–98.

Clouston, Al. *"Come 'ere Till I Tells Ya": A Collection of Newfoundland Humour.* St. John's: The Author, 1978.

Coffin, Tristram P., and Roger DeV. Renwick. *The British Traditional Ballad in North America.* Austin: University of Texas Press, 1977.

Coldwell, Joyce. "Treasure Stories and Beliefs in Atlantic Canada." Ph.D. dissertation, Memorial University, 1977.

Colombo, John Robert. *Windigo: An Anthology of Fact and Fiction.* Saskatoon: Western Producer Prairie Books, 1982.

Creighton, Helen. *Bluenose Ghosts.* Toronto: Ryerson, 1957. Reprinted Toronto: McGraw-Hill Ryerson, 1976.

Creighton, Helen. *Bluenose Magic: Popular Beliefs and Superstititons in Nova Scotia.* Toronto: Ryerson, 1968.

*Creighton, Helen. *Folklore of Lunenberg County, Nova Scotia.* Ottawa: National Museum, Bulletin 117, 1950. Reprinted Toronto: McGraw-Hill Ryerson, 1976.

Creighton, Helen. "Folklore of Victoria Beach, Nova Scotia." *JAF*, 63(1950), pp. 143–46.

Creighton, Helen. *Maritime Folk Songs.* Toronto: Ryerson, 1961.

Creighton, Helen, and Edward D. Ives. "Eight Folktales from Miramichi as Told by Wilmot MacDonald." *Northeast Folklore*, 4(1962), pp. 1–70.

Creighton, Helen, and Doreen H. Senior. *Traditional Songs from Nova Scotia.* Toronto: Ryerson, 1950.

Desplanques, M.A. *English-French bilingualism on the Port-au-Prince peninsula, Newfoundland, with special reference to the role of folktale narration.* Université de Haute-Normandie, Institut d'anglais, 1983.

Doerflinger, W.M. *Shantymen and Shantyboys.* New York: Macmillan, 1951.

Dorson, Richard M. "Canadiens." *Bloodstoppers and Bearwalkers.* Cambridge: Harvard University Press, 1959, pp. 69–102.

Dorson, Richard M. "Canadiens in the Upper Peninsula of Michigan." *Archives de Folklore*, 4(1949), pp. 17–27.

Dorson, Richard M. "Dialect Stories of the Upper Peninsula." *JAF*, 61(1948), pp. 117–50.

Dorson, Richard M. *Folktales Told Around the World.* Chicago: University of Chicago Press, 1975, pp. 429–77.

Dundes, Alan. *The Morphology of North American Indian Folktales.* Helsinki: Folklore Fellows Communications 195, 1964.

Dunn, Charles W. *Highland Settler: A Portrait of the Scottish Gael in Nova Scotia.* Toronto: University of Toronto Press, 1953.

Eberhard, Wolfram, ed. *Folktales of China.* Chicago: University of Chicago Press, 1965.

Einarsson, Magnús. "Icelandic Pular." In *Folklore of Canada.* Ed. Edith Fowke. Toronto: McClelland & Stewart, 1976, pp. 287–90.

Einarsson, Magnús. "Oral Tradition and Cultural Boundaries: West Icelandic Verses and Anecdotes." *Canadian Ethnic Studies,* 7:2(1975), pp. 19–32.

*Elbaz, André E. *Folktales of the Canadian Sephardim.* Toronto: Fitzhenry & Whiteside, 1982.

Fanning, W. Wayne. "Storytelling at a Nova Scotia General Store." *Culture and Tradition,* 3(1978), pp. 57–67.

*Fauset, Arthur Huff. *Folklore from Nova Scotia.* New York: American Folklore Society, 1931.

Fauset, Arthur Huff. "Folklore from the Half-Breeds in Nova Scotia." *JAF,* 38 (1925), pp. 300–15.

*Fiddler, Chief Thomas. *Killing the Shamen.* Ed. James R. Stevens. Moonbeam, Ontario: Penumbra, 1985.

Fiddler, Chief Thomas. *Legends From The Forest.* Ed. James R. Stevens. Moonbeam, Ontario: Penumbra, 1985.

Fowke, Edith, *Folklore of Canada.* Toronto: McClelland & Stewart, 1976.

Fowke, Edith. "Folktales and Folk Songs." In *The Literary History of Canada.* Rev. ed. Vol. 1. Ed. Carl Klinck. Toronto: University of Toronto Press, 1975, pp. 177–87.

Fowke, Edith, *Folktales of French Canada.* Toronto: NC Press, 1979.

Fowke, Edith, "In Defence of Paul Bunyan." *Explorations,* pp. 189–99.

Fowke, Edith, *Sea Songs and Ballads from Nineteenth-Century Nova Scotia.* New York: Folklorica, 1981.

Fowke, Edith, "The Tale of Anson Minor: An Ontario Camp Legend." *Canadian Folklore canadien,* 3(1981), pp. 1–9.

Fowke, Edith, and Carole H. Carpenter. *A Bibliography of Canadian Folklore in English.* Toronto: University of Toronto Press, 1981, pp. 28–61.

Fowke, Edith, and Carole H. Carpenter, *Explorations in Canadian Folklore.* Toronto: McClelland & Stewart, 1985.

Fowke, Edith, and Alan Mills. *Canada's Story in Song.* Toronto: Gage, 1965.

Fraser, C.A. "Scottish Myths from Ontario." *JAF*, 6(1893), pp. 185–98.

Fraser, Mary L. *Folklore of Nova Scotia*. 1931. Reprinted Antigonish: Formac, 1975. pp. 69–77; 94–100.

Frye, Northrop. "Conclusion." *The Literary History of Canada*. Ed. Carl Klinck. Toronto: University of Toronto Press, 1965, pp. 821–49.

Gard, Robert, *Johnny Chinook: Tall Tales and True from the Canadian West*. London: Longmans, Green, 1945. Reprinted Edmonton: Hurtig, 1967.

Gedalof, Robin. *An Annotated Bibliography of Canadian Inuit Literature*. Ottawa: Indian and Northern Affairs Canada, 1979.

*Gedalof, Robin, ed. *Paper Stays Put: A Collection of Inuit Writing*. Edmonton: Hurtig, 1980.

Gillis, Jas. D. *The Cape Breton Giant*. Halifax: Allen, 1926.

Goldstein, Kenneth S., and Robert D. Bethke, eds. Special Issue: "Monologues and Folk Recitations." *Southern Folklore Quarterly*, 40(March/June), 1976.

Green, John. *On the Track of the Sasquatch*. Agassiz, British Columbia: Cheam, 1971.

Greenhill, Pauline. *Lots of Stories: Maritime Narratives from the Creighton Collection*. Ottawa: National Museum, CCFCS Mercury Series 57, 1985.

Greenleaf, Elisabeth B., and Grace Y. Mansfield. *Ballads and Sea Songs of Newfoundland*. Cambridge: Harvard University Press, 1933.

Greenough, William Parker. *Canadian Folk-Life and Folk-Lore*. New York: Richmond, 1897, pp. 46–63.

Halpin, Marjorie and Michael M. Ames, eds. *Manlike Monsters on Trial: Early Records and Modern Evidence*. Vancouver: University of British Columbia Press, 1980.

Halpert Herbert. " 'The Cut-Off Head Frozen On': Some International Versions of a Tall Tale." *Canadian Folklore canadien*, 1(1979), pp. 13–23. Reprinted in *Explorations*, pp. 159–73.

Halpert, Herbert. *A Folklore Sampler from the Maritimes*. St. John's: Memorial University, 1982, pp. 1–35.

Halpert, Herbert, "Tall Tales and Other Yarns from Calgary, Alberta." *California Folklore Quarterly*, 4(1945), pp. 29–49. Reprinted in *Folklore of Canada*. Ed. Edith Fowke. Toronto: McClelland & Stewart, 1976, pp. 171–89.

Hendry, Allan. *The UFO Handbook*. New York: Doubleday, 1979.

Hoe, Ban Seng. "Folktales and Social Structure: The Case of the Chinese in Montreal." *Canadian Folklore canadien*, 1(1979), pp. 25–37.

Hunter, Don, with René Dahinden. *Sasquatch*. Toronto: McClelland & Stewart, 1973.

Ives, Edward D. "The Burning Ship of Northumberland Strait." *Northeast Folklore*, 2(1958), pp. 64–65; 2(1959), pp. 53–55.

Ives, Edward D. *Larry Gorman: The Man Who Made the Songs*. Bloomington: Indiana University Press, 1964.

Ives, Edward D. "Lumbercamp Singing and the Two Traditions." *Canadian Folk Music Journal*, 5(1977), pp. 17–23.

Ives, Edward D. "The Man Who Picked the Gorbey: A Maine Woods Legend." *JAF*, 74(1961), pp. 1–8. Reprinted in *Explorations*, pp. 174–88.

Jackson, Kenneth, "More Tales from Port Hood, Nova Scotia." *Scottish Gaelic Studies*, 6(1949), pp. 176–88.

Jackson, Kenneth, "Notes on the Gaelic of Port Hood, Nova Scotia." *Scottish Gaelic Studies*, 6(1949), pp. 89–109.

Janes, L.W. *The Treasury of Newfoundland Stories*. St. John's. Maple Leaf Mills, no date.

Jansen, Wm. Hugh. "The Esoteric-Exoteric Factor in Folklore." *Fabula*, 2(1959), pp. 205–11. Reprinted in *The Study of Folklore*. Ed. Alan Dundes. Englewood Cliffs, NJ: Prentice-Hall, 1965, pp. 43–51.

*Jolicoeur, Catherine, *Le Vaisseau Fantôme: Légende étiologique*. *Archives de Folklore*, 11(1970) Passim

Kane, Alice. *Songs and Sayings of an Ulster Childhood*. Ed. Edith Fowke. Toronto: McClelland & Stewart, 1983.

*Kerfont, Angela, *Folktales from Western Newfoundland*. Coll. and ed. Marie-Annick Desplanques. Mont-Saint-Aignan: Université de Rouen, 1985.

Kirshenblatt-Gimblett, Barbara. "Culture Shock and Narrative Creativity." In *Folklore in the Modern World*. Ed. Richard M. Dorson. The Hague: Mouton, 1976.

Kirshenblatt-Gimblett, Barbara. "A Parable in Context: A Social Interactional Analysis of a Storytelling Performance." In *Folklore: Performance and Communication*. Eds. Kenneth S. Goldstein and Dan Ben-Amos. The Hague: Mouton, 1975, pp. 105–30. Reprinted in *Explorations*, pp. 289–319.

*Kirshenblatt-Gimblett, Barbara. "Traditional Story-Telling in the Toronto Jewish Community: A Study in Performance and Creativity in an Immigrant Culture." Ph.D. dissertation, Indiana University, 1972.

Klymasz, Robert B. "The Ethnic Joke in Canada Today." *Keystone Folklore Quarterly*, 15(1970), pp. 167–73. Reprinted in *Explorations*, pp. 320–28.

*Klymasz, Robert B. *Folk Narrative Among Ukrainian-Canadians in Western Canada*. Ottawa: National Museum of Man, CCFCS Mercury Series 4, 1973.

Lacey, Laurie, ed. *Lunenberg County Folklore and Oral History: Project '77*. Ottawa: National Museum of Man, CCFCS Mercury Series 30, 1979. Passim.

Lacourcière, Luc. "The Analytical Catalogue of French Folktales in North America." *Laurentian University Review*, 8(February 1976), pp. 123–28.

Lacourcière, Luc. "Oral Tradition: New England and French Canada," Quebec: Archives de Folklore, Université Laval, 1972. 20 pages. Mimeo.

Lacourcière, Luc. "The Present State of French-Canadian Folklore Studies." *JAF*, 74(1961), pp. 373–82.

Lacourcière, Luc. "Le ruban qui rend fort." *Les cahiers des dix*. 36(1971), pp. 235–97.

Laws, G. Malcolm, Jr. *Native American Balladry*. Philadelphia: American Folklore Society, 1964.

Leach, MacEdward. "Celtic Tales from Cape Breton." In *Studies in Honor of Stith Thompson*. Ed. W. Edson Richmond. Bloomington: Indiana University Press, 1957, pp. 40–54.

Low, Margaret. "The Motif of the External Soul in French-Canadian Folktales." *Laurentian University Review*, 8(February 1976), pp. 61–69. Reprinted in *Explorations*, pp. 266–76.

*MacDonell, Margaret, and John Shaw. *Luirgean Eachainn Nill: Folktales from Cape Breton*. Stornoway: Acair, 1981.

McGrath, Robin Gedalof. "Inuit Literature." In *The Oxford Companion to Canadian Literature*. Ed. William Toye. Toronto: Oxford, 1983, pp. 390–91.

MacLean, Angus Hector. *God and the Devil at Seal Cove*. Halifax: Petheric, 1976.

*MacLeod, C.I.N. *Stories from Nova Scotia*. Antigonish: Formac, 1974.

MacNeil, Neil. *The Highland Heart in Nova Scotia*. New York: Scribner's, 1948.

Monteiro, George. " 'Histoire de Montferrand: L'Athlète Canadien' and Joe Mufraw." *JAF*, 73(1960), pp. 24–34.

Mowat, Farley. *And No Birds Sang*. McClelland & Stewart, 1979.

*Norman, Howard. *Where the Chill Came From: Cree Windigo Tales and Journeys*. San Francisco: North Point, 1982.

Palmer, Roy. *Everyman's Book of British Ballads*. London: Dent, 1980.

*Patterson, G. James *The Greeks of Vancouver: A Study in the Preservation of Ethnicity.* Ottawa: National Museum of Man, CCFCS Mercury Series 23, 1976.

Petrone, Penny. "Indian Legends and Tales." In *The Oxford Companion to Canadian Literature.* Ed. William Toye. Toronto: Oxford, 1983, pp. 377–83.

Pocius, Gerald L. "Frank Williams, Newfoundland Joke-Teller." *Lore and Language,* 2(January 1977), pp. 16–29; 2(July 1977), pp. 11–21; 2(January 1978), pp. 11–19; 2(July 1978), pp. 6–15.

Quilliam, Tom. *Look 'Ere Me Son. A Collection of Newfoundland Stories.* Grand Falls, Newfoundland: Helme, 1977.

Radin, Paul. *The Trickster: A Study in American Indian Mythology.* 1956. Reprinted New York: Greenwood, 1969.

Reader, H.J. *Newfoundland Wit, Humor and Folklore.* Corner Brook, Newfoundland: Author, [1967].

Robins, John D. "Paul Bunyan." *Canadian Forum,* 6(1926), pp. 146–50.

Rubin, Ruth. "Yiddish Tales for Children." In *Folklore of Canada.* Ed. Edith Fowke. Toronto: McClelland & Stewart, 1976, pp. 291–94.

Rudnyc'kyj, Jaroslav B. *Readings in Canadian Slavic Folklore.* 2 vols. Winnipeg: University of Manitoba Press, 1961.

Rudnyc'kyj, Jaroslav B. *Ukrainian-Canadian Folklore Texts in English Translation.* Winnipeg: Ukrainian Free Academy of Sciences, 1960.

Salo, Matt T., and Sheila M.G. Salo. "Memorates and belief stories." Appendix, *The Kalderas in Eastern Canada.* Ottawa: National Museum of Man, CCFCS Mercury Series 21, 1977, pp. 223–53.

Scholem, Gershom. "The Tradition of the Thirty-Six Hidden Just Men." *The Messianic Idea in Judaism.* New York: Schocken Books, 1971, pp. 251–56.

Scott, John Roper. "Personal Experience Narratives Among Professional Sailors: Generic Keys to the Study of an Occupation." Ph.D. dissertation, Memorial University, 1985.

Shaw, Walter. *Tell Me the Tales.* Charlottetown: Square Deal, 1975.

*Sidney, Mrs. Angela. *Tagish Tlaagu: Tagish Stories.* Recorded by Julie Cruikshank. Whitehorse: Council for Yukon Indians and the Government of Yukon, 1982.

Smith, Paul. *The Book of Nasty Legends.* London: Routledge & Kegan Paul, 1983.

Smith, Paul, ed. *Perspectives on Contemporary Legend.* Sheffield: University of Sheffield, 1984.

Smith, Susan. "Urban Tales." In *Folklore of Canada*. Ed. Edith Fowke. Toronto: McClelland & Stewart, 1976, pp. 262–68.

*Spray, Carole, *Will o' the Wisp: Folk Tales and Legends of New Brunswick*. Fredericton: Brunswick Press, 1979.

Stone, Kay. "I Won't Tell These Stores to My Kids." *Canadian Ethnic Studies*, 7:2(1975), pp. 33–41.

*Stone, Kay. *Prairie Folklore*. Winnipeg: University of Winnipeg, 1976. Mimeo.

Stone, Kay. "Romantic Heroines in Anglo-American Folk and Popular Literature." Ph.D. dissertation, Indiana Univeresity, 1975.

Sulte, Benjamin. *Histoire de Jos. Montferrand: L'athlète canadien*. Montreal: Beauchemin, 1905.

Taft, Michael, *Tall Tales of British Columbia*. Sound Heritage Series Number 39. Victoria: Provincial Archives of British Columbia, 1983.

Tallman, Richard S. "The Tall Tale Tradition and the Teller: A Biographical Contextual Study of a Story-teller, Robert Coffil of Blomidon, Nova Scotia." Ph.D. dissertation, Memorial University, 1974.

Tallman, Richard S. " 'You Can Almost Picture It': The Aesthetic of a Nova Scotia Storyteller." *Folklore Forum*, 7(1974), pp. 121–30.

Tallman, Richard S. "Where Stories Are Told: A Nova Scotia Storyteller's Milieu." *American Review of Canadian Studies*, 5(1975), pp. 17–41.

*Tarasoff, Koozma J. *Traditional Doukhobor Folkways: An Ethnographic and Biographic Record of Prescribed Behaviour*. Ottawa: National Museum of Man, CCFCS Mercury Series 20, 1977.

*Teit, James, ed. *Traditions of the Thompson River Indians of British Columbia*. Boston and New York: Houghton, Mifflin, 1898.

*Teit, James A. "Water-Beings in Shetlandic Folk-Lore as Remembered by Shetlanders in British Columbia," *JAF*, 31(1918), pp. 180–201.

Thibadeau, Joe. "Ontario Yarns from Joe Thibadeau." In *Folklore of Canada*. Ed. Edith Fowke. Toronto: McClelland & Stewart, 1976, pp. 167–70.

Thomas, Gerald. *Les Deux Traditions: le conte populaire chez les Franco-Terreneuviens*. Montreal: Bellarmin, 1983.

Thomas, Gerald. "Folklore in French." In *The Oxford Companion to Canadian Literature*. Ed. William Toye. Toronto: Oxford, 1983, pp. 264–67.

Thomas, Gerald. "The Folktale and Folktale Style in the Tradition of French Newfoundlanders," *Canadian Folklore canadien*, 1(1979), pp. 71–78.

Thomas, Gerald. "Newfie Jokes." In *Folklore of Canada.* Ed. Edith Fowke. Toronto: McClelland & Stewart, 1976, pp. 142–53.

Thomas Gerald. "Stories, Storytelling and Storytellers in Newfoundland's French Tradition: A Study of the Narrative Art of Four French Newfoundlanders." Ph.D. dissertation, Memorial University, 1977.

Thomas, Gerald. "A Tradition under Pressure: Folk Narratives of the French Minority of the Port-au-Port Peninsula, Newfoundland (Canada)." *Studia Fennica 20: Folk Narrative Research,* Helsinki, 1976, pp. 192–201.

Thompson, Stith. *Motif-Index of Folk Literature.* 6 vols. Bloomington: Indiana University Press, 1966.

Thompson, Stith. *Tales of the North American Indians.* Bloomington: Indiana University Press, 1929.

Trueman, Stuart. *Ghosts, Pirates and Treasure Trove: The Phantoms that Haunt New Brunswick.* Toronto: McClelland & Stewart, 1975.

Trueman, Stuart. *Tall Tales and True Tales from Down East.* Toronto: McClelland & Stewart, 1979.

Wareham, Wilfred. "The Monologue in Newfoundland." In *The Blasty Bough.* Ed. Clyde Rose. St. John's: Breakwater, 1976, pp. 196–216.

Waugh, F.W. "Canadian Folk-Lore from Ontario." *JAF,* 31(1918), pp. 78–82.

*Wintemberg, W.J. *Folk-Lore of Waterloo County, Ontario.* Ottawa: King's Printer, 1950.

Wintemberg, W.J. "French-Canadian Folk Tales." *JAF,* 17(1904), pp. 265–67.

Wintemberg, W.J., and Katherine H. Wintemberg. "Folk-Lore from Grey County, Ontario." *JAF,* 31(1918), pp. 83–124.

Wooley, Ruth E. "A Comparative Study of Some French-Canadian Tales." M.A. thesis, Indiana University, 1927.

Acknowledgements

"Old-One." Reproduced by permission of the American Folklore Society from "*Folktales of Salishan and Sahaptin Tribes*," Memoir of the American Folklore Society, No. 11, 1917, pp. 80–81. Not for further reproduction.

"Crow Makes the World," from *Tagish Tlaagu: Tagish Stories* (Whitehorse: Council for Yukon Indians, 1982), by permission of Angela Sidney and Julie Cruickshank.

"The Moon" and "The Mosquito and the Thunder." Reproduced from "*Traditions of the Thompson River Indians of British Columbia*," Memoir of the American Folklore Society, No. 6, 1898, pp. 91 and 56.

"A Wolf, a Fox, and a Lion" and "Once Upon a Time There Was a Shepherd," from the Carla Bianco Collection (tapes 28 and 33). Published by permission of the Canadian Centre for Folk Culture Studies, National Museum of Man, National Museums of Canada.

"The Race Between Turtle and Frog." Reproduced by permission of the American Folklore Society from "*Folktales of the Salishan and Sahaptin Tribes*," Memoir of the American Folklore Society, No. 11, 1917, p. 111. Not for further reproduction.

"The Talking Nightingale," and "A Miracle in Montreal" from Elbaz, André E., *Folktales of the Canadian Sephardim* (Markham: Fitzhenry & Whiteside, 1982), by permission of Fitzhenry & Whiteside.

"The White Bear," from *Folktales from Western Newfoundland* (Publications de l'Université de Rouen, 1 rue Thomas Becket, 76130 Mont-Saint-Aignan, France, 1985), narrated by Angela Kerfont, edited by Marie-Annick Desplanques, by permission of Publications de l'Université de Rouen.

"The Magic Chest," from Klymasz, Robert B., *Folk Narrative Among Ukrainian Canadians in Western Canada*. National Museum of Man Mercury Series, Canadian Centre for Folk Culture Studies Paper No. 4. Ottawa: National Museums of Canada, 1973, pp. 39–44.

"The Blacksmith and Beelzebub's Imps," from Wintemberg, W. J., *Folk-Lore of Waterloo County, Ontario*. National Museum of Canada Bulletin 116, Anthropological Series 28. Ottawa, 1950, p. 63.

"The Fox Wife," from Gedalof, Robin, ed., *Paper Stays Put: A Collection of Inuit Writing* (Edmonton: Hurtig, 1980), by permission of Robin Gedalof McGrath and Hurtig Publishers Ltd.

"The Two Brothers," from Patterson, G. James, *The Greeks of Vancouver*. National Museum of Man Mercury Series, Canadian Centre for Folk Culture Studies Paper No. 18. Ottawa: National Museums of Canada, 1976, pp. 73–75.

"The Shoemaker in Heaven" and "Old Man Gimli," from Stone, Kay, ed., *Prairie Folklore*. By permission of Kay Stone.

"Mac Crùslain," from MacDonell, Margaret, and John Shaw, *Folktales from Cape Breton* (Stornoway: Acair Ltd., 1981), by permission of Acair Ltd.

"The Scotchman Who Loved an Irish Girl." Reproduced by permission of the American Folklore Society from *"Folklore from Nova Scotia,"* Memoir of the American Folklore Society, No. 24, 1931, pp. 124–25. Not for further reproduction.

"Little Claus and Big Claus," from Creighton, Helen, *Folk-Lore of Lunenburg County, Nova Scotia*. National Museum of Canada Bulletin No. 117, Anthropological Series No. 29. Ottawa, 1950, pp. 140–45.

"The Lobster Salad," by permission of Wilfred Wareham.

"A Catch Tale," from Spray, Carole, *Will o' the Wisp: Folk Tales and Legends of New Brunswick*. (Fredericton: Brunswick Press, 1979), by permission of Carole Spray and Brunswick Press.

"The Seal-Woman." Reproduced by permission of the American Folklore Society from *Journal of American Folklore*, 31, 1918, pp. 191–92. Not for further reproduction.

"The Wrong Chill Windigo." Excerpted from *Where the Chill Came From*. Copyright © 1982 by Howard Norman. Published by North Point Press and reprinted by permission. All rights reserved.

"Steer North and North East," from MacLeod, Calum I.N., *Stories from Nova Scotia* (Halifax: Formac, 1974).

"The Ghostly Sailors," from Peacock, Kenneth, *Songs of the Newfoundland Outports*, Vol. 3. National Museum of Canada Bulletin 197, Anthropological Series 65. Ottawa, 1965, pp. 873–74.

"Buried Treasure: The Pot of Gold," from Doucette, Laurel, ed., *Cultural Retention and Demographic Change: Studies of the Hebridean Scots in the Eastern Townships of Quebec*. National Museum of Man Mercury Series, Canadian Centre for Folk Culture Studies Paper No. 34. Ottawa: National Museums of Canada, 1980, pp. 111–13.

"Young Lad," from Fiddler, Thomas, and James R. Stevens, *Legends from the Forest* (Moonbeam: Penumbra Press, 1985), by permission of Penumbra Press.

"How I Learned to Make Bread" and "The Frank Slide Disaster," from Broadfoot, Barry, *The Pioneer Years* (Toronto: Doubleday Canada, 1976), by permission of Barry Broadfoot.

"St. Peter's Day: Memorable Gatherings," from Tarasoff, Koozma J., *Traditional Doukhobor Folkways: An Ethnographic and Biographic Record of Prescribed Behaviour*. National Museum of Man Mercury Series, Canadian Centre for Folk Culture Studies Paper No. 20. Ottawa: National Museums of Canada, 1977, pp. 93–94.

My thanks to the following friends and colleagues who have supplied items not previously published: Rita Cox, Luc Lacourcière and Margaret Low, Ban Seng Hoe, Kelly Russell, Sheldon Posen, Alice Kane, Barbara Kirshenblatt-Gimblett, Jeanne Pattison, Judy Smith, Carole H. Carpenter, Chris Rutkowski.